Copyright © 2021 by Maddison Cole

All rights reserved. No part of this publication may be reproduced, stored or transmitted in any form or by any means, electronic, mechanical, photocopying, recording, scanning, or otherwise without written permission from the publisher. It is illegal to copy this book, post it to a website, or distribute it by any other means without permission.

This novel is entirely a work of fiction. The names, characters and incidents portrayed in it are the work of the author's imagination. Any resemblance to actual persons, living or dead, events or localities is entirely coincidental.

Maddison Cole asserts the moral right to be identified as the author of this work.

Maddison Cole has no responsibility for the persistence or accuracy of URLs for external or third-party Internet Websites referred to in this publication and does not guarantee that any content on such Websites is, or will remain, accurate or appropriate.

Designations used by companies to distinguish their products are often claimed as trademarks. All brand names and product names used in this book and on its cover are trade names, service marks, trademarks and registered trademarks of their respective owners. The publishers and the book are not associated with any product or vendor mentioned in this book. None of the companies referenced within the book have endorsed the book.

First Edition.

Ebook ISBN:B09DSR2XBB

Paperback ISBN: 9798482916346

Editing: Tiffany Purdon

Cover Design: Jessica Mohring at Raven Ink Covers

Formatting: Emma Luna at Moonlight Author Services

AUTHOR NOTE

The writing in this book is the Queen's English, but please don't hold the fact I'm a Brit against me! I can't help it, but I have worked hard to make sure you understand what I am talking about. If anything confuses you, give me a shout!

TRIGGER WARNING

The 'I Love Candy series' features a feisty female lead and her broody harem. Candy is spontaneous, impulsive and reckless, which makes this book inappropriate for under 18's. She gives as good as she gets, causing chaos and usually leaves you wondering who is bullying who! Expect excessive amounts of steam, violence and cursing throughout. This series is an RH trilogy with a HEA…eventually.

CRUSHIN' CANDY

I LOVE CANDY BOOK ONE

MADDISON COLE

"Sup," I nod to the crackheads and hobos loitering across the cell benches. The metal grate slams shut behind me and I throw a wink back at Captain Knobstick. He became my main interrogator four arrests ago and even though he can never make a charge stick, I feel like we've really bonded. The balding man is eye-line with me at 5' 8", with a wide gap between his front two teeth and a dead caterpillar living on his upper lip. Grimacing at me, he walks away whilst trailing his baton across all the bars. Music to my ears, I sigh to myself. Digging out the piece of gum wedged between my back teeth and cheek, I cross the space and pop a bubble at the gangly girl quivering in the corner.

"You're in my seat." She actually flinches, her dull hair shaking around her ankles since her knees are pulled up to her chest. I wait a whole ten seconds before growling to make her shift aside, taking my favourite spot. Turning away from the others, I lie back on the bench and lift my PVC-covered legs to lean them against the wall. There's a small whimper from the girl and if she starts to cry, I'll be putting her out of her misery. Only with a mild concussion, but everyone would thank me for it . Except maybe her.

"First time huh?" I blow a large pink bubble before popping it. I think she nods amongst her trembling, her wide doe eyes swinging to me like a gazelle spotting a lioness. Well, rawr to you too.

"Y-y-yeah, but it wasn't my fault! I swear! I was just trying to finish my college essay before the deadline at the Starbucks on Vine Street, when a masked person barrelled straight into the table. My coffee spilled all over my laptop and I was so worried about my essay, I didn't even notice the drugs that had been stashed in my bag until the police dogs caught up to me."

Twisting my head properly to the side, I lift my hands in circles to hold them over my eyes and squint. My mask often rides up during a healthy jog from the cops, and I'll be damn it is her. Giggles slip through my chewing until I'm in full hysterics on my back once more. What are the chances my ignorant partner in crime would be in the same holding cell as me? I ran for fucking miles. Cardio has always been my best friend though, along with the gym, doughnuts, rainbow sprinkles and a load of bullshit other reasons I need to keep cardio on my good side.

The smile is hurting my cheeks until I suddenly realise what else her presence means and the laughter dies. An abrupt and painful death. I go slack and impossibly still on the bench, with my eyes staring at a spot on the ceiling. Fuck, that means my plan to stalk her and break into her student dorms some point tomorrow to retrieve my stash is royally fucked. Instead, it's living the life with its illegal friends in an evidence locker beneath my feet somewhere. Big Cheese is not going to like this.

"Oh well," I say, making my neighbour flinch again. I'll blame Gangly Girl for not knowing better and he'll just add it to my lifetime worth of debt. Running his errands is all I have to live for anyway so I might as well keep them coming.

Even the thrill of being arrested has lost its appeal. No matter what tactics I use, being interrogated just doesn't fill my veins with the same sense of adrenaline. What does it take for them to pull out the big guns - call the secret service, waterboard me, attach electrocution clamps to my nipples, or something?! I reckon I'll have to find a way to pay for it myself at this rate, but I already know I'm too much of a Dom to let a man completely overpower me.

"I've missed the deadline now," a soft voice sounds. Despite thinking about her, I'd forgotten my accomplice was still sitting next to me. She tucks her head into her knees and begins to sob. Rolling my eyes, I lean up and flick her in the temple.

"Don't they teach you anything useful at that college of yours? Police dogs are trained to scent fear, not drugs. You must have had something to hide or you wouldn't be here." This catches her off guard, her glazed-over brown eyes looking to the others for how to respond. Good luck with that one, this lot are too high or dejected to care.

"He seems rather focused on you," a gruff voice sounds inside my head. I twist to look at Angus on the bench above my head, his eyeless sockets focused on a guy across the other side of the cell. On second look, he does seem to be staring. Heavy dreads sit upon his youngish face, his smooth, chocolate skin and dark eyes, something I would usually be all over if it weren't for his fixed scowl.

"Apparently so," I agree. "Can't blame him though." I blow a kiss to get some sort of reaction. Nothing. When I can't peg where I slightly recognise him from, I tuck my hands behind my head and return to looking at the ceiling when Gangly Girl braves speaking to me again.

"W-who are you talking to?"

"Angus," I tut. The little fucker hops his way over my face and sits on my chest, a cringe worthy noise sounding with each moment. Like leather being stretched. *Shudder*. Noticing the girl's large eyes are still focused on me and waiting for more, I sigh. "He's the pink gummy bear that follows me around and fills my head with his terrible wisdom. Like a mascot who always leads me wrong, or the little squishy devil on my shoulder." I leave out the part about him having the voice of a chain-smoker or how he curses like a blind seamstress.

"Why's he called Angus?" her small voice asks. I lean forward up on my forearms at this, briefly swiping one arm to knock the little shit to the floor. No one's ever asked me that before. Usually I get shrink referrals or avoided completely, which is what I was hoping for but now I'm intrigued.

"Because he's pink, spews shit and puts the 'G' in anus." I smirk, remembering how clever thirteen-year-old me thought I was coming up with that when he first appeared. Gangly Girl nods to herself, not seeming too bothered by me as she looks away. On second thought, I reckon she's feeling so lost in pity and despair, nothing else matters. I know that feeling. Maybe if life hadn't fucked me anally with a dirty stick, I might have been like her. Innocent, rigid, boring.

Nah, fuck that. I'll take all the shit to be me. I'm Candy fucking Crystal - not my legal middle name but the rest is authentic. My mother was a stripper before one too many years of drugs took its toll on her, and I was the product of one of her clients. No idea who, and I couldn't care less. She'd never wanted to be a mom, but after the legal system and dozens of group homes raised me, she thought I'd run into her arms and plead to join the family business. No thank you. I love my body, from my cute set of abs to my long legs. My neon pink hair hangs just past my shoulders, my left arm and chest inked with exaggerated caricatures of superheroes . But they're mine. Not someone's lying husband in a seedy club. Mine.

Anyways, where was I? Oh yeah. Swinging my legs around, I take pity on the girl I've decided is my protégé.

"Here," I pull my gum in half with my teeth. "Chew this." When she doesn't immediately open, I lunge forward and pry her mouth open, not without gaining some teeth marks on my fingers though. Feisty, I love it. Popping the gum in her mouth, I clamp her jaw shut and give her my best death stare until she begins to chew.

"Good girl," I pat her on the head. Next, my eyes fall to her top. It's navy and fits nicely, except from the excess lace covering the top of her bust up to her neck. What is this girl, a nun? Expecting her to put up a fight, I swing myself around to straddle her, trapping her arms at her side by my thighs. Ripping the top half off, she bucks and shrieks but it's no use. Master Splinter taught me everything he knew whilst I was growing up and the library let me stay late to watch Teenage Mutant Ninja Turtles on a weekend. It beat going back to the group home and I gave those bookcases a run for their money.

The metal grate slides open, Captain Knobstick shouting my name along with the satisfying sound of a taser. Oh yeah, it's on.

"Candy, you're free to go. Don't make me use this on you." I give my apprentice one last look over and smirk, happy with my work. Rising from her lap, I slowly spin to face the clammy officer opposite.

"How about you give me one spark for the road and I promise not to be back for at least....a month?" Angus sucks in a croaky breath. I know mate, big words but if that's what it takes, I'll do my best to stick to it. Knobstick is slowly shaking his head, the way he's pursing his lips making the caterpillar dance. Maybe I'm wrong, it might be a hairy worm instead.

Hanging my head low, I walk by defeatedly and wait for the grate to be closed. I lean mournfully on the other side, bidding my student goodbye with the promise I'll find her to finish what I started. Her eyes nearly pop out of her head and I then realise the threat that could be inferred in my words. To ease her mind, I blow her a kiss but somehow, I think I've had the opposite effect. Knobstick nudges me along, my eyes locking with the guy who is still staring at me with every step I take. There's a few dreads cut short at the back of his head and it suddenly comes to me.

"Dude!" I grip my side as laughter roars out of me, my finger pointing at him through the bars. I remember now! There was a downtown scavenger hunt last year and a handful of his dreads declared me Scumbag of the year. I got a mini trophy and an ounce of weed, it was an awesome day. Sure, I probably should have asked him first, but he was being wheeled into an ambulance to have his stomach pumped at the time. It's not my fault he can't handle his poison of choice or that the paramedics are so easily distracted by their vehicle having a bitch fit. Whether I tampered with the wires or not was neither here nor there - I won something for the first time in my life!

Knobstick throws me back just as the guy collides with the other side of the bars, the tears streaming from my eyes making my reactions slow. Making my way into the stairwell leading back up to the precinct, I can't hold back the streams of laughter that echo around the walls. I needed that pick me up.

The station is mostly deserted, since it's stupid o'clock in the morning. I'm escorted all the way to the front desk, a large-set woman sitting on the other side of the glass eyeing me closely. I briefly wonder why bother with the red lipstick since her uniform is crinkled and her greasy hair is in a messy bun that I reckon she's slept in for a few days, until I see her expression soften at Captain Knobstick. I raise an eyebrow, noticing the shy blush entering his cheeks until the wedding band on his finger catches my attention.

My hand twitches, the taser on his belt so close and Angus egging me on in my head to do it. Teach this cheater a lesson. Jab him right in the sternum and let the volts shock the deceit right out of him. Short-circuit his heart. Hide his lifeless body in the back of a bin truck. Wait, what? Shut the fuck up Angus, I'm inside a police station for fuck's sake.

Willing my hand to relax, I return my attention to the adulteress on the other side of the glass. I can't ignore the small rush of adrenaline I briefly felt however, like the kiss of an old acquaintance in all the right places. A leather jacket and a brown envelope is dumped on the counter before me, my name scribbled across the front messily. Without moving an inch, I maintain eye contact with her.

"Where's my bat?"

"We can't return potential weapons to those who have been in our custody," she drawls. I squint slightly, fully prepared to not only take down Knobstick but every fucker in this place if I a) I don't get my bat back in the next five seconds and b) if so help me, there happens to be a scratch on it. A chill shudders through my spine, my breathing hard to keep controlled. There's a time and a place to utterly lose one's shit, and this isn't it. Instead, I pull on all of my reserves to speak low and calmly.

"I've been in your custody long enough to know there's a photo of a pretty blonde and twin girls on his desk," I jerk my chin to the officer tensing beside me, "and unless you've reallllllllly let yourself go and had a full facial reconstruction, it's not you. How about you fetch my bat, and I won't start screaming the word affair on repeat until your ears bleed?" All of the colour in her face drains but she doesn't move straight away. Shrugging, I tuck away my gum and open my mouth wide on an inhale. "AF-"

"Okay! Okay, fine," she hisses. Reaching beneath her desk, she produces my beloved bat with barely any effort at all. I smile sweetly, smoothing my hand over every memorised crevice in the wood.

"See, that wasn't so hard." Grabbing the brown envelope, I spin and leave with a backwards wave. I'll be back before they get too comfortable. It's pitch black outside, not a single star shining down on New York City tonight. Thankfully it's the height of summer so the air is balmy enough to not need to put my jacket on as I skip down the stone steps. I'm not too far from my current place of residence but I hail a taxi anyway, not wanting to get myself in more trouble walking around with my bat in my hand in the dead of night.

Dropping into the back seat, I lean over to strap Angus in before taking my phone out of the envelope and switching it on. The home screen has barely loaded when it starts to vibrate with the incoming of a stream of messages. All from the Big Cheese and all coded, of course.

> **Big Cheese: Where are you? Dinner has gone cold.** (AKA the warehouse I was stealing the haul from is now empty.)

> **Big Cheese: Found you. Mom was worried sick.** (AKA I know you're in jail, again.)

Big Cheese: Don't forget your cousins are in town, I'll send a car round to pick you up so you aren't late tomorrow night as well. (AKA my presence is required at the mansion and there will be an audience for my public spanking.)

"Dammit!" I slam my hand into the passenger head rest, causing the driver to skid to a stop and send me flying forward. Shit, should have worn my seatbelt. Muttering an apology, I settle back and toss my phone into the seat beside me.

Pulling up a little further down my street, because letting others know your address is a rookie mistake, I hop out and hold the door open long enough to let Angus squelch his way out.

"Hey, that's $21!" The cabby shouts at me through the window when I go to walk away. "Night's rates!" I look over my shoulder, my worldly possessions huddled in my arms.

"You really should have checked that I had money before accepting me as a rider," I shrug. Walking away, he makes a fuss of cussing and beeping his horn before speeding away. Wow, road-rage much. Closing in on my place, a minibeast crosses my path and hisses at me. I scowl at Sphinx, my landlady's little shit of a hairless Egyptian cat. He's missing one eye and wrinkly like foreskin, but I do appreciate his 'stroke me or die' attitude. Scooping him up by the collar, he makes a screeching noise until I dump him in my leather jacket and start to scratch his tummy. Prickly on the outside, pussy on the inside - I get that.

I make it to the main building, shoving Sphinx into the cat flap before taking the hidden steps around the side down to the basement level. My keys are in the envelope, with a fluffy pink pom-pom and little plastic gummy bear attached. I smirk at Angus who has jumped up onto my shoulder, juggling my bat as I unlock the door.

"Home sweet home," I breathe in the scent of damp as I step inside.

"Shithole, sweet shithole more like," Angus adds unhelpfully. The lightbulb flickers overhead when I switch it on so I just leave it off. Dumping everything on the plastic table in the centre of the living room/kitchen/dinner combo, the weight of the day suddenly falls over me. My skin-tight leggings and corset go next, the air wrapping my body in a welcoming embrace. Grabbing the handle on the wall, I tug my fold away bed down onto it's squeaking metal legs and drop onto the thin mattress.

"Good night shitface," I mutter into the material, intending it for Angus. Sleep has just begun to claim me when his reply filters in, a small smile pulling at the corner of my mouth.

"Sweet dreams fucktard."

CANDY

There's a car with blacked out windows waiting for me on the corner of the block by nightfall, the driver not bothering to get out and open the door for me. Must be Nigel. Passing around the front of the Mercedes, I plant a smudgey lipstick kiss on the driver's window before getting into the back. Sure enough, it is Nigel sitting in the front seat.

He's one of Cheese's bodyguard/drivers. Tall and muscled with his dark hair cropped short and jawline razor sharp. Fuck yes, I'd ride his face any day. Unfortunately, Nigel is still pretending he's not interested in my invitation to join me back here. Even after the time he reported me for getting started without him during an opium high, I saw the way he watched me in the rear-view mirror. He's a guard dog on a tight leash, but that doesn't stop him from being starved.

"You're looking especially hungry tonight, big fella. Come back here and have a lick of some Candy. I promise the sugar rush will be worth it," I wink, spreading myself across the seat like a buffet. He ignores me, putting the Mercedes in drive but even Angus agrees that I'm looking especially delectable. I should hope so, since I drank a whole bottle of lime vodka before venturing outside tonight. Big Cheese doesn't scare me, nothing does. But intimidate, yeah he sure does that.

I decided to have my hair tied back tonight in a high ponytail with a few tendrils left out to frame my face. My makeup is simple, a bit of eyeliner, mascara and a pop of pink on my lips which is now smeared across the window. I don't own many clothes, but what I do have is all black, mostly leather and usually revealing- like this one piece catsuit. The high, choker neckline covers my front except for a teardrop cut out over my cleavage and exposes my entire back, right down to the floral tramp stamp I have at the base of my spine.

Big Cheese lives a state over, giving me plenty of time to sink into the seat and contemplate my life choices whilst staring out of the window. I never used to question myself; it was all act now and think never. When in doubt, I've let Angus take over and it usually ends with someone bleeding out and rasping for help. Only those who deserve it, but I'd be lying if I said I was some kind of vigilante. I hurt others because I'm bored and usually this feeling of numbness leads to a life being lost by my hand.

I'm not a bad person, I just do bad things in search of the high I crave. Their screams are my heroin, their pleads my opium. It reminds me I'm not the only one suffering and it could be oh so much worse. But increasingly, lately, nothing I do stops me from becoming lost amongst it all. I need direction. A goal. Ooh, maybe a holiday. I heard the Irish aren't fussy and those accents, yep it's decided. I'm booking a flight first thing tomorrow.

In no time, we're pulling into the driveway large enough for two tanks. A guard permits us entry from his booth, opening the tall gates which will seal me inside once we've passed through. The mansion is a mix-mash of white columns, grey brickwork, iron flourishes and glass lined balconies. Out back there's a pool, bar, and hot tub. Everything a mob boss needs for his mob crew. Oh, did I leave that part out? Yeah, Big Cheese is exactly as his name states and more.

Nigel pulls up in front of the double door entrance, speeding off the second my feet touch the tarmac so Angus has to leap out the back door and belly flop onto the ground. Poor little dude. Waiting for him to dust off his gummy body, we walk up to the entrance just as the doors open. A leggy brunette in a floaty dress with twisted lips and sharp eyes greets me.

"You're not coming in dressed like a slut," she hisses. Sticking up my middle finger, I shove past Tanya and let myself in. Many of Cheese's higher crew members stay in his mansion, enjoying an extravagant life the rookies like me pay for. Sure they've paid their dues and worked up from the bottom, but then something happens where their heads double in size and a bunch of the most prestigious cocks you've ever met suddenly appear. Like Tanya. She thinks she's the head bitch around here, but when I'm around there's no such thing.

"I was ordered to come and this is how I'm dressed. If you want to run along and tell him you've turned me away, be my guest." Turning back with my eyebrow raised, a silent stare-off commences between the two of us. Beneath the crystal chandelier, her blue eyes twinkle and I try to imagine what she'd look like if she took the stick out of her ass. Like she isn't constantly sucking on a sour mint, I reckon. Angus creeps up onto my shoulder, watching intently for the moment her eyelids flick closed. "Aha!" he shouts in my head and I lash out, my open palm cracking across her cheek.

"What the fuck?!" Tanya squeals, holding her face in shock.

"You blinked so I got slapsies," I shrug. A chuckle sounds from the staircase, my eyes skating to Riley over my shoulder.

"Always causing trouble, huh Candy?" He smirks. Closing the distance between us, I scrunch my nose up at his black shirt and grey dress trousers. Looks like everyone got an invite to this so-called 'dinner'. Riley is around my age with dark hair cropped short at the sides. His nose is too straight, there's a butt cleft in his chin and the way he slides an arm around my waist makes me think of him as all round slimey, but I suppose he is handsome by regular standards. Just not Candy standards.

"Touch me again and you'll lose your hand," I growl, shoving him aside. Riley's smile only widens, the words 'challenge accepted' visible in his eyes.

"Look, you're already on thin ice with the big man and dinner won't be ready for another half hour yet. How about you cut your losses and find something to change into upstairs?" I snarl at his gentle tone, treating me like a child on the verge of a tantrum. Looking between him and Tanya, I chew my gum whilst making a decision. Usually I'd storm through this place and get my wrist slapped so I can leave, but Riley's right. For once. If Big Cheese cuts my monthly allowance, I can kiss my Irish vacation and basement apartment goodbye.

Striding away, I make my way up the stairs in hunt of something 'more suitable.' Angus questions my motives the entire way but I don't answer him. Looking in a few rooms, I find railings of floral summer dresses like the one Tanya was wearing and formal fitting gowns. Ugh, no way. Trying a room which distinctly smells like it belongs to a man instead, I smile at the array of suits I discover in the oak wardrobe. This, I can do something with.

I'm elbow deep in clothing when I hear the door open behind me. Ignoring whoever it is, I pull a few hangers out and sling them over my arm when a body presses into me from behind.

"What are the odds you'd come to my room?" Riley's hot breath moves over my neck. I suppress a shudder, not wanting him to get the wrong impression, but the bulge pushing against my ass tells me it's too late.

"You'd better step back if you know what's good for you," I growl. Instead of heeding my advice, Riley spins me around and shoves me against the door of his wardrobe. Lashing out to slap his cheek, he smirks and grabs my wrists, wrenching them behind my back so my chest is pushed out. I throw my head forward to strike his, causing the smirk on his face to slip . His hands release me to wrap one around my neck and he starts leaning towards my mouth. Oh hell no. Slamming my palms into his shoulders, I refuse to let his lips anywhere near me.

"This is your last warning Riley. Back. The fuck. Off." He doesn't back off. Riley tries to kiss me once more and this time, I let him. My arms drop away as I relent to his touches, even reach for his belt buckle whilst curling my tongue around his.

"Knew you'd come around," he mumbles into my mouth as I work my hand into his pants and grip his shaft until it's straining to be freed. Putting enough space between us for Riley to see me lick my lips seductively, he allows me to guide him towards the four-poster bed in the centre of the room. Before he sits, I wiggle his trousers down until I'm crouching before his dick. It's a pretty nice dick actually, girthy with a network of ribbed veins running along the length of it. Oh well.

Whipping the specialised hunting pocket knife out of my boot, I grab the end of Riley's dick firmly and make a clean slice all the way through the base before his eyes are able to focus. The scream that leaves him is so high-pitched, it could have been mine and I panic at the noise. Someone is surely going to hear him so I shoot up, fumbling with his severed dick before stuffing it into his mouth. He sputters and gags on himself, which gives me a strange sense of satisfaction, until he passes out and flops onto the bed. Well, that stopped the noise issue but now I'm looking at a gaping, bleeding hole where Riley's dick should be and a body I can't just leave here.

There's an ottoman beneath the window so I dive into it, pulling out a cluster of bedsheets. Shoving them onto his wound, I then yank a cord out the back of his TV and use it to secure the sheets around his bare ass. All that's left to do is drag Riley into his personal bathroom, flush his detached cock down the toilet and shut the door.

"Everything okay in there?" A voice makes me flinch as I re-enter the bedroom. It's only Penny, the housekeeper. She's a harmless, frail woman who always wears an apron and white frilly hat by choice. "I thought I heard a scream?"

"Oh, yeah. That was me. Accidently caught myself shaving, all good now though." Penny steps closer, her eyes widening at my appearance and I twist to catch sight of myself in a mirror. There's blood sprayed all over my face like something out of a horror movie. I still and then fake a laugh. "It looks worse than it is. Those damn moustache hairs, am I right?" Penny nods shakily, trying to find a smile while she backs away.

"Well, just to let you know dinner is almost served. But you take your time Dear." I thank her, slipping back into the bathroom to wash my face off. Riley is beginning to rouse, muttering something I can't make out so I kick him in the face to knock him out again. It's easier for everyone this way. The world loses a rapist and he gets the benefit he doesn't deserve of bleeding out blissfully unaware. You're welcome.

I make it downstairs just as the first course is being carried from the kitchen to the main hall. Slipping by the butlers, I find my seat via place tag, right beside the Big Cheese himself, Mr. R Leicester. His suit is as sharp as his blue gaze, like two spears of ice stabbing into my chest each time I chance a look. On the outside, I'm cool as a cucumber obviously, but Angus knows the truth. Big Cheese is the only one who I'm emotionally connected to, and that scares the shit out of me. He, along with around twenty others are already present, making my entrance that much more obvious.

"I thought you were sent to change," Cheese scowls. I frown at my new outfit, courtesy of Riley's closet. A white shirt which I've left mostly open and fixed tight with a hair tie at the back, hidden beneath a slim blazer jacket. I've rolled the sleeves up to my elbows and popped the collar high. I couldn't find anything appropriate that would fit for my bottom half, so I opted for a pair of black boxer shorts to poke out the bottom and match my boots.

"She did," Tanya sniggers from opposite me. Luckily the table is soon distracted with their fancy, rabbit food starter that I push around the plate.

"Can we get on with the reason you've gathered everyone to watch my humiliation so I can hit a drive thru on the way home for some real food?" I ask.

"First of all, that shithole of yours isn't a home," Cheese begins. "It's a forgotten hole in the ground you choose to live in. Please tell me, Candy, what do you do with the money I give you each month?" Leaning over Angus in my lap, I open my mouth and let my piece of candy drop out onto a napkin.

"Eat junk food mostly. Hit the casino, skydive. Whatever takes my fancy." It's the truth for the most part, except for the stash I've hidden away in a metal tin. For what, beats me. Seemed like a good idea to have a stash just in case I decide to leave this life behind and make a run for it. Big Cheese won't let me go willingly, so if I find a reason to live, it'll be a complete disappearing act. If. "And secondly?" I prompt when he doesn't continue.

"Secondly, I bailed you out yesterday for the last time."

"You said that last time," I sing with a wide smile. Picking at a piece of flaky fish, I let Angus examine my fork before popping it into my mouth. Ew, no. I immediately spit it back onto the plate, earning a symphony of groans from the rest of the table.

"Candy." Cheese uses that tone which slices through my being. In one sharp word, I'm reminded my collar is tight enough to suffocate and the muzzle on my face will never be loosened, no matter if I succeed or fuck it all up. Clenching my jaw, I lower my head slightly in submission, all humour evading me.

"You've always been a liability but I thought you'd have worked your way through it by now. I've gathered everyone here to hear this from me first hand. You're being benched until further notice Candy. Consider yourself at the bottom of the rankings again, just like you were when I picked you up off the street."

"You can't bench me, I have the Stromboli job tomorrow. I've been working recon for weeks." I scoff, braving a look upwards. His expression remains stoic but everyone at this table knows not to answer back when given an order. Cheese isn't one to act irrationally. He's cool, calculated. I'll wake up with a few fingers missing in the morning and god knows, I need my fingers.

"Don't worry about the job, I've taken care of it." Cheese states, carefully placing down his knife and fork having finished his fishy first course. When I was recruited by a mob boss, these weren't the dinners I was expecting. More like fighting rings where we wrestle for scraps and drink the blood of our fallen foe. I look around the rest of the crew, ignoring the various warning looks to keep my mouth shut.

"What, so you've replaced me? Me?! This is ridiculous. It was just a lousy arrest."

"Not just one arrest, fourteen this year to be exact. And it's only August." I roll my eyes at his statistics. I'm not a numbers person, I'm a fall back person. Taking the hit is what I do best, and in fact that's fourteen arrests I've managed to worm my way out of so to be honest…Where's my motherfucking medal?

"Well, if that's all, I'll be on my way then. I don't want you to waste any of your pretentious food or honoured company on a liability like me." I push myself upright, the chair screeching against the wood floor. Cheese merely shoo's me away with his hand, telling his men to stand down. After all, I'm just some insolent child he created, right? Wrong. I'm Candy motherfucking Crystal. The baddest bitch around because her morals are non-existent and she does whatever her imaginary, gummy version of the Devil tells her to.

"Oh, and Candy?" Cheese's voice reaches me just before I exit. "Send Riley down, we have business to discuss." My eyes fall on the empty seat and the way no one questioned his missing presence. Most likely because I was seen in his room and came down here in his underwear. I know I was probably feeling scared at them finding him, but that's not what's at the forefront of my mind. Instead, it's the bored tone which I'm being addressed with.

"That seems like a job for a higher ranking member of your gang I'm afraid. But when the appropriate person for the job does seek him out, make sure they have my catsuit laundered and returned to the shithole I reside in." I swing around with a flick of my ponytail, finding Nigel leaning against the doorframe.

"Drive me back. Now." There's no questions asked, probably

because like the others, Nigel is happy to get rid of me. That's my life, rejected at every turn.

"Not by me Sweetcheeks," Angus speaks up, trailing behind. I smile weakly at him, slipping into the back of the Mercedes when it's pulled around. Numbness claims me, a flutter to my chest I'm uncomfortable with making me frown.

The one person I had in the world who remembers I exist has turned his back on me. Replaced me. Did I deserve it? Probably, but I didn't think he'd do it. Not after the stunts I've pulled over the years. Cheese has always given me more chances, kept me close by while the others struggled to get his attention. I just had to be regular old me and that was enough, until now. But if I'm not me, who am I?

It's only then I realise I have a steak knife from the dining table held tightly in my hand, the blade biting into my palm. I marvel at the rivets of blood making their own network of veins down my forearm. The thump of my heart quickens at the sight, my eyes glued in fascination.

It's been years since I thought about my childhood and the ways I managed my inner anger. The easiest way is to let it out, physically. Funnily enough, a therapist gave me the idea. She called it 'self-actualisation,' I called it phase one of losing my fucking mind. Pulling my thoughts back to the present, I swivel the knife and press it against the soft muscle of my inner thigh.

"Tell me to stop," I breathe for Angus' ears only. Nigel is too busy driving with the radio turned up to hear me, not that I want a spectator right now.

"Only you know what will make you feel better Candy." I grit my teeth, suddenly realising I'm missing my gum. The one thing that might have distracted me enough to not listen to the gummy bear version of Yoda sitting beside me.

On a long exhale, I press the blade deeper into my skin until it splits. Like a dam breaking, a rush of adrenaline floods my system like a full bodied orgasm. I push harder, biting down on my lip to keep myself from calling out. I don't need the unwanted attention, this moment belongs solely to me.

A gasp leaves my lips as I feel the slice all the way down to my toes. My body hums with pleasure, the pain sparking a need within me I'd forgotten. A need to feel, a need to bleed. All of my pent-up anxiety releases through the cut and before I know it, I've added more and more and turned onto the other thigh. The last is the highest and deepest, just below the true Candy Crush Saga. This time a moan spills from me and I slouch back in the seat, dropping the knife onto the floor.

"Feel better?" Angus asks. I nod my head and groan a 'uh huh' whilst slipping into the blissful aftershock of blood loss. Inside I'm all flutters and tingles, from my lips to my fingers and toes.

"Jesus fucking Christ Candy. What did you do?!" Nigel suddenly shouts into my ear. I jolt upright, having clearly drifted off and not realised we'd arrived already. A silly smile grows across my face, my hand gripping Nigel's shoulder to ease myself out of the vehicle.

"I vented Nige, you should try it sometime."

"Holy shit, look what you've done to my seats!" I leave Nigel to fret over his upholstery, mentally hi-fiving myself for no longer being highly strung. Walking away with a slight stagger to my step, I can already feel the burn of a sting blossoming around my thighs. It's going to hurt like a bitch in the morning, but what better way to feel alive than through suffering?

"Are you sure about this?" I ask Angus right as I'm about to clip the red wire. I'm sweating through my ski mask, pausing with the pliers hovering in place.

"Yes I'm sure, it's always the red one," he hisses at me from my shoulder. He's been the mastermind behind all the preparations today and he sounded so confident, it was easier to just agree. Now though, I'm having a rare moment of self-doubt.

"No, I mean are you sure I should hijack this heist? If Big Cheese has already lost faith in me, what's the point in trying to get back on his good side?" All these years I've been telling myself there's a reason Big Cheese is the only person who messages my phone. Who bails me out every time without fail. Who drops by my basement in the middle of the night to pick up his haul and threaten me to do better next time. Out of the many people he must have at his disposal, he chooses me for the big jobs. A niggling voice that isn't Angus' says that's because I'm expendable and whoever he chose for today must be reliable enough to call in when it's all gone to shit.

"Because he's the closest thing to family you've got. So get in there, grab those diamonds, show Cheese how amazing you are and then…then we're gonna fuck him with his own moustache." My eyes slide to the gummy evil genius, seeing his eyebrows furrowed and a cruel smile on his squishy face.

"But…Big Cheese doesn't have a moustache?"

"Exactly," he growls. "After this job, he'll realise how valuable you are and retire, become too frail to shave and that's when we're gonna fuck him so hard with his own moustache, there will be follicle splinters in his colon and grey fur in his shit."

"Yeah, okay. Let's do that." I nod, done with thinking. I let the mist of instinct settle over me and snip the damn wire, ready to take this operation back for myself. A low beep sounds, deactivating the alarm system into the building. Acting fast, I grab my bat and slink across the roof like a cat in my all black, spandex outfit, making quick work of picking the heavy fire-door lock. Once I hear a click on the other side of the door, I slip the tension wrench and pick back into the hidden phone pocket of my leggings. The tags labelled them as ideal for jogging but I saw their full potential. Master thieving pants.

Once inside the building, I keep to the tunnels where only the electricians and plumbers would usually go. I don't expect to encounter anyone in the middle of the night, but I keep my guard up just in case. Without access to expensive software, I had to scope out this old-style building for the past two weeks. Acquiring the blueprints from some guy called Dan at the local drug den, I studied every inch before casing the building in real life. Even went inside a few times, taking note of the entrance lobby and double elevators that lead to the jewellers I'm here to rob on the top floor.

Angus covers me as I sneak from one corridor into the next, keeping close to the wall. Finding the vent I was looking for, I need to stand on a janitor's trolley to undo the screws with the edge of my pick and then twist them out by hand. I leave the top left one in, swinging the grate aside to throw the bat in before pulling myself up. With the screws squeezed tightly in my fist, I wriggle inside like a worm, bending in half to yank the grate back into place. Easing my fingers through the bars, I loosely fix one screw into the bottom right to cover my tracks and ensure I have a speedy exit when needed. Only then do I start to shuffle my way through the vent system, taking two lefts and a right so I should be directly over the jeweller's showroom.

I don't have time or the tech to mess about with cameras so I'm going for a drop in, grab and hide in the vent until it's safe to leave, approach. There's a cereal bar tucked into my cleavage so I'll be good to camp out until said opportunity arises. Steadying my breathing, I start to pull myself the final distance to the next grate until a voice stops me in my tracks.

"Alarms are disabled and Ace is covering us on the cameras. Let's get this job done quickly and with as little evidence as possible." The deep voice below me sends a flutter of ice through my chest, my lungs beginning to scream as I dare not breathe. The replacement. He, or rather they, must already be here. Slowly edging forward, I peek down through the metal bars to see two men. Both are wearing skull masks which cover half of their faces, black jackets with the hoods pulled up, cargos and leather gloves. One man, standing behind the glass counter, is currently trying on several thick gold chains and assessing himself in the mirror.

"Pack it in Jack, we have business to attend to," the largest of the pair growls. His is the voice I heard before. Thick biceps push against the cotton of his top, the material pulled tightly over his firm physique. I try to imagine what kind of face that voice would suit, but it's hard to tell.

"Yeah, yeah. Spade's on it already. All I can do is stand around and look pretty until we're ready to bust a move," the one named Jack replies. He's tall and lean, although there's a six pack also pushing against his shirt. His cargos are riding low on his hips, giving me a hint of that perfect V women crave as the fluorescent light bounces off him. I can't see the third man they spoke of from this angle, which can only mean one thing. He's tucked away at the back of the room where the locked safe holds the diamonds. My diamonds.

"You can't let them take this from us," Angus' gravelly voice states. He wriggles up beside me, peering at the sight below. "They've taken care of the alarm and cameras so there's no need to sneak around anymore. Get down there and take what's ours." I don't waste the time to second guess Angus; his advice has never steered me wrong before. Well, almost never. Wriggling over the vent until my boots are above it, I grip the Candy Crusher in my hands and roll onto my back. 3, 2, 1...

Smashing my heels as hard as I'm able at this angle, the grate gives way and I quickly shuffle to drop down at the same time the metal clashes against the ground. I'm in a low crouch, ignoring the glint of a gun I notice as I swing my bat at the nearest, masked man. The biggest, evidently. I catch him right in the jaw, throwing my boot into his sternum and swinging against whilst I have the element of surprise. It doesn't last as a body collides with my side, knocking me to the ground.

"Shit looking out Angus," I snarl at the pink gummy bear, uselessly standing and watching nearby. Keeping my bat in my hand, I shove the butt upwards and hear the crack of it connecting with something made of bone. A strangled cry sounds and the drag of metal chains scrapes across my neck as the body rolls off me and slumps to the floor. Sorry, not sorry Jack. Pouncing to my feet, I duck to avoid the fist of the big guy and set my sights on 'Spade.' I don't get a good look at him since I'm busy running and leaping over the counter dividing us.

His fist cracks into the side of my face but I'm way ahead of him, flicking my bat upwards to have a meet and greet with his groin. It always amazes me how quickly one bat can fully disarm a man, his body dropping like a sack of shit at my feet. I bend and snatch the gun from the holster on his hip, flicking off the safety and raising the barrel just in time to stop the big fucker from joining me on this side of the counter. I smirk to, myself, not having been able to plan this better. The diamond drawer is fully open already, inviting me to take what I came for.

"You have no idea who you're fucking with here," Jack's voice pipes up, muffled and nasally. He strides across the room, holding his nose through his mask. His eyes are so green, they're glistening as they assess the length of my body. "Holy shit, she's a girl," he chuckles. The man by my feet moves and I shift the focus of the gun to him instead.

"You, get up." He grumbles something at me, taking his time and using the cabinet to push himself to his feet. This one has piercing blue eyes, one's that are currently picturing the many ways he'd like to kill me I reckon. In any other circumstances, I'd pull up a chair and want to hear all about them, but I can't lose focus on the job at hand. "There's two bags of red diamonds in that drawer. Push one of each into the cups of my bra and I swear, if I feel anything other than plastic touch my nipples, I'll shoot your dick off." I take a moment to unhook my stash of gum and have a victory chew. I've so got this.

Instead of instantly obeying, Spade stares at me intently and then begins to laugh. Full on laughing in my face, causing my confidence to plummet so I hook the gum back behind my teeth.

"I don't get what's so funny," I protest. The other two across the counter have begun to laugh as well, although Jack hisses at the pain it causes him. Lowering the gun to Spade's crotch, I step forward to show I'm serious but he holds his finger up to give him a second.

"Stealing the exact same haul as us on the same night? You must be Leicester's fuck-up." I gasp, those words sinking into the depths of my soul to haunt me later. Leicester's fuck-up. Angus yells at me that there's no time for this but they've already started echoing inside my mind. Leicester's...fuck-up. Not only did he replace me, he told them why. Does everyone know? Am I just a running joke between Big Cheese's crew?

"Candy! Concentrate!" Angus finally snaps me out of it, my eyes narrowing on Spade. I can tell he's smirking by the crinkle beneath his left eye and the way he's now leaning against the cabinet comfortably with his arms crossed.

"Yeah, well. If I'm the fuck-up, then how come it's your blood all over the crime scene?" His blue eyes narrow and I don't hesitate. Moving the gun a few inches over, I shoot his thigh, drop the gun, grab the diamonds and bolt. Screams of agony and anger fill the air behind me, and now it's my time to laugh. Throwing myself over the counter by the open door, I pass through and slam it closed as a body connects with the other side. All that's in front of me is a long corridor with an elevator at the far end.

I don't waste time, with my bat in one hand and the bags of diamonds in the other, I run for it. Halfway down the hall, I've managed to shove the bags into my bra as a voice shouts behind me.

"Stop, Bitch!" It's the big guy who I've yet to find a name for. The elevator doors slide open of their own accord on my approach, an alarm that sounds like the ice cream van tune sounding in my head. They've got a hidden guy in control of the cameras, which means I'm being watched and the stupid shit thinks I'm going to let him trap me in an elevator until the police arrive. I may be naturally blonde, but not *that* dumb. Shoving myself into the fire escape door just to the left, I find myself hurtling down staircase after staircase.

The door slams open behind me, the heavy pounding of footsteps echoing all around until I can't tell how close or far my chaser is. Jumping over the edge of the railing, I land on the next stairwell and lose my footing. Bang. Thud. Ow. I collapse in a heap on the ground, pain working its way through my body and blossoming in my ribs. I choke on my next breath, whizzing and holding my sides.

"Yep. You're the fuck-up alright," the voice says over me, a military-style boot kicking me in the stomach. "That's for Jack. This is for Spade." My mask is ripped off my head, a handful of my hair going with it. There's only a small pause before a blunt object smashes into my face. I'd know the sweet kiss of my Candy Crusher anywhere, but it's not usually being used on me. One more hit is lights out and not even Angus' plea to get the fuck up can help me.

The sound of sirens makes me flinch, my instincts screaming to run if it weren't for the agony that slices through my skull. I grip either side of my head, trying to hold it together and manage to crack an eyelid. The air is sticky, warm enough to take me a full minute to realise I'm outside. Red and blue flashing lights whizz past, allowing a blanket of darkness to fall over me. The rancid scent of a nearby gutter makes me gag, all the shit and rotten egg vibes hitting me full force. I'm in an alley, by the looks of the brick walls closing in on me. My back is propped against a dumpster, my mask lying in my lap. What the fuck happened?

I suddenly remember the events that led up to this point and reach inside my bra, finding it empty except for my God's gift of double C's. Those fuckers even took my emergency cereal bar. Animals. Gently lowering my hands onto the ground, scared to make any sudden movements, I reach out in search of my bat. My bat! My eyelids burst open, the swirling in my gut overpowering the vice tight grip on my head.

The diamonds I couldn't really give a fuck about; I wanted to prove I was worth something and failed. But my bat is one of three prized possessions I have. Angus and my bubblegum subscription being the other two. When one is missing, I'm at a total loss. Incomplete. Inconsolable. I might as well throw myself off the nearest bridge if I have to live without the Candy Crusher.

But I have a better idea. I'm going to find it and then make those bastards pay for ever touching her polished pine surface. I'll become their pink-haired demon, hellbent on haunting their nightmares until the sickening taste of Candy overpowers and chokes them in their sleep. They'll be begging me to take the bat back and arrange a bi-weekly varnishing by the time I'm done, but no. Their blood will be embedded in her every crevice to serve as a reminder to all others who even think about taking her away from me. Don't fucking touch my bat.

There's a threshold between the decent part of town and the slums. Not a physical one drawn across the concrete, but more like a shift in the air. An entity that sends a chill down your spine and sets alarm bells off in your head to run for it. I know because I just crossed it. Not for the first time; I know these deprived streets as well as the upper class ones, and to be honest I prefer it here. It's where I fit in.

Each house on the streets either side of me has some sort of fault. A hole in the roof, garbage strewn all over the front yard, the outer door hanging off its hinges. The critters have free reign over the trash cans because the bin men have stopped coming to this side of town. A few too many dead bodies were crushed in their truck and they went on strike. One house still hasn't had their windows fixed from a police raid a few months back. There was so much coke stashed inside, it made the national news.

My phone begins vibrating in the back pocket of my skin tight black jeans for the hundredth time. I yank it out to deny the incoming call, then wait for the voicemail to come through so I can delete that too.

'*After the mess you've caused, you should be here kissing my goddamn feet-'* boop, delete. I turn the device off and slide it back into its cubbyhole, popping gum bubbles as I walk the streets. There won't be a soul about at this time, not with the sun directly overhead and the addicts still passed out from the night before. I wholly believe vampires are real and places like this are their hangouts. No sunlight, no witnesses, a sea of unconscious bodies to drink from. Bloodsucking heaven.

A car blears its horn behind me, someone who is clearly too lucid to be an addict shouting for me to get out of the road. I look over my shoulder, seeing a collar and tie behind the wheel. Parole officer. Flicking up my middle finger, I slow my pace right down and roll my hips side to side like a walking belly dancer. When I'm not intimidated by the engine revving, the red BMW half mounts the pavement to speed around me.

"That's a driving violation!" I shout, smiling to myself the entire time. I don't know why I've been so sentimental lately about feeling lost and not having a purpose. Clearly my purpose is to piss people off and I'm damn good at doing it. Exiting from the main road, I take to the back streets and hop over a few fences to get to my destination.

A run-down shack which even the wooden panels holding it upright are trying to escape. The tiles on the roof are loose and hanging precariously over the drain pipe, reminding me of an arcade machine with the coins lined up perfectly to drop over the edge. One nudge of my hip and they could all come crashing down. Completely at odds with the rest of the building is a modern back door fitted with a triple lock. Jumping over the broken porch steps and landing on the top one, I bang my fist on the new addition.

"Open up Fletch, I haven't got all day." That's true, since the longer I ignore Cheese's phone calls, the sooner he'll send his goons to find me. There's the creak of a floorboard inside and I share a look with Angus. "I can hear you in there, don't make me destroy your new, pretty door." Cracking the door but keeping on the chain, Fletch's dirty face comes into view.

"B-back up, Candy. There's no way in hell you're coming in here after last time." He really tries to keep the stammer from his voice, bless his cotton socks and sliders. Popping my gum, I shove all my weight into the door and break off the chain so I can stride inside.

"Don't be such a pussy Fletch. I'm here on business from the Big Cheese himself."

"L-L-Leicester sent y-you?" his stammer returns as the colour leaks from his face like those two go hand in hand. I think I'd rather keep my mouth shut in favour of a good complexion but that's not going to happen. Neither confirming or denying his question, I drop onto the lumpy, olive green sofa. I've spent many a night tripping out the other side of my face in this exact spot. "W-well get on w-with it then. Y-you're not w-welcome here."

"Fair enough." Rolling my eyes, I sit forward and dig my elbows into my jeans. "There's a group of men I- we need to find. They go by the names Jack, Spade, Ace and I don't know the other one. Help us out and I'll grant you protection the next time you or your cousin try to pass off coke mixed with washing powder." Fletch begins to fidget, as if embarrassed by his past transgressions. To be honest, I thought it was funny as shit and my nasal passage had never felt cleaner the first time he got me. The second and third time I was sneezing Fairy Non-Bio for a week and that wasn't as fun.

"I d-don't know anyone b-by those names," he lies. I'm like a human lie detector, which is easy because no one ever tells the truth. "N-now get out!" Twisting my lips, I hold up a finger at him to wait while I twist and talk to Angus.

"I'm feeling quite a bit of hostility here Ang."

"Well, you did pull out all of his cousin's teeth with pliers while she was passed out last year." Angus snickers.

"Okay first off, she stole my last piece of gum. Plus I paid for her to have a full new set AND you're the one that told me to do it!" Angus' laugh is dirty and filled with pure evil.

"No teethy, no chewy, no stealy," he chokes out. I remember him saying that exact phrase over and over whilst I was doing it too. I left them all under her pillow for the tooth fairy so I really don't see what the big deal is. When will people understand that just because I have nothing of value to them doesn't mean my possessions aren't valuable to me?

"Anyways, back to today's business. Obviously he's lying, so how shall we make him talk?"

"I-I don't know the g-guys you're looking for!" Fletch protests from across the room, clearly having been eavesdropping on mine and Angus' conversation. Rude. To be fair, it was a long shot but Fletch has a hobby for knowing everyone and their personal brand of poison, and then exploiting it. Rising to my feet, Fletch steps back into the adjoined kitchen to give me a wide berth .

"Shame. I won't be able to report back how helpful you were." There's a bunch of begging and wailing from the fully grown man which I ignore, heading towards the back door when a female voice stops me.

"I have the info you want, but it's going to cost ya," a female voice halts my steps. I turn to see Remi standing at the bottom of the stairs. She's like a pixie at 4 ft 10, but has all the attitude to make up for it. Her brown hair is shaved on one side with a red bandana tied over. Licking her tongue over her teeth, I get a glimpse at the pearly whites.

"Woah, nice dentures Remi! They look better than the real thing." In fact, now that I've seen them, I'm wondering where my red carpet is. I should have been welcomed inside with a glass of champagne for fixing the rotting mess that was in her face. She doesn't seem impressed for some reason, pursing her lips and giving Fletch a hard look that says 'keep your shit together'. "Okay whatever. Name your price. "

"We want a sit down with Leicester. The streets have dried up, there's no customers for us around here anymore. Sure we've done some dodgy shit to get by, but it just goes to show we're committed to getting jobs done." I raise my eyebrow at the speech I bet Remi was practising upstairs since I arrived. Too bad I can see straight through her.

"In other words, you've pissed off the wrong person and you want Big Cheese's protection." The clench to her jaw confirms my suspicions. Leaning against the kitchen counter, I pop my gum and nod slowly. "Fine, I'll get you a sit down but the rest is on you. Now tell me what I came for."

"No fucking way, arrange the sit down first. Then we'll talk." Remi tries to stand straighter in an attempt to look taller, but ends up just pushing her chest forward. As much as I appreciate a good rack on another woman, I don't bat for that team. Aww, man now I'm thinking of bats and start to flex my fingers at the memory of them wrapped around the Candy Crusher. Clenching my hand into a fist, I push the desperation coursing through my veins deep down and shrug.

"Seems to me, you have more at stake here so I'll find my information elsewhere," I bluff. I don't even get to do my dramatic turn with a hair flick included before Remi bites back an answer, stealing my fun.

"Fine. The men you're looking for are part of an elusive biker gang who call themselves The Gambler's Monarchs. They own a bar further down the west coast called The Devil's Bedpost. If it were anyone else, I'd warn them about the heightened security and shotguns displayed on the walls, but you can walk right in." I pout my bottom lip and flutter my eyelashes. Remi pretends she doesn't find me completely adorable but I know the truth. Just to the left of her blank stare, I spot a car pulling up through the window and my heart sinks. A black Mercedes with tinted windows.

"Thank you for your cooperation," I bow my head. Slipping my phone out from my jean pocket, I place it onto the wonky dining table. "I'm going to leave this right here and rest assured, once you turn it on, Cheese will call it almost instantly." Fletch is eyeing me closely and I can't help but jolt at him, his high-pitched screech music to my ears. Exiting via the back door, I race across the yard and throw myself over a wooden fence. Peering through a hole in the slats, I see Nigel creeping around the side of Fletch's building, a pistol in his hand.

"What are you waiting for? Fucking move your ass!" Angus growls. Springing into action, I keep to the back roads whilst running at top speed. Gunshots pierce the air behind me, drawing me to a shift stop. I've lost sight of the building I recently vacated, but with Nigel's marksmanship, I'm certain those bullets wouldn't have been for him. I suppose Remi got her request, she'll just have to wait until Cheese ventures to Hell for their sit down. I'm debating whether to hide out until it's dark to grab the dentures right out of her mouth, after all I paid for them so I have the right to pawn them, until another black car swings around the corner and spots me.

"Shit," I curse at myself. My boots skid out on the dirt track beneath my feet as I scramble into the tightest alley I can find, the Mercedes flying past. I use a dumpster to hoist myself into the next backyard, saluting a few midday risers enjoying their morning joint on the back porch. The next yard presents a minefield of potted plants, most of which being pot itself. I dodge at least half of them, the sound of shattering clay beneath my boots filling the air behind me. Oops.

Hopping the last fence in the row of houses, I glue myself to the wood and shuffle sideways. Angus is humming the Pink Panther theme tune as I move. Reaching the corner of the house I'm pressed against, I brave a look at the main road. Activity has picked up, probably due to the commotion I've caused and no doubt the police will arrive soon, but luckily there's no mad bodyguard or black Mercedes in sight.

Pulling my hood up to cover my hair, I bounce lightly before darting across the street into the alley opposite. There's a bus station not too far from here if I stick to the unconventional routes where vehicles can't follow. Opposing gang markings have been sprayed everywhere possible, even on the shit-brown sofa that has been left out here to rot.

I hear the crunch of wheels turning around the corner up ahead and slide behind a pair of mattresses leaning against the fence. Fuck, it smells like someone died on these, but I manage to resist gagging by holding my breath. It wasn't one of Cheese's men, but not being seen by anyone is for the best. People tend to let their mouths run wild when faced with the barrel end of a gun. Once in the clear, I keep moving. Keep dodging and ducking, sticking to the minimal shadows as the sun beats down from directly overhead. Eventually, I make it to the edge of town with the bus station in view.

Ignoring the main building, I stride around the outside and spot which bus is heading back towards my basement. Even if I'd had the money on me to buy a ticket, I prefer to save my cash for the things that matter. Like gum or cheesy fries. The last of the passengers are getting on board while the driver chucks their bags into the underneath compartment.

Sneaking past the bus, I peer around the corner to wait for the perfect moment. It arises in the form of a tall blonde, with a cocky smirk and drool-worthy dimples. He catches my eye, winking cheekily before throwing something to the right of the driver. Whatever it was bangs on contact with the ground, making the driver flinch and spin around. He dives left, shooing me to jump into the cab with his body colliding in after. We hastily grab a bag each, covering ourselves although I'm sure my laughter can be heard through this duffle. Nevertheless, the driver pulls the lid shut and encases us in darkness.

"How long you riding the baggage express for, love?" The man's voice has a British twinge and is as smooth as his appearance, melting through me like butter on a crumpet. Shoving the bag aside, I can make out his outline by the thin spears of light penetrating the metal shell around us.

"First stop is in forty minutes, I'll walk from there." He doesn't answer but I can feel him smirking. The engine turns over with a deep rumble, juddering straight through my body as the bus edges forward. The man has turned onto his side to face me, his chest bumping mine with the movement around us. I slowly chew my gum, needing to distract myself from the sensations sparking within.

"Forty minutes is quite a while," he says. Another moment passes, another bump in the road making my jeans zipper rub against me in the most delicious way. Is it hot in here or am I just heating up with the force of an inferno? Everywhere my clothing rubs my skin feels taunted, the apple-infused breath of the stranger dousing my rising irritation.

"What's that you're chewing? Trident?"

"Hubba Bubba," he responds and I groan. Fuck me sideways, a man after my own bubblicious heart. He leans forward, blowing a bubble in front of my face. I can't resist gnashing it with my teeth, causing it to pop between us. Wrapping my tongue around the remaining gum, I draw it into my mouth and push the wad behind my back teeth. I'm saving that for later.

The next jostle of the bus sends me flying into his body, our lips crashing together. Like the spark for our fuse, the moment unleashes a whirlwind of passion I'm used to feeling. Men are literal knob sticks, their sole purpose a measly three inches hanging between their legs. Yet I can already feel the bulge digging into my thigh is way bigger, the man attached to it touching me in all the right ways. His apple flavoured tongue devours mine, his thighs pinning me in place while his hands slide under my hoodie and vest to find me braless.

"You were just waiting for me, weren't ya love?" he mutters into my mouth. I don't bother answering, shoving him over until I'm on top and digging my tongue back into his mouth. Bras are my enemy, all tight straps and underwire, but I'm fine with letting... whatever his name is, think I was hanging around hoping for him to join me in the bag compartment of a random bus. On that thought, I break away and steady myself on his firm chest. I can feel this is going to be good and I don't want to be screaming 'Man' at the top of my lungs.

"Give me something to call you by," I demand as his thumbs brush over my pierced nipples. Our jeans are rubbing together, my panties becoming drenched with need.

"Jasper."

"Candy," I reply. I probably should give something false, but no one believes that's my name anyway and there's nothing else that would suit me. I'm sickeningly sweet to the core, ready to slip past your defences and smile innocently as I shoot you between the eyes. It's a cutthroat world I've learnt to master, and people will know my name as I continue to do so.

"At least the name I gave you was real," Jasper smirks. We turn a tight corner, sending the pair of us hurtling across the metallic box. A suitcase thuds me in the back as I roll to a stop. Shoving it aside, Jasper presses down on me from behind and gently curls his hand around my neck.

"Tell me, Candy, are you as delicious as you sound?" Pressing my hand over his, I force his grip tighter before shuffling my jeans down over my ass.

"Why don't you fucking find out?" Using one hand, Jasper frees himself and I feel a dull thud hit my lower back. I bite tightly on my lip, arching my back until my ass is firmly pressed against him. His fingers flick over my clit, making me gasp at the sensation. My body is primed, practically singing for him to take me, yet he slowly plays with my pussy like an addictive new fidget toy. I whimper, nudging back further for more but he chuckles at me.

"So impatient." Releasing my throat, his thumbs pry me open and his cock crashes through my wetness all the way to the hilt. I scream out, my body tightening as I adjust to the sheer size of him. He does it again, the tightest of his grip and my jeans biting into my thighs keeping me in place. I smoosh my cheek against the ground, trying to wriggle forward like a worm to relieve the pressure building up inside me. His cock is like a battering ram, holding me hostage while my g-spot takes a beating.

Suddenly, the bags are sliding this way again and Jasper takes advantage of the turning, shifting me onto my side. Curled up with his arm holding my knees to my chest, he begins to fuck me like a man possessed. Pink spots burst beneath my scrunched eyelids, the pain of his size giving way to a pleasure unlike anything I felt before. Up to now, my best orgasms have been with Peter, my vibrating rabbit, but I can feel the build-up of this one already.

"So. Fucking. Tight," Jasper grinds out. I twist my head for my mouth to meet his, my teeth biting at his tongue, lip and jaw, anywhere I can. How dare he blindside me into a quickie in the baggage compartment when he knew full well he had a demon dick in his pants. My toes curl in my boots, my nails digging into the skin of his forearm. His thrusts are relentless, his apple breath washing over me in heavy pants. I reach between us to rub my clit furiously, too used to getting myself off and needing that friction to push myself over the edge.

"Oh, fuuuuuck!" My screams are drowned out by the roar of the engine, my climax crashing through me like a whip. My pussy squeezes around Jasper so tightly, he has to stop moving while I ride wave after wave. I pulse against the ridges of his dick, my hips rolling in time with the sensations. Knocking my hand away, Jasper releases my legs and circles my clit with his fingers, letting me flatten out and moan continuously. "That was fucking incredible," I sigh to myself.

"Don't get comfortable love. We've still got about half an hour left until your stop, you ain't seen anything yet."

CANDY

I duck behind a trash can, watching as the bus pulls away. My lips are still tingling from the last kiss Jasper gave me, his cheeky smirk peering out from between the bags as the trunk was shut. I unhook the mixture of raspberry and apple gum out from behind my teeth, churning the flavour around my mouth. What a man. What a demon dick. I reckon the best part of him is the fact I won't see him again. The dark gave us a sense of anonymity, the tussling of the bus heightening our pleasure.

Even when the brakes were slammed on and sent us flying into the rear panel, he managed to stay nestled deep inside me with the blaring horn masking his laughter. Deep being the key word. As I straighten from my hiding place and begin to walk, I have to hold my lower abdomen. Essentially, my uterus has just taken one hell of a beating, a feeling which will stay with me for a while yet.

My basement apartment is a few miles back and the sun has begun to dip low by the time I've hobbled to the end of the block. Sphinx, the fugly little shit, is waiting to welcome me back with a hiss until I shoo him along with my boot. Making it to my place, my boots ring out on the stone steps down to the front door. My key is hidden in the lantern which doesn't work, to the left of the door.

"Home sweet home," Angus pipes up. I was wondering where he'd got to but wasn't concerned. He usually gives me some privacy when things turn heated, either alone or with others. His squishy pink form shuffles into the basement ahead of me, although my attention is on grabbing the items I need. It's no coincidence Cheese's men were at Fletch's earlier, and if I'm being honest, I'm surprised to see my place isn't turned upside down.

Grabbing my only backpack, I pry the loose bottom out of the kitchen cupboard and begin to fill it with the necessities. The cash-filled metal tin, my hidden stash of gum, multiple boxes of fuchsia hair dye. Moving towards the hanging rail, grabbing some toiletries and snacks on the way, I quickly roll up two pairs of PVC trousers and several black vests. Shaking out of the baggy hoodie, I shrug on my leather jacket and share a nod with Angus.

I pause briefly at my front door, needing a deep exhale. This is really it. I figured I'd be under Big Cheese's thumb for my entire life. It's not like I have anywhere to go or anything else to do. Not until my bat was stolen. Now I've got to rain payback down on some thieving fuckers, and then who knows. If I can grab a fake passport along the way, maybe I could be in Ireland by the weekend. Sipping on whiskey with a short, ginger leprechaun whose name I can't pronounce.

Opening my front door, I make it one step outside when something solid connects with my face. Crashing into my cheek, I collide with my door before catching myself. Several boots surge at me, hands grabbing and fists punching all over my torso. I stupidly reach for the Candy Crusher out of my backpack on instinct, leaving my ribs wide open. Knuckles pummel into me until a shoulder finally takes me down, a strike to the face putting me out of my misery. I'm still awake, but the ringing in my ears and double vision help to ease the pain.

I'm shifted onto my front and my arms are wrenched behind my back, secured with a cable tie if I'm not mistaken. Being rolled over again, I get my first clear view of the man hovering over me. Nigel.

"If you wanted to get kinky Nige, you only had to say. This seems a little excessive," I choke out. The coppery taste of blood seeps into my mouth, probably from where my lip and jaw are throbbing. He grimaces, slapping a piece of duct tape over my mouth before hoisting me up. The backpack still on my back falls forward to knock into the back of my head as my ass is sticking up by Nigel's face. A bodyguard thoughtfully hangs back to close my door, the rest of them nowhere to be seen from this angle.

Throwing me into the back seat of his car, the door is slammed shut and the lock clicks. My head clenches with the threat of a killer headache but I manage to hold it at bay. It can have it's wicked way with me later, but for now I need to focus. Nigel stops outside the blackened out window to have a mother's meeting with his pals, like the stupidest kidnapper in history. Dragging my legs up onto the seat, I sit on top of them so I can pry my pocket knife from my boot. The zip tie doesn't take long to cut, although I keep my hands behind my back for show after tucking my knife away.

Nigel eventually slides into the driver's seat to eye me in the rear view mirror. I cock my eyebrow, sitting awkwardly on my bag with my hands holding each other. Putting the vehicle in drive, he starts a procession of Mercedes' as if I'm the Queen. Biding my time, I let him escort me out of town while images of me slitting his throat start running through my mind. My pocket knife is still in my hand, the blade running the length of my fingers. I'm just getting to the good bit in my imagination when Nigel indicates to turn right instead of left at the usual junction.

I perk up on my knees now, more interested in where he is taking me if not directly to the Big Cheese himself. The further we drive, the less buildings are around. Keeping off main roads, even the street lamps can't comfort me as the darkness above sets in. Angus hops up onto the door handle, balancing whilst trying to get a better view of outside.

It's when we begin to ascend that the worry starts to really settle in. The road becomes narrower, barely big enough for one vehicle so we're screwed if another comes the opposite way. A short metal railing protects us from the lengthening cliff face, in some parts anyway. In others, it seems a vehicle has gone over the edge and taken that section of the railing with it.

Nigel switches his full beams on, giving me a view of the road ahead. There's a break in the railing coming up on a corner. Leaning forward, I begin to retch and squeal behind the duct tape, causing him to slow right down.

"What the fuck are you doing?!" he shouts. I continue to make as much noise as possible, imitating a movement I've seen Sphinx do many times. Back curved, head bowed, shoulders raised. Nigel curses, switching his hazards on to warn the others behind to slow down before reaching back and ripping the tape off my mouth. "What the hell is wrong with you now?"

"Gum hair-ball. I'm gonna heave all over your carpet if you don't let me spit it out of the window." He tuts and turns back around, starting to speed up again. I gag, letting my tongue hang out. My acting is so good, I do start to feel vomit working its way up my pipes. On my next hurling sound, Nigel mumbles something about me being the bane of his life and slides open the window closest to the cliff's edge. I shuffle sideways, leaning up on my knees to stick my head out of the window.

"See ya," I smirk quickly, kicking upwards and throwing myself out. My side hits the road first, the concrete bruising whatever ribs Nigel and his friends didn't. I grab for the ground but my hands meet air as I bounce over the edge and free fall. The sky is pitch black up ahead, only the shadow of Nigel running in front of his headlights visible as I sail downwards. Toward what, I have no idea. Angus is by my side, pretending to breaststroke through the air before a pink parachute bursts out of his back and he waves me goodbye. Little fucker.

My back smashes into a formidable surface, making me cry out as icy cold water grabs me and yanks me further beneath. My mouth fills with water, my arms flailing to breach the top and splutter it back out. There's nothing but black everywhere I look, the sounds too loud to process what is coming from where.

A wave strikes me with the force of a hammer, pushing me beneath the water once more. I roll and tumble, unable to fight against the current. Something jagged slices against my leg, the wound instantly stinging like a bitch. Thrown into what I'm guessing is the side of the cliff, due to the sheer size of the rock, I pry my fingers into any gaps I can and drag myself upwards.

Finally finding the surface and able to breathe again, I move as quickly as I can to keep moving upwards before another wave comes to batter the shit out of me. The rock cuts into my hands with each pull. Every small movement feels like weights are dragging me back down, my body too cold and numb to respond properly.

After an eternity of slugging up the side of the cliff, my hand lands on a flat surface. The other copies, my biceps shaking with effort to heave my body up onto it. The ledge isn't big, barely wide enough for me to huddle onto, but as I shuffle all the way back, I notice a tiny outcrop overhead sheltering me. Like a miniature cave built for someone Angus' size, wherever that shithead is. I'll be having some serious words when he gets down here.

My clothes are glued to my body but I can't bring myself to peel them off, the thought makes me shiver more. Manoeuvring each arm out of my backpack, I manage to just about cross my legs and settle it on my lap. My cereal bars are soggy as shit, but I eat the whole box of them regardless, the energy having been zapped out of me by the cold.

After a while, the crash of the waves becomes therapeutic and my body eases against the rock. Falling asleep would be foolish, but passing out doesn't seem like it's in my control at this stage. Not with the blood leaking from my palms and leg, or the deep rooted agony of my ribs in this crinkled position. No, not in my control at all...

CANDY

It's funny how much perspective the daylight can bring. I'm glad no one was around to witness my dramatics from last night, although I did leave a few tourists stunned when I crawled up onto the shore from the sea. It turns out all of my climbing in the dark barely got me a few meters above sea level, and with the dawn of a new day, the sea became utterly tranquil. There wasn't a wave in sight when I eased myself back into the water, keeping close to the cliff just in case I saw a shark fin. A few bends and about a mile of swimming later has brought me here, wherever the fuck I am.

The short, older woman appears through the beaded curtain separating her rooms. I thought she was joking when she ushered me into her wooden beach hut, but it's like wonderland in here. An external canopy hanging over two deck chairs is the same blue and white stripes as the walls inside. The main room is a slim oblong shape with a kitchen unit and small bathroom off to the side. My mind nearly exploded when she removed the centre section of the bed and flipped it around into a dining table with bench seats. Each piece of art is cleverly concealing a shelving unit or cupboard; I know because I've investigated every single one. There's a freaking sewing machine and reams of material stashed behind the seashell framed mirror, which also doubles as a sewing table.

"So you full on live here? Like...permanently?" I ask. The woman smiles wisely, fixing us some tea. Her hair is pure silver, falling down her back in two long plaits. A flowy floral dress covers her petite body, right down to the brown sandals on her feet. There's something fascinating about her but I can't quite decide what it is.

"She's free," a gruff voice pipes up from the bench seat beside me. I twist with a scowl, glaring at Angus' stupidly innocent expression.

"There you are, you little shit! Feeling good about yourself, are ya? One hiccup with the mob and an unplanned skydive and you bail on me?! Some friend you are." I sit back with a huff, folding my arms as the woman slowly lowers herself down opposite.

"Drink your tea," she smiles. "Everything looks better after some tea." Angus mutters something about poison but I'm not listening to him right now. Instead, I relax into the cushion and watch the sea through the hut's open doors. The beach is getting busier now, various colours of umbrellas being plunged into the yellow sand while kids rush to strip down to their bathing suits and run into the water. My clothes are on the retractable washing line outside, swaying gently in the much needed breeze.

Even though I'm firmly ignoring him, Angus is right. This woman, Liz, is freer than I have ever been. The hut isn't large or grand, but it's hers and the look of pride in her eyes says it all. And despite the space only being big enough for one of us to move around in at a time, she blindly welcomed me in. No questions, no judgement. It's refreshing.

"How long have you lived here?" I ask over the rim of my mug.

"Almost fifteen years now," she smiles, her pale eyes dulling slightly. "My husband and I couldn't conceive. As much as we tried, it just wasn't meant to be. Then, when he passed, I couldn't continue living the life we'd built together without him there. But not living at all would be an insult to his memory, so I chose to start fresh. I've never been the housewife type anyway. All I need is the necessities and this view." We stare out at the sea again, the ripples glimmering under the sun of yet another glorious day. "You're welcome to stay for as long as you need, I can teach you to spear fish for dinner."

"Ahh man, that sounds epic," I grin. Spotting the spears leaning just inside the door, sudden visions of me spearing Liz through the chest burst to life in my mind. A voice which is usually dormant speaks up, echoing around the inside of my skull. *'Kill her. Dump her body in the sea. Take her hut and freedom for your own.'*

"Is everything okay?" Liz asks, noticing my frown. Her hand gently touches my arm and I flinch, spilling my tea all over her table/bed. Jumping up, I stagger backwards until my foot drops out of the doorway. I reach out for the door frame, causing one of the spears to fall and land perfectly in my palm. The glint of the metal draws my attention, the razor sharp tip filling me with trepidation. I used to joke with Angus that I have internal tourettes , and that all the things my brain says are bad suddenly become my obsession. Like an impulse. And a blade like this, it's something special. I need to know how much damage it can cause, how much blood it takes to cover the entire handle. *'Do it. Relish it. Feel it.'*

"Candy," a female voice breaks through my thoughts. I look up to see Liz has risen too, slowly creeping forward with her hand outstretched. It would take merely one jerk of movement to slice the vein in her wrist. My conscience wouldn't mind, it's tainted anyway but something tells me this time would be different. This one would stick with me, grate on me. Forcing myself to take a step back, I drop the spear at her feet.

"You're a good person, Liz. You need to be careful who you welcome into your home." In a flash, I grab my backpack from the floor and yank my damp clothes off the washing line, stuffing them inside. My boots are also hanging by their laces until I unhook them and stuff them under my arm. In a flimsy white robe, I bolt across the beach as fast as my bare feet can manage amongst sinking into the sand.

Reaching the promenade, I spot a series of outdoor showers divided up by concrete slabs. They're mostly empty due to the crowds only starting to arrive, but some hardcore surfers have rested their boards against the side after catching some morning waves. I keep running until I reach the end of the block, spotting a folded towel, pair of denim shorts and pink bikini top piled up beside a shower in the middle.

One by one, I dart around the dividers before peering over to see if the next one is free. Catching up with a tall blonde who is standing beneath the spray, I perv on her as she starts wrestling with her wetsuit and quickly shrug off the robe. Throwing it over the concrete block when she's not looking, I grab her clothes and drag them on just enough to cover my nips and minnie moo before making a full on run for it. I do the shorts button along the way and fix the tightness of the bikini top once hidden behind a thick tree trunk.

Digging around in the denim pockets, I find a twenty, a hair band and a cube of cherry gum. Fucking score. Fixing my hair into a high ponytail, I stuff my feet into my still wet boots. They squelch as I walk but it's better than getting blisters on the red hot sidewalk. All that survived in my backpack from my impromptu swim is my metal tin of money luckily. I'll need that mula to replace the year's supply of gum and hair dye I lost. There's a commotion to my left about some girl's clothes being stolen so I veer right, jaywalking across a four-lane road. Tyres skid around me, making my ears ring.

"Watch where you're going, assholes!" I shout at the drivers, flipping them off as they blast their horns at me.

"How fucking inconsiderate," Angus pipes up from where he's hanging off my backpack strap. Making it to the other side, I let my nose do the directing, following the mouth-watering smells to a series of food trucks parked in a long line. I halt at the strong scent of onion, ordering myself a monster hot dog with all the toppings. The cute trainee gives me a large Pepsi max for free, his number scrawled across the side of the cup.

"Oh, you are way too innocent to handle someone like me," I chuckle, walking off. Munching away, I'm just thinking to myself how this day has turned itself around when I see a glimpse of a funfair through a gap between the trucks. No fucking way! Stuffing the hot dog into my face one last time, I chuck the rest and hastily manoeuvre around the people strolling by. Crossing the road is as successful as last time, my focus centered on the sounds of screamed laughter and flashing lights up ahead. My feet can barely keep up with myself and soon I'm at the entrance gates.

I used to sneak out of the group homes almost every night, which rapidly got me kicked out and placed elsewhere. One was near a funfair just like this one, and even though I spent most of the night nudging the coin machines to pay out until an attendant caught on, I loved the atmosphere. A body barges past me, tutting loudly and I zero in on him. Six foot one, brown hair that resembles dry noodles sitting on top of his head, camo jacket. I'll be seeing you later.

Letting my giddiness rise, I enter the funfair grounds and take my time to just walk around. I want to see every ride, soak in the smiling faces. This is where people come to let their inner wild child out, to spend a shitload of money to win pointless shit and laugh about it. It's like coming home. Rides whizz overhead, a Ferris wheel looms over the sea at the end of the pier. A couple steps into a sphere with leather seats and harness, holding hands tightly as the security checks are performed until they're shot into the air like a slingshot. Grinning to myself, I pinch a piece of popcorn from the top of someone's bucket when they aren't looking and make my way into the arcade.

The sounds are louder here, the colours brighter. It's like looking at my brain from the inside, all fluorescent lights, rigged games and the odd creepy clown looming in the corner. I stop by the whack a mole, showing a bunch of kids how to get on the scoreboard and leaving my reel of tickets for them to collect. One day, they'll write my biography and pinpoint the arcades as where it all went wrong.

Rewarded and congratulated for battering a dead mole with a hammer repeatedly, what's not to love.

Meandering through the machines, I stop abruptly in the middle of the aisle as my jaw drops. "Angus!" I shout, dodging everyone in the way until I'm standing in front of a claw machine against the back wall. Inside, a sea of gummy bear teddies in all colours are littered across the bed of beady white shit, a bright pink one lying in the middle. "Oh my em gee, It's you!"

Finishing a couple of quarters out of my back pocket, I bend down to fake tying my boot whilst twisting the silver knob on the machine twice. An old hack I picked up watching a 'street magician' do it once, to trick the machine into thinking it's having a maintenance check. Standing, I use the joystick to ease the claw directly over Angus' stuffed doppelganger and watch as it lowers before clamping into place. A small crowd gathers around to gasp as he drops into the prize pit and I scoop him up into my chest.

"You never try to squeeze me like that," Angus grumbles. I roll my eyes as I walk through the crowd, swaying to the music playing in the background. Noodle head who barged past me earlier catches my eye, his wallet sticking out of his back pocket. I don't even need the money, but I do need to prove a point. Sashaying closer, I wait until he's bent over a Pac-man machine before sliding it straight out of his jeans. Not having space to conceal it in these tiny shorts or the bikini top, I slide it under my backpack and hold it there as I hastily exit.

"What the- where's my wallet?!" I hear behind me, smiling into the fluffy head of Angus 2. Rounding the rides and mile long queues snaking around them, I come to the pier railing overlooking the water below. Flicking open the wallet, I pocket the cash and ignore the various cards. A debit card, driving license, ID, Walmart rewards card, nothing important.

Checking a hidden compartment in the back, I find a playing card. The four of clubs. On the other side in black, bold lettering is 'The Devil's Bedpost,' and an address printed below. Twirling the card between my fingers, I chuck the wallet into the sea and frown in thought. How had I forgotten all about the Candy Crusher?

"Well, you did almost die," a gruff voice answers my thought.

"Don't be dramatic Angus. A bit of free falling into a stormy sea and a dash of hypothermia never killed anyone." Pushing off the railing, I spot a few men in security outfits looking my way. Noodle head is nearby, hunting through the crowd for who-knows-what. Shrugging, I duck into the crowd before he reaches me and sneak my way off the funfair grounds. It's a shame to leave so soon but I'll return, right after I've played a real life version of whack a mole. One I'm going to call whack the bastards who stole my bat.

CANDY

Hoisting myself up using the licence plate, I settle my butt on the hood of a red pick-up truck. I've been saving the cube of cherry gum in my pocket all day, but now my stomach is beginning to rumble, I pop it into my mouth. Best way to stay skinny is to trick my stomach by constantly chewing. A few life or death chases is always helpful for my figure too. Angus is sulking in my backpack with his teddy twin, unless they're doing something else in there...

The Devil's Bedpost isn't anything like what I thought it would be. Remi mentioned it being simply a bar, but there's nothing simple about the building across the parking lot. This is a four storey nightclub dropped in the middle of nowhere.

A huge panel hangs at the very top with the club's name printed in shining chrome and surrounded in lights. Vertical panels on the outside have been painted a slick black with playing cards embossed into the wood. Hidden spotlights beneath the outcrop brighten the entrance, a revolving glass door with matching chrome handles. Unnecessary yet impressive. But it's the row of motorcycles along one side that catches my attention.

I worked a job for Cheese once which involved hot wiring

motorbikes and riding them to an abandoned locker. His men would head back a few days later to take the bikes apart and rebuild elsewhere when the trail for them had gone cold. Best part of the job was that I learnt to ride on the beastliest machines out there. After the MTT Turbine Streetfighter, any bike I could have afforded for myself paled in comparison so I didn't bother wasting my money. These bikes though, I reckon I could get pretty far using one of those as my getaway vehicle.

Keeping a sweet, custom-painted Harley Davidson Dyna in my sights, I slide off the truck and sneak around the car park. There's not many other vehicles around now that the moon is directly overhead. It took me all day to find this damn place, on and off buses and walking until my boots had dried. I slipped my leather jacket over the bikini top as the chill of night set in and let my hair loose from its tie.

A couple of guys burst out of the swinging doors as I duck behind the bike, singing and swaying all the way to the pick-up. I try to spot the designated driver between them, thinking I'm in for a treat if they ram into the building on my behalf. He then presents himself, striding out of the saloon with his strides way too controlled for my liking. Spoil sport.

The engine revs as I turn my attention back to the black and purple beauty before me. Running my hand over the plush, leather seat, a delicious shudder rolls through me. The thought of riding this metal monster has my nipples standing to attention, rubbing against the nylon bikini top. The truck's headlights pass just in time for me to locate and unhook the connector box containing the wires. I then squint to make out the parallel ports and figure out which wire I'll need to cut in a hurry. Keeping it in my palm, I then push the box back into place so it's sticking out. Job done.

On the other side of the porch walkway, the lights inside the bar turn off, plunging me into darkness. I shuffle to press my back against the wood, waiting patiently in the shadows for the perfect time. It's an ideal night, cloudless with the stars sparkling. Not a sound can be heard except for the chirping of crickets in the random potted bushes around. It baffles me why anyone would put so much money into a bar this far away from civilization. The back yard is practically a desert with mountains visible in the distance. Diverting from the main road, the only way in and out is by the beaten-up dirt track I walked miles down to get here.

I suppose that's the point, I muse to myself. Anyone who comes here does so for that reason alone, meaning no stragglers stop by unannounced. Until now. Knocking my boots together, I pull my phone out of the backpack's side pocket, willing it to switch on. No such luck. Even if it wasn't waterlogged, I reckon it'd be out of battery anyway. Blowing a large gum bubble, the pop echoes around the empty lot. Okay, I'm bored - time to move.

I've already done some recon, finding a total lack in the security system department. That's men for you; they think being 'man of the house' is enough until a pink-haired assassin jumps through the window while they are snoring and anally fucks them with a knife. I haven't done that yet, but I sure thought about it. Leaving my backpack (and Angus) tucked beneath the Dyna, I pull myself onto the railing and monkey climb up the column. Reaching the overhanging porch, I roll onto my back and listen for any sounds around me. No snoring greets my ears and I scowl at the sky.

My body is flat beneath the row of windows on this level which look down onto the bar. Even without clear vision, I can tell the décor is mostly black or dark wood like the exterior, with glints of chrome throughout. I can make out a hit of a seating area, but the only lighting I have to go by is emanating from behind the bar in the form of several glass door fridges and a series of spotlights hanging above the mirror wall. Further up still, the moon reflects off a metallic moose head hanging like a hunter would showcase his latest kill, and laying across the antlers is the Candy Crusher herself!

Adrenaline surges through me, the need to have her in my hands making me twitch. I reach for the pocketknife I keep in the sole of my boot when I notice the window down the end is slightly open. Army crawling over, I pry my fingers inside and unhook the latch it was left on and clearly forgotten about. Maybe I should take that as a sign. No alarm, window on the latch. These guys must have a reputation to not be fucked with, but I never cared much for gossip. I prefer what I know and what I can see. And I see my bat.

Carefully opening the window, I shrug off my jacket before slugging inside. There's a sheer drop to the ground below, but the wooden slats across the ceiling give me the best idea. Grabbing my jacket, I hook one arm over each side of a slat and wrap the material around my wrists.

"That's a terrible idea," Angus' muffled shout from my backpack fills my head. "I love it!" Smirking, I exhale and throw myself off the ledge. The jacket holds, but then I just hang there like a dead sloth with his talons stuck. Kicking my legs back and forth, I drag the material and shuffle forward bit by bit. My arms are being wrenched from their sockets and my ribs are screaming in agony but small giggles escape my lips. I'm getting closer. Halfway now.

I kick my legs high, swinging back with all my might to edge along faster. She's so close, I begin to salivate because I'm going to run my tongue all over that fine piece of pine. My chewing gum drops out along the way but I don't care. All of my energy is focused on victory dancing along the dirt road out of here. On the next swing, my sweaty hand slips through the leather and I lose my grip. The jacket fails me and I'm falling until my back collides with something solid. The breath is knocked out of me, causing me to wheeze and lie still, my chest heaving with short pants.

Releasing my grip in the offending piece of clothing I'll never wear again, I feel around me and realise I'm on something long and firm, just a little larger than the width of me. The fucking bar. Luckily this place is closed because I'm spread out and temporarily immobile, fighting to draw a full breath into my lungs. Heaving myself up on a groan, my eyes are pinned on the moose shaped bat holder up above. There seems to be a railing above the mirror, suggesting there was once or will be curtains hung at some point.

"Someone will have heard that," Angus' voice breaks through

my thoughts again. He likes to state the obvious when I'm half dead.

"Thank you, asshole," I hiss. Forcing myself to stand, I leap across the gap between the bar and the counter, smashing a few bottles at the same time. My boots crunch loudly as I plaster myself to the mirror, reaching as high as my tip toes will allow. There's no plan for when I reach the railing, in my mind I'll do some epic backflip and magically land beside the moose, clinging to the wall like Spiderman.

My fingers just graze the metal, making me curse and stretch even harder. I'm well aware these ribs are never going to heal properly unless I give them time to, but quitting isn't an option. The Candy Crusher has kept me safe so many times, now it's my turn to save her. Once I figure out how to get her down, I'll head upstairs and let her reap all the vengeance she likes. The idiots blissfully sleeping won't know what hit them. Well I'll tell ya, blunt force trauma - that's what.

ACE

"She knows this is a two-way mirror, right?" Jack muses out loud across the poker table, although no one bothers to answer. We're too busy staring at the pair of inked tits currently smashed against our hidden window in a bikini top two sizes too small. I bet my black eyed and broken nosed friend wishes we'd installed that waterfall feature he begged for over the bar mirror last year. Taking the cigarette out from between his lips, he flicks the ash into the tray. "Guess I'd better put her out of her misery."

"Get fucked," Malik growls. "If anyone is about to throw the trash out, it'll be me." He tosses his hand into the centre, revealing a three of a kind and rises slowly to lean on the table. Malik has spent years grabbling for control over his short fuse, and most of the time he's successful. But then something unplanned crashes into our bar and plummets him back into old habits. His shoulders are bunched and the vein that pops out of his temple when he's furious is on full display. He's going to be pissed all night for sure, although I knew she was coming all along.

The hidden cameras tripped my phone's alarm the moment she stepped on our land and I've been secretly watching her under the table since. I could have told the guys, but I knew they'd race to scare her off and I was curious to see what she does. Besides, seeing Malik's face now is everything.

"She clearly only wants her bat back. Just give it over and she won't be our problem anymore," I state, rolling my eyes.

"She shot me in the fucking leg!" Spade chimes in. Another reason I didn't announce her arrival. With a thick cast on his femur, Spade has been even more pissy than usual. "If the bat means that much to her, I say we strap her down and make her watch it be shredded."

Shrugging, I skid my chair back and head over to the mini bar we've installed back here. Pouring a double shot of whiskey, I turn to watch Malik and Jack rush to storm out of the room first. *Another day, another problem,* I sigh to myself. I'm the quiet one out of the four of us, preferring to lose myself in a video game than the shit Malik gets us into.

Downing the drink, I refill the glass and head back to offer it to Spade before he gets any ideas of hopping up on his crutches and joining in. I have no doubts that he could, considering he rode his own Ducati to hospital after the robbery, but the nurse gave him strict instructions to rest. Whether the bullet went straight through or not, the wound needs a chance to heal before he does himself more damage.

"Here," I mutter, offering out an Airpod. Spade pushes it in his ear whilst I use the other, propping my phone against his now empty glass on the table. I've got the whole building wired in case someone we've pissed off tries to strike back against us.

Using night-vision on the camera installed in the corner of the mirror, Spade and I have a perfect view of Malik rounding the pink-haired intruder just as she jumps and catches hold of the railing. He grabs her waist and she immediately flails around in his grip like a worm having a panic attack. Kicking wildly, her boot smashes into his jaw, temporarily stunning him. He tries to grab at her again, but ends up aiding instead as she manages to stomp on his shoulder and give herself the boost she needed. Pulling herself up with her boots stomping up the mirror, she hooks her leg over and disappears from my view.

Swiping the screen, I scroll through the different viewpoints until settling on one from across the room. Wobbling slightly, she sits herself upright with the pole between her thighs and uses the metal moose fixture to pull herself up to standing. Grabbing her bat with a squeal, she then runs her tongue up the side of it and hooks herself over the moose so she's sitting on his face with her legs spread wide across the antlers. *Lucky moose*, I smirk to myself. Catching myself, I immediately wipe the grin off my face before Spade notices.

Outside of the four of us, I avoid other people as much as possible, women in particular. I'm all for brief entertainment via a camera but in reality, this girl seems like a whole load of trouble we don't need. She's as unpredictable as the night at the jewellers, and despite myself, I'm as intrigued watching her through the surveillance screens now as I was then. It's like porn I suppose, addicting to watch yet bland in real life. Swinging her bare legs, the pink-haired imp giggles to herself while resting her cheek on the bat.

"You're only making this harder on yourself," Malik calls out, flicking the lights on so he can see her. His back is to the camera but I can tell he's fuming. It's visible in the rigidness to his stance as he stands directly underneath her, probably in hopes she'll fall. Laughter rings out in response, the crazy chick switching positions so both legs are dragging over one side like a hammock. Jack appears from wherever he's been hiding up to now, a double-barrelled shotgun resting over his shoulder.

"I say we play fairly," his nasally voice echoes into the microphone. "One shot and a stamp to the face and we'll let you go. Tit for tat." Our intruder doesn't seem bothered by Jack's appearance, in fact she hasn't even looked down. She's too focused on stroking her bat and muttering to herself.

"If we're being technical," she shouts back, "I already received a beating for your nose job before I woke up in whatever random alley you dumped me in." I feel the heat of Malik's gaze glaring at me through the mirror before I look up to see it. I may have left out that tiny detail, since I had to hang back to wipe the hard drives and saw her body lying in the stairwell. With the police on their way, I couldn't bring myself to leave her there so I'd thrown her over the back of my bike on the way out. I don't know why and I didn't think I'd have to explain myself, but I hadn't expected her to show up here either.

"As for the shooting part, I reckon separating me from my beloved has been traumatic en-" My focus shifts back to the screen as her voice cuts abruptly. She's rolled over across the antlers, her gaze fixed on Jack. "You!"

Throwing herself out of her cubby hole, she squeezes her thighs around the bat and grabs the railing at the last moment to swing down onto the bar. Ignoring Malik, which makes him bristle further, she creeps towards Jack like a crazed monkey. I can see her through the mirror again now, her face shifting between multiple expressions. "What the fuck happened to your face?"

"Erm...you did, you bloody lunatic!" Jack spits, his British accent bleeding through his irritation. Grabbing the gun tightly in his fist, his knuckles turn white but he has yet to aim it at her. He's clearly as confused as the rest of us. So much so, when she reaches out to thread her fingers through his blonde hair, he lets her. She traces the length of his jaw, using her thumbs to push his mouth up into a smile to inspect his dimples. Only then does she jerk back, reaching for her bat and jumping down on the other side of the bar.

"Wait. You're one of them? Did you follow me to the bus station? Are you...the spy who shagged me?"

"I have literally no idea what you're talking about," Jack drawls. She raises her bat the same time he lazily flicks the gun around for the barrel to face her. Malik steps in closer, the three of them facing off in a triangle with the bar in the middle.

"Oh, I see how it is. Your buddy is here now so you've got to act all cool. Go ahead and pretend you didn't ride in the baggage compartment or gutter punch me in the cunt yesterday. But you could at least remember my name."

"I don't know your name, Crazy Girl?!" Jack argues but Malik signals for him to be quiet. His eyes are fixed on the girl who's interest has shifted back to her bat, picking a piece of invisible dust from the tip and flicking it away. My guess is either Malik's calculated nature can't figure out the woman before him or he's trying to piece together the puzzle of what's happening here like the rest of us. Spade nudges me at this point, drawing my attention away from the scene unfolding before me. I frown at him, until he mouths a name that makes my gut drop. Oh shit. Shooting to my feet, I push Spade back down when he tries to join and run through the connecting double doors.

"Jasper!" I shout. The ball drops, causing Jack and Malik to surge forward but they're a second too late. Pinkie has already made a dash for the exit. A gunshot rings out as Jack aims for her, just as she lunges aside. The bullet shatters the glass of the revolving door and she dives through, yelling a 'thank you' with her middle finger raised high. By the time Malik has hurdled over the bar and I've run to join his side, getting my shoe stuck on a piece of gum on the way, we burst into the night to find she's disappeared.

"Where the fuck is she?!" Malik barks at me. I feel my pockets for my phone, realising I've left it on the table. Jack slams through the middle of us, running into the night with his shotgun reloaded and raised. We follow him down the porch steps, taking opposite directions.

My role amongst us isn't usually a physical one, but with Spade out of action and our chance at finally finding Jasper on the line, I'll do what it takes. We've been after Jack's twin for years now, ever since he double crossed us and took our fortune with him. Despite all of my hacking, I haven't been able to find a trace of him and we'd begun to wonder if he was even still alive.

I cross the parking lot, looking beneath the odd vehicle which has been left to be collected tomorrow. A single rock being kicked has me spinning around at the exact moment the headlights of Malik's bike light up and the engine revs. Skidding out on the dirt road, the back wheel catches my bike next, causing them all to fall one by one like dominos. Then, she shoots forward into the night with her cackle trailing behind. I merely stand there until the crack of a shot explodes beside my ear.

"Jesus fucking Christ, Jack!" I shout, pressing my hands against my ears. A high-pitched ring slices through me, the shear agony throbbing through my head flooring me. I vaguely realise Jack has ditched the gun and jumped on his bike, chasing after her while Malik picks me up from the ground. Fury churns in his dark eyes from the light leaking out from inside but he waits until I can partially hear before speaking.

"This is the first real lead we've had since Jasper left. Get on your computer and find him before the trail goes cold."

"And the girl?" I ask, dreading his answer. We've done a lot of shit to get by, shit I'm not proud of. But I refuse to hurt a woman, not again. Malik's expression softens a fraction, his hand patting my shoulder. He knows my reasons and better yet, he knows my boundaries. The fact he can still tap into his protectiveness while the anger is riding him this hard shows the guy who saved me from myself is still in there. And he's still looking out for me.

"I want to know everything there is to know about her. Then, you leave her to me."

CANDY

"Hoooo weee!" I yell, taking yet another corner too sharply. I stick my leg out to stop myself from toppling completely, straightening up again to mimic the road ahead. I'd forgotten how fucking good riding a motorbike feels. Exhilaration licks at my skin as I surpass 100mph, the adrenaline of my life being on the line reminding what it feels like to live again. I'm completely at the mercy of fate, and fuck if it isn't freeing. All it'll take is a deer to cross my path now and that jerk of the handlebars could be it for me. What a way to go. She'd better be at my funeral though, murderous horn-y bitch.

A full yellow moon is hanging low in the sky, leaning towards the mountain landscape where I'm headed. As much as I'm enjoying myself, I've yet to shake my tail. Beaming headlights reflect against my wing mirrors, the sound of another engine gaining on me destroying the peaceful night. So inconsiderate .

Pushing the Dyna even harder and breaching 115mph, the bite of the oncoming wind has goose bumps rising all over my body. My nipples are rock hard, my thighs going numb as the bike purrs between them. But the adrenaline keeps me going. The firmness of the clutch strokes my palm like a caress, and the rush of blood pumping around my heart warms me from the inside out. My mouth is upturned in a permanent smirk even if my lips feel blue.

The roar of the other exhaust closing in on me draws my attention back to the mirrors. As sweet as this ride is, she won't be able to out-speed a Ducati. Not in a standard race anyway, but there's no rules out here. Reaching behind me, I pull the Candy Crusher out of my backpack. Her solid weight in my hand is pure harmony as I ready up to whack this mofo into next week.

"Bridge!" Angus barks. He's been shouting orders at me from inside my backpack since I retrieved it but I'm firmly ignoring him. He's not the one who's been attacked, shot at and ghosted by someone who was nine inches deep in me yesterday. I didn't stick around to find out what had the guys so riled up or ask how Jasper/Jack disguised his busted nose from me. The power of make-up I guess.

Seeing his approach is imminent, I throw my bat out to the side. She connects with something but not as hard as I was hoping and the rider is still closing the gap between us. Swinging the Candy Crusher again, the rider grabs her and tosses her aside like a piece of cheap wood. She's anything but cheap. I stole her from a driving range in the most expensive hotel complex in LA and then used her to fight my way past security on the way out. We've been partners ever since.

"Take the motherfucking bridge!" Angus yells and this time, I listen. The fork in the road is upon us as I swerve left so hard the bike bows all the way over. Bracing my leg on the ground, I push the bike straight as I shove myself off to land heavily on the ground. Rolling like a salmon lost in the current, I run out of tarmac and drop into a roadside ditch. Quickly hopping to my feet, I jump up just in time to see the Dyna veer off the side of the bridge and crash into whatever is waiting below.

"Yes!" I cheer, fist pumping myself with both hands. I'd forgotten I wasn't alone until the screech of tyres spinning around broke through my celebrations and a set of headlights landed on me. Dammit. Grabbing my backpack which came loose in the fall, I start to run back the way I came, staying inside the ditch. The gravel shifts beneath my feet, but I scramble the best I can, slinging the bag onto my back. Pumping my arms, I feel the weight of the bike crash into the ditch behind me before I hear it.

The road is mostly dark, leaving me to bound blind ahead until my eyes land on the Candy Crusher laying in the road. The moonlight shines down on her like a beacon. Flinging myself sideways, the brush of air flying past me tickles the back of my legs. That fucker was going to run me over! Grabbing for the road, I hoist myself up and roll across the tarmac. The engine dies at the same time as my hand closes around the bat's handle, the sound of feet pounding towards me reaching my ears.

Spinning around, I whack the oncoming attacker in the side before I notice who it is. Of course, Jasper had a taste of the Candy and is now addicted. I have that effect on people. He keeps coming and I keep smacking any body part I can. He grips my wrist, twisting sharply until I drop the bat to the ground. I try to lunge after her but his body blocks my movements. Wrapping his arms around mine like an elastic band made of steel, I writhe in this restrictive version of a hug.

"What the fuck are you doing?" I snarl. Bringing my knee up between us, his thighs clamp down and bar me from driving his cock back into his body. Beatings I can handle, abuse is my middle name (not literally, it's Martha), fucking is my jam, but hugs trigger something within me. He's too close, his breath across my shoulder opening the chasm of despair deep inside I sealed a long, long time ago.

Take it from a girl who grew up to learn that every foster parent that tried to hug me only wanted something in return. A pay cheque. A sneaky favour causing a distraction at the corner store while he emptied the cash register. A piece of me I would never get back. Yeah sure, Cheese used me too, but only on my terms and he sure as shit never tried to lay a hand on me. Compared to the scum I'd been dumped with, Cheese was my goddam guardian angel.

"Get the fuck off of me!" I stomp my foot down onto his, my

boot crushing into his flimsy Converse. He doesn't even flinch so I turn my attention to his face instead, throwing my head around in an attempt to catch his broken nose.

"Stop moving," he orders. His voice is as cold as the night which is fully settling on me, making me shiver. This makes him hold me tighter and I hate him for it. "Once you've calmed the fuck down, you're going to listen to what I have to say." If that's the condition, then I'll make sure I never calm down.

Leaning ever-so-slightly into his chest, I use his hold to support me while I kick my legs wildly. My toe caps meet his shins numerous times, my body flailing and thrashing like a woman possessed. If this bikini top wasn't so snug, it would have slid aside by now. My efforts don't gain a single reaction from the terminator holding me in place. After a while, I run out of energy. My kicks don't pack as much oomph and my body goes limp.

"Just fuck off Jasper," I whine. Sighing I just hang there in his arms like a slug succumbing to the ring of salt I can't escape. Damn men and their stupid muscles.

"First off, I'm not Jasper. The name's Jack, and the fact you confused my twin and I insults me deeply. Secondly, now you've chilled out, I need to do something." I glance up at the face staring straight down at me. Twins? I didn't see that coming but now all I can picture is being squished between the identical pair.

The moon has cast Jack's features in shadow but the likeness between the two of them is uncanny. Blonde hair which is longer on top and pushed back, stunning green eyes I wish I could get a better look at. I was with Jasper in the dark too and memorised the sharpness of his jaw by touch, as well as his biceps, hard chest, chiselled abs and everything south. I wonder if Jack is equally endowed.

Suddenly his hands are moving, making me flinch at first. Their warmth runs the length of my arms up to my shoulders. Tingles wake in response to everywhere he touches. One hand travels to my nape, holding me while his eyes explore my face. I don't like such close scrutiny but I don't move either.

Tilting my head up with his free hand, he slowly drags his thumb over my lips. They're basically numb but I somehow breathe life back into them for this, whatever this is. Steading myself on his chest, Jack tucks my hair behind my ear and leans closer. My eyes flutter closed on instinct, his stubble grazing my cheek to whisper in my ear.

"You're not the only one who can use sex appeal as a weapon." Angus shouts my name the same time alarm bells blare inside my head, but it's too late. Holding me in place, Jack puts a margin of space between us for his fist to plough into my face. My knees give out with the force of it, my lowered defences being my downfall. Through blurred vision, I vaguely register Jack bending down to scoop me up and over his shoulder. I flop around with his long strides, mustering the strength to weakly punch his ass.

"Bring my fucking bat. And bag," I mumble. Fading in and out, I next find myself in a similar position as before with Jack's body propping me up. Leather bites into my wrists as they're bound together and slung over his head, the metal of a belt clasp digging into my palm. The engine of his Ducati roars to life, the vibration zapping straight through me. Warmth has blossomed around my nose and mouth, something thick dripping over my lips. As the bike jerks forward, my mouth smashes into Jack's white t-shirt and leaves a dark smudge across his shoulder. Oh, I'm bleeding. That makes sense.

There's a funny line between pain and pleasure, one I like to toe often. Usually the pain comes in the form of nipple clamps or electrocution play, but beggars can't be choosers. Right now, I'm bound to a bastard that might just be as feisty as me. Pulling my legs higher, I wind them around his hips and pull myself closer to straddle him properly. Twisting my hands, I slide them into his hair and watch the tick beat in his clenched jaw. I reckon Jack was as carefree as his twin once upon time and I wonder how far I'd have to dig to find it. Not that I plan on doing it, but I don't have anything else on my calendar presently.

"I know what you're doing, Crazy Girl," he remarks. I smirk, licking my lips clean of the blood that settled there.

"That's weird, because I never do." Jack leans to fly around a corner, his arm instinctively wrapping around me to stop me from falling off. Straightening up, he lets go and avoids my raised eyebrow. We surge forward with the wind whipping around us, my hair flying around my face. "It's Candy, by the way."

"What is?" Jack nudges my head aside with his chin when I keep getting in his eyeline.

"My name. Figured you might want to know what to put on my gravestone for when you toss me off this bike."

"What kind of stripper gave you a name like that?" he asks, ignoring the other part.

"A stripper," I shrug. Crossing my ankles around his back, I tighten my grip and yank his head down to look at me. "So what do you say Jacky? Are you going to throw me into the hands of fate or are you going to follow me to Hell?" His bruised eyes try to focus on the bike's direction but I tug him back to mine. I recognised the billboard we passed a minute ago, this road is all straight anyway but I want to see if he has the balls to keep up with me. When he doesn't respond, I roll my eyes and lean back as far as the belt on my wrists allows.

"Your twin is so much more fun than you," I sigh. His gaze flickers and then narrows, his lip rising on one side in a snarl.

"Fuck you," he growls. Twisting the clutch, the Ducati howls as it surges faster, the tyres tearing over the tarmac. Jack's hand grips my hair tightly and yanks me forward until my nose meets the end of his broken one. Staring directly into my eyes, we plummet into the dark together in a silent death pact. Hands of fate baby, it's the only way to live. Tilting my hips forward, the tiny denim shorts rub against his jeans, the bulge there thickening beneath me. He's definitely as feisty as me and identical to his twin in every way.

A light appears on his face, growing in brightness. I wait for the moment he looks away to call him a pussy but it doesn't come. Instead, those orbs of green remain fixed on me as a set of full beams shines all around us. Sticking my tongue out, I run it across his bottom lip and grind my hips into him again. A horn slices through the air, followed by the cursing of a driver who had to toy with the roadside ditch to pass. Lunging at me, Jack takes my bottom lip into his mouth and sucks hard. I groan, pushing my chest into his until he releases me.

"That's enough craziness for today," Jack states. I feel the change of terrain under the tyres at the same time I watch the seriousness settle back over his features. All traces of the reckless man I just saw vanish, right down to the rigidness of his shoulders beneath my hands. Yanking my arms over his head, he pushes me back into the handlebars and shoves my thighs off his. Skidding to a halt, he kicks down the stand and hops off the bike without looking back.

"She's all yours."

JACK

Striding past Malik, who hasn't moved from the spot where I last saw him outside The Devil's Bedpost, I enter through the empty frame where our glass door should be. I won't hear the end of that when he's finished with Candy the fucking nutcase outside. I don't know what happened back there or how she managed to get into my head, and I'm refusing to think about it. Leaning over the bar, I grab a bottle of beer and head into the back.

Not finding anyone in our games area, I take the elevator up to the third floor. Spade, Ace and I have our rooms on this level with King Malik taking the whole penthouse-style floor above. At first we let him get away with his superior shit because it was both him and his money that picked the rest of us out of the gutter. We let him boss us around, decide how we live, even give us our nicknames, because we had no other direction to follow. But then Jasper had to go and fuck it all up. For all of us.

Bypassing my room, I head straight into the nerd's fetish lair that is Ace's. He's hunched over his keyboard like I knew he would be, Spade watching the various computer screens from the bed. I drop down beside him, jolting his leg and making him hiss.

"Sorry bro," I pat him on the back. Despite us having every reason to be furious, we share a grin. Sitting here like a pair of wounded soldiers whilst being bested by a girl with bright pink hair. After the vigorous training schedule we all keep to and the jobs we've pulled off before, she shouldn't be anything but a blip on our radar. Yet here we are.

"Give me some good news Ace. You've found him, right?" Sitting back in his gaming chair, I already have my answer before he's swivelled around to face us. Like Spade, Ace is around 5 ft 11 and hits the gym hard, but that's where the similarities end. Ace's brown hair flicks in all directions and his baby face is perfectly smooth, while Spade has a dark mohawk to suit his mocha skin. Where Spade's eyes are stark blue and all-seeing, Ace's chocolate coloured puppy dog eyes are more likely to avoid anyone nearby. He prefers to watch life through a screen, remaining as a spectator rather than actually taking part.

"He must have known which bus stations have cameras. We've got him getting in, but not coming out." Reaching back, Ace taps his keyboard for the surveillance footage to start playing on the top corner screen. Jasper is talking to the bus driver and hands out a wad of cash before slinking back across the parking lot. Lurking nearby, he waits for Candy to pop her pink head around the corner of the bus before returning, faking a distraction to usher her into the baggage compartment. He targeted her, but why?

"He must have been watching the night of the robbery. It's the only way he'd have known about her connection to us," Spade fills the silence with the obvious. I can't take my eyes off my twin, striding around as if he owns everywhere his timberland boots land. It riles me that we share the same face, my enemy staring back at me every time I look in the mirror. Kicking the backpack at my feet, I flop back on the mattress.

"The girl however," Ace's voice perks up a little.

"Candy," I supply, slinging my arm over my eyes without jarring my nose. She's the last thing I want to think about right now, as if her mischievous grin isn't already imprinted on the inside of my brain.

"Yeah, Candy. There's a shitload of records on her. Criminal ones to be exact, although she's never been properly charged. Seems Leicester bails her out before it gets that far, even when there's evidence stacked against her." I grunt at Leicester's name. If he could handle his lap dogs better, we wouldn't be in this mess. Spade's out of action for months, my beautiful face is damaged, Malik is probably cutting her limb from limb somewhere in the basement and it'll be yet another struggle to get him to lighten up again.

"What else?" Spade asks, as if the rest matters. It doesn't. She's insane, she's dangerous and she needs to go.

"Well her history is as colourful as her hair I guess," Ace replies. Despite myself, I sit upright as he spins around in his chair, his hands flying over the keyboard. Ace can hack any system we need him to and then some.

Files pop up all over the screens along with a series of mugshots from the past decade. Huh, she's a natural blonde. There's a noticeable difference in each one, but the cocky smirk remains the same. Her hair colour changes from blue to purple to pink, the progression of a spotty teen turning into a beautiful woman displayed for us all to see. Large brown eyes stare down the camera lens, her nose petite and slightly upturned at the end. Her creamy skin is flawless and in any other lifetime, she could have been on the front cover of any magazine. Our pasts define us unfortunately.

"Mom works at 'The Naked Tease' in New Jersey as a finance consultant. She was their star attraction once but it looks like an injunction was put on her while still pregnant. The court files are redacted but someone was adamant she wasn't keeping her baby. Strange though, because Candy became a ward of the state at birth and from there, it's all the standard shit. Foster parents, group homes, eventually she became a runaway. Managed to stay off the radar until being picked up for aggressive assault at seventeen and it's all downhill from there."

"Cry me a river," I scoff. Grabbing her backpack, I tip the contents over the bed. There's not much to see; a gummy bear teddy, an old coffee can, some crumpled clothes that smell like rotten fish. Huffing, I pick the bat off the floor and hook it around the back of my shoulders. "I'm keeping this," is all I say, exiting the room. Spade's voice trails out into the hallway.

"You know she won't stop until she has that bat. Wherever it is, she'll follow." I do know that, yet I feel compelled to keep it near. Who knows why. Maybe I need the excuse to beat up a girl who deserves it, maybe I'm bored. Or just maybe, a teeny tiny part of me that resonates with her recklessness is eager for her to mix shit up around here.

Entering my room, I use the bat to flick my light on. I have the corner room facing the mountain range in the distance. In the daylight, I'll be able to squint through the bay window and make out the bridge Malik's bike is currently lying beneath. I can't imagine how pissed he is right now but the idea of it makes me giddy. He's had this coming—he can't control every aspect of his and our lives and not expect something to go wrong.

The three of us on this floor have basically the same room but our tastes dictate the décor. My bed is circular, hanging in the centre of the room by a thick rope from each corner like a giant swing. Satin sheets and a mound of cushions complete my favourite space, as does the huge flatscreen TV on the pinstripe feature wall. The other walls are all white whilst the ceiling and furniture are jet black like a zebra's wet dream.

Kicking off my converse, I pad across the tiled floor into my personal bathroom. Well, personal now as it adjoins the room next door, the one which remains locked and abandoned. Dumping the bat over the sink, I suddenly see myself and freeze. The right side of my white tee is smeared in dried blood from the shoulder to my chest. My hair is a fucking mess of blonde flicks, my eyes thickly bruised and don't get me started on my nose. If it doesn't heal straight, Candy will have more to worry about than Malik's temper.

Carefully peeling the t-shirt off and stripping out of my jeans, I growl at the semi I'm still sporting from earlier. My traitorous cock has a thing for the bad girls but even he should know better this time. Besides, no fucking random chicks in this building - Malik's rules. Sneering at myself one last time, I twist the taps on my huge claw foot bathtub and jump straight in while it's filling. My toes tap impatiently, my fingers drumming on my chest.

I've become complacent with going through the motions, I had forgotten what adventure feels like. To take risks, to act on instinct. The day I'd found Jasper had bounced changed everything, our group dynamic being the main victim. But it wasn't just the group he left, it was me. His own flesh and blood who had been there with him since the womb. You can't fake a bond like that, but apparently you can end it. I've resisted thinking about him for years, and all at once it's like his memory is life like walking these halls and mocking me. The twin that's still stuck here while he's out there, loving life and sleeping with crazy chicks whenever he feels like. As if Malik doesn't understand you can cut off a dog's balls but you can't take away his urges.

The longer I sit, the more pent up I become. What makes him so special, we're genetically the same person. Whatever Candy saw in him, she'll see in me too. Not that I want her to. But now I'm stewing over how she looked at me on the bike, as if I amused her and not in a good way. Her smirks mocked me, her sense of spontaneity putting me to shame. For one brief moment, I let her see the man I used to be. Now he's there, just beneath the surface and I don't know how to suppress him again, if I even want to.

My eyes trail toward the bat sitting across the sink, Spade's words churning in my mind. She won't leave without it and I'm not done investigating why this girl intrigues just the slightest bit. So let her come, I'm ready.

CANDY

"How accommodating of you," I tease. The chiselled man remains to give me a blank stare as I pull on the oversized t-shirt he just threw at my face. My butt went numb on the cold, stone floor a while ago but the shackles on my ankles keep me pinned in place. Not sure why these guys need an array of restraints and weapons, or why they'd bring a prisoner down to the basement where they're all stored but I'm not complaining. Shows confidence I suppose. I'm either dealing with some professional hitmen or just super kinky mofos.

"I can't stand looking at your lack of decency anymore," he grumbles, arms folded across the room. From the glimpses I've caught, he's the perfect specimen of a man. Handsome with a dark edge, corded muscles pushing against the fabric of his shirt and slacks.

"Oh yeah, sorry about that. Can't help being irresistible I'm afraid. Would make my life so much easier if I could." Unhooking the back of the bikini top and lifting it over my head, he acts disgusted and turns his head to the side but I see him looking out the corner of his eye. Pulling the grey t-shirt over my head, I make a knot at my hip. My nipples are pushing against the cotton and the low V-neck does wonders for my cleavage. "So what are we gonna do now? I'm tied up, completely at your mercy. You can skip over the ego trip and get to the bit where you reveal the entire plan so I can start finding a way out."

"You're delusional if you think anything that happens in my house does so without my approval first. You'll sit here and do as you're told until I figure out how best to handle you." I snort at the word 'handle', as many have tried and failed before.

"I mean, I don't want to tell you how to run 'your house' or anything," I finger quote in the air. "But if I were you, I'd be more worried about how I'm going to fish my motorbike out of the river." There's only a single, naked bulb hanging in the basement, but I still manage to see the vein pop out of his temple. He doesn't react as such, but it's there in the sudden tense to his jaw. His fingers flex before unbuttoning the cuff of his dark shirt and slowly rolling his sleeves up to his elbows.

Turning to the rack of restraints, he picks out two adjoining metal loops, one much bigger and thicker than the other. I chew on the inside of my mouth, missing the aid of my gum as he continues to not say a word. That's new. Normally these types of situations are all about boosting my captive's little dick syndrome until I find a way to slip out unnoticed or they release me of their own accord. They'll try to front it out, saying shit like 'you're too damn annoying' or 'do you ever shut the fuck up', but I know my charm is what wins them over. This dude, though, isn't saying a word and my gut is starting to twist uncomfortably.

Striding towards me purposefully, he lunges to grab my neck and clasps the metal hoop around it. He then attaches the smaller one to a fixture on the wall behind me I hadn't noticed. I claw at his arm, leaving gashes in his perfect skin but he doesn't seem to care, grabbing my face tightly so my lips smush together.

"Bitches need to be kept on a short leash." He shoves me back, my head bashing into the stone as he crosses the basement to the far corner. Angus would have a few choice words for him if he wasn't trapped in my backpack somewhere. Since I'm now unable to lean forward and follow the guy's movements, I twist as far as I can to just about make out the chest freezer he's leaning into. Pulling out an industrial size bag of ice, he then tips it into a large wooden barrel to my right. Strange time to set up for trade, I think to myself. It must be almost daybreak by now.

"I've figured it out," he states, leaning against said-barrel. Crossing his ankles, he's going to crease his pressed suit pants but I'm not about to tell him that. "From now on, everything you do to one of us or our property is done to you. We'll see how long it takes before you give up and leave us alone, if you're still alive that is."

"Sorry to burst your bubble there Al Capone, but I don't understand what giving up means. Could I get a definition, or an example maybe? I'll take an interpretive dance if you're in the mood." Ignoring me, he turns and braces his arms on the barrel.

"Understand this, Barbie. Until you cry and beg, I'm going to rain hell down on you. You hurt my men, I hurt you. You ditch my bike in a freezing, cold river....well..." My eyes widen as I realise what he's doing but it's too late.

Pushing his bulky weight against the barrel, it dips in my direction and the contents pour out with the force of a tsunami. Throwing me back into the wall, the liquid slap knocks the breath from my lungs before the cold consumes me. Ice cubes scratch at my face as it keeps coming and coming, a flashback to the cliff dive causing me to panic. I flap around, trying to protect my face whilst my pulse grows erratic. The barrel finally falls and crashes on the stone floor, the rest of its contents pouring around my ass and legs.

Scraping the droplets from my stinging eyes, I find myself plunged into darkness as the light is turned off and the top door closed. With my heart hammering in my chest, I gulp down air and that's when the scent hits me. Vodka. I'm not opposed to a good drink, but the sheer volume of it now makes me gag. It's in my nose, the back of my throat, everywhere. Calming myself when there's no other sign of life or threat, I begin to shiver. Soon, the cold starts settling into my bones and the darkness all around has me curled up into a ball, my head awkwardly resting on my knees.

If that model-worthy man seriously thinks this is enough to break me, he clearly has no idea who he's dealing with.

A hand gripping my hair jerks me awake and I lash out, my open palm meeting a face I haven't seen yet. His eyes are hooded, the light swinging gently behind his mohawk. His hand tightens on my hair and he seems to be battling with his self-control so I take the opportunity to size up his body. He's huge in muscle mass, the biggest I've seen since arriving here. There's a defined shape to his bunched biceps, his shoulders are broad and the strong line of his jaw is striking.

"Are you all drop dead gorgeous or do you keep the Quasimodo lookalikes hidden from the general public?" He's thrown off by my question, the pinch of my hair loosening slightly. Leaning down further, I briefly think he's going to kiss me until he picks up a crutch from the ground and straightens. A black cast is poking out from beneath a pair of casual shorts, following his leg all the way down to a medical boot on his foot. Ouch.

"I heard you were a smooth talker." I grin at this, my irritation from a lousy wakeup call vanishing. I sit upright, suddenly realising my neck is free of that metal contraption. Gasping, I stroke the length of my throat and roll my head around on my shoulders. This is soon followed by a stretch, my arms way above my head and my chest pushed out. The smile on my face says it all; best morning stretch ever (if it is morning). "Get up. Malik has a job for you," the one that must be Spade grumbles.

It's at this point I realise my ankles are also free and use the wall to pull myself up. Now dry and somewhat sticky, the vodka has become one with my skin, saturating me in a fermented smell. Any other instance, I'd be licking myself like a cat to savour the sweet alcohol that's been wasted. Right now however, my head is spinning as if I have a hangover without the usual deep seated ache of a damn good night.

Spade begins to hobble towards the steps before venturing up them. One. By. One. I'm pretty sure I saw a snail crawl up the handrail quicker. Waiting at the bottom, because I can't be assed with all this stop start stop start bullshit, a familiar gruff voice sounds inside my head.

"How far do you think we could shove one of those crutches up his-"

"Don't even talk to me," I hiss. Spade halts near the door, twisting back to question me with a twitch to his eyebrow. Angus hops up onto the bottom step, his squidgy pink body squeaking like a chew toy as he drags himself up to the next.

"Being mad at me isn't going to help." Spade busies himself with unlocking the door while I crouch down to talk to this abandoning bastard.

"Well if you weren't such a fucking nubbin, I might be able to forgive you. How come every time I get myself into a pickle, you seem to vanish like Snobby Susan who found a gherkin in her MacDonald's burger. It's how they come Susan, go to subway next time!"

"I...feel like we're getting off track," Angus says, trying to pull his gummy version of a puppy dog face. It's not going to work this time.

"I don't even know why I bother keeping you around anymore." Standing, I stride up the steps without looking back but the lack of squidging tells me he hasn't bothered to follow. It's hard breaking up with a part of myself, but that part's an asshole. Spade is waiting just outside the door, not saying a word as I pass with my head held high. The basement is at the back of the kitchen, the tall refrigerator calling to me. Crossing the room on my wrecked, leather boots, I yank the door open and my mouth immediately begins to water. Oh my.

"Take whatever you want from the second shelf up," Spade grumbles and starts to hobble away. "Malik is waiting for you in the parking lot. Don't make him wait long if you know what's best for you." Shrugging, I'm soon alone with the goodies laid out before me. In the early days when Cheese first picked me up, he used to let me stay over at the mansion when I needed to lay low for a while. My room had a mounted TV like the rest of them, and I'd spend my days watching Law and Order reruns with my body weight of snacks. Other than the fact I have a sweet tooth, those days taught me all about the art of deduction. A gift I will use right now.

The bottom shelf of the fridge is filled with comfort food; leftover pizza, sliced meats, cheeses, and a tub of cookie dough. That's someone who wants easy snacking with little prep, probably more of a hoard and hide away type. The next shelf, which I've been granted access to, is a mess of packets and half eaten meals - lazy and lean would be Jack. I'd bet my life the next is Spade's with the bottles of protein shakes and stacks of steaks piled up. Which leaves the top for Malik, OCD heaven.

Reaching up on my tiptoes, I pull out a carefully prepared sub in paper wrapping. I don't even want the bottle of water from beside it when there's a door filled with milkshakes staring at me, but knowing it's his makes it worth the blandness. I pull myself up onto the sparkling kitchen counter and unwrap the sub, taking my time to savour the meatball filling.

"What's' taking-" Malik bursts through the back door as I'm halfway through, freezing as he spots me. "Is that my sandwich?" I shrug, answering with a mouthful of food.

"Was on the second shelf up." I don't know if he buys it or not, his face giving nothing away. Instead, he storms across the room and tears the sub from my hand. I hold on as tight as I can, a tomatoey meatball popping out and rolling down Malik's white shirt sleeve. He stills, staring at the stain and I take my chance. Lunging forward, I gnash my teeth into the sub, taking a huge chunk out of the side when Malik tugs me off the counter and shoves me outside.

The sun blinds me, forcing a hiss through my teeth. Heat wraps around me, beating down on my sticky skin. The grey t-shirt has dried but tugs rigidly as I move towards the motorbike in the middle of the parking lot. The Dyna! She's in rough shape, caked in mud and moss with random bits of junk thrown all over the place. A pair of shrivelled sneakers hang from the handlebars by the tied laces. Strips of magazines and labels are strewn over the seat and I'm sure clumps of actual shit are wedged in the exhaust. Smells like it at least.

"You got her back. Guess we're even then," I say, beginning to walk away. There's no one else around but the few vehicles suggest people are already inside. I'll just grab what belongs to me and be on my way then. A hand grips the back of the t-shirt, holding me in place.

"I don't think so. You're staying until you clean every millimetre of my bike. Once you're done, we're going to have a chat about Jasper, because I don't believe in chance meetings. Then, and only then, will you get your bat back in decent condition and I'll never have to see your face again." Looking back, I now see the bucket of soapy water, sponges and array of bottles around the other side of the bike.

"You do like the sound of your own voice, don't ya?" Puffing out my cheeks, I click my tongue and draw the pretend gum back into my mouth. That was a perfect bubble popping moment, and I have a wicked imagination. After all, I've been dog poor before. Malik narrows his eyes before releasing me and walking away. I follow his tight buns in those navy slacks, all the way to Jack sitting on the porch steps watching. He quickly mutters something about his sandwich and not letting me out of his sight. I blow Jack a quick kiss, rounding the bike to look at the tubs of polish and wax.

Hours later, I'm pushing my way through the revolving door which has been fixed in record time. The bar is a bit busier now, although I kept a fair few customers hanging around outside to watch the show. I've never been one to disappoint, or miss an opportunity.

Malik is behind the bar with another guy, the one I saw briefly before Jack cocked the shotgun at me last night. He's super cute, in a shy way. He tries to avoid my gaze, but those chocolate brown eyes betray him. I want to drag my fingers through his tousled brown hair to see if it's as smooth as it looks. The hint of a tattoo poking out of his fitted tee causes me to think there's more to him than meets the eye, as does his apparent curiosity of me.

Jack follows me inside, having stayed out there the entire time. He didn't say a word. Just watched me intently. Planting myself on a bar stool, I lean over to take a drink Malik has just poured. He turns back with a mini umbrella to find an empty cocktail glass in its place and I merely shrug at him.

"What? I'm parched. Hard work is thirsty work." Rolling the kink out of my shoulders, I place my hand on Jack's shoulder and use his body to push myself up onto the bar. Swivelling on my ass in these tiny shorts, I pull the knot of the t-shirt higher so my stomach is exposed. The cute bartender rushes to move glasses out of the way when I lean back, lying flat between the three of them.

"What the fuck are you doing?!" Malik whisper-shouts. He probably doesn't want to draw the attention of his customers but it's too late for that. They've seen enough outside.

"I'm getting ready. You said whatever I do to one of you or your properties will be done back to me." Looking around, I spot Spade lounging on a sofa nearby. He raises a glass of whiskey slowly, his eyes focused on the rise and fall of my chest. Aw, it must have been a while. Putting my fingers in my mouth, I whistle loudly to call him over.

"Jack, what is she talking about?" Malik growls. That vein in his temple has come out to play again. "Did she clean my bike or not?"

"Oh it's clean," he smirks. Taking the glass from Spade as he arrives, Jack leans over me to refill it from the bar tap. "I think she took the term 'spit and shine' a little too literally though." Pure horror settles over Malik's face, his eyes not knowing who to glare at. He doesn't even know what I used to polish the seat with yet.

"It's called a loophole," I smirk. "But I'd rather you didn't deliver my punishment on this one. Let one of your sex-starved submissives do it instead." Malik seems stunned into silence so I twist my head to Spade and start lifting the t-shirt higher. "Go ahead, spit away and rub your gooch all over my face."

Jack leans forward as if he's been waiting for such an invitation before I'm dragged off the bar quick enough to get whiplash and manhandled into a back room. Malik twists my arms sharply behind my back, shoving me face-first into a poker table. Despite his aggression, the bulge rammed against my ass tells a whole different story. I shimmy my hips, giggling as he jerks away from me.

"I won't let you ruin everything I've built here," he seethes. I roll over and sit on the edge of the table, swinging my legs.

"And I won't let you control me. Give my shit back and I'll be gone." I can see by the tick in his jaw he won't be doing that. Malik thrives on power and isn't going to give in. Not only does he now have my bat, he's got my money and I won't make it anywhere else without it so I might as well take my chances here. Sighing, I roll my eyes back and forth across the ceiling.

"You know, you're going about this all wrong. If I wanted information out of someone, I'd treat them a bit better. Provide a bed and food. Access to a toilet wouldn't go amiss." The dark eyes from across the room don't waver from mine, the tightness of his lips suggesting he's deep in thought.

Now I have the chance to see him in the light, Malik is much more striking than I originally thought. The cut of his jaw is razor sharp with an equally angular beard line. The hair is trimmed close to his tanned face, as it is on the sides of his scalp. Long, dark flicks fall past his eyebrows in a carefree manner, but I can see he's sprayed them that way deliberately.

Malik doesn't move a muscle while I explore him with my eyes. Usually, people are easy to read, which is why I like to shake things up, but he's like a breathing statue. I wonder what it would take to make him smile, or laugh, or moan. The door opens then, Cutie walking in to stand at his master's side, his eyes downcast. Folding his arms, the t-shirt sleeve rides up over his bicep and I see more of the tattoo there being revealed. 'Ace' is printed under a playing card I can only see half of.

"Deal with her," Malik orders, storming out of the room. I smirk, bobbing my eyebrows and opening my legs when those chocolate browns flick my way. Ace doesn't take my offer, instead directing me towards an elevator I hadn't noticed behind me. Guess I'm here for a little while yet. Now I've just got to find out something about Jasper other than the fact he's blonde and has a monster-sized cock.

SPADE

Sliding my Beats headphones over my ears, I crank Eminem up full volume before lifting the weight bar from its holder. Ideally, I'd have a spotter but since none of my so-called brothers will let me work out, I have to do it in secret. Lowering the bar to my chest, I start pumping and counting. I won't stop until sweat is running into my mohawk and I've forgotten the world exists. The four walls of my room are driving me insane, this fucking cast on my leg is rubbing on my last nerve.

At least the person who gave it to me isn't around, right? Fucking wrong. She's being set up in Jasper's old room for some unknown reason. If I'd been the one chasing her down last night, this would be a completely different story. One where I'm exerting myself by digging a six foot by six foot hole until dawn instead of bench pressing in secret. Even Malik hasn't fully lost his temper yet, trying to hold onto his zen bullshit by any means necessary.

When my irritation doesn't cease, or rather only rises, I dump the metal bar back into its hooks and sit upright. I need heavier weights. The stand isn't far, but I'd need to stay on my feet whilst lifting and dragging them over here. Rubbing the back of my neck, I think fuck it and push myself up on one leg. Using the bar for balance, I shuffle towards the weight stand. Rounding the stand, I lower myself to the floor and rest my back against it. With one leg, I heave my body backwards and hear the satisfying skid of metal against rubber tiles. This is a workout in itself but soon the stand is next to the bench and I heave myself back onto it.

From sitting, I can now load up the weight bar before resting back and lifting it from the hooks. That's so much better. I can actually feel the strain pulling at my shoulders, the veins popping out of my arms in a spiderweb effect.

My dulled pain threshold is a godsend usually, but sometimes I just want to *feel* something. I used to treat it like a magic trick as a kid, becoming such a regular in the ER, children's services would visit randomly to check my mom's dickhead husband wasn't hurting me. When he was being a real cunt, I'd tell them he was and he would get a few nights away in custody. I love my mom but her choice in men makes it hard to stand by and watch, so I left. Irony is, I've turned into just as much as an asshole anyway.

Pumping the bar in time to the music blaring into my ears, I welcome the burn. Ace has his tech, Malik has control, Jack...well Jack does whatever the fuck he likes, but for me - the gym is my sanctuary. The place I leave my stress at the door and let loose. My blood is pumping, my heart pounding. This is the build up to bliss, where everything fades away except the inferno inside, chasing away the shadows that try to keep me up at night. Those fuckers can find someone else to taunt.

Thrusting the bar high in the air, a smile is about to grace my lips when the music in my ears suddenly changes. My hand slips and I just manage to steer the bar away from my face. It bashes into my chest before I can catch it, pinning me in place on the leather bench. I sputter out a cough, trying to shake the headphones off. The music pains me more than the weights pushing down on my torso. *'Hey Barbie. Hi Ken. Wanna ride? Sure Ken.'* I holler out, thrashing around until the bar is lifted and I can get that offensive music away from me.

"What the fuck Spade?!" Ace shouts. "You're supposed to be resting!"

"Where is she?" I snarl. Grabbing the crutches from beneath the bench, I shove past him and move towards the door. I don't actually need his response, I can hear the pounding of the music down the hall. Leaving Ace to deal with the weights, I hop towards Jasper's old room to find the door locked. Slamming my fist on it, I then head next door into Jack's room instead.

He raises his head from his mound of pillows, wearing the nose splint he's not supposed to take off. When his nose heals crooked, I'm going to spend every day of my life taking the piss out of it. His bed swings as he sits upright, eyeing my gym shorts and loose vest.

"Were you just working out? You know you're not-" Ignoring him, I shuffle to the bathroom door and throw it open. The music hits me tenfold, offending my ears as steam billows out. Beyond the speaker system and pounding of the shower, I hear Candy singing about being a Barbie girl. Her pink hair is just visible inside the steamy cubicle, and sensing Jack's presence lingering at my back, I edge inside and slam the door closed.

Locking it, I then turn my attention to the music system built into the wall, turning that shit off. She wouldn't have been able to access my Spotify playlist without the password, which means Jack gave her free reign. I'm not sure what's got into him, or how he can go from shooting at someone to giving them music access in less than 24 hours, but I'm putting an end to this madness.

Candy's ass presses against the cubicle as she bends over to get the body wash, causing my dick to jerk. I grab him and squeeze in warning but there's no hiding what's already started in these gym shorts. Swallowing thickly, I lean the crutches against the wall and pull myself up onto the counter beside the basin. Reaching around, I turn off the music and as suspected, she bolts upright.

"Who the fuck turned off the music?!" She wipes a circle clear on the glass, peering through to spot me. I see the ghost of a smirk before she slides the door open, revealing herself to me. Holy hell, I thought I was ready, but I really wasn't. Her arms and chest are tattooed with demented characters, her perky nipples pierced. I'm surprised by the outline of her abs pushing against her taut, creamy skin. Despite this, there's a small indent in her waist and flare to her hips. Further down, she's completely hairless and I find myself licking my lips.

"Oh, hey handsome. I'd ask you to join me but I'm guessing you can't get wet," her chin jerks to my cast. Fucking cast. Cocking my eyebrow at her, I keep my hand casually over my crotch so she can't see how much my body wants to say screw it and join her anyway. "It's okay. I'll just get wet enough for the both of us."

Stepping back, Candy unhooks the shower head and runs her hand down the length of her body. My eyes widen, the turn of events taking me by surprise. I know there was a reason I came in here, but at this precise moment, I can't seem to remember it. Rolling her nipple between her fingers, her wet hair glides into her cleavage with the flow of the water. There's a rattle by the door before it's thrown open, revealing Jack standing there with the butter knife he used to jimmy the lock. Dropping it with a clang, he strides in and closes the door behind him.

"Who said you get all the fun?" Jumping up on the other side of the basin, Jack leans against the mirror. Candy doesn't seem to notice or care, her hand too busy travelling the length of her body. Holding the shower head over her tits, she gasps as the spray hits her nipples just right. Water cascades down her, pooling in her hand as she rubs her clit in small circles. Keeping my breathing slow and deep, I recognise the burning inside as the one I was trying to achieve in the gym. The serenity of nothing or no one else mattering beyond this room presenting itself to me in the form of a pink haired minx.

Lifting her leg, Candy braces herself on the side of the cubicle, giving us a full view of her beautiful pussy. Pink and compact like the rest of her. Lowering the shower head, her head falls back with the contact of the water, a moan spilling from her lips. There's no hiding my cock now as it strains against my boxers. The urge to jump up and take her right here and now is riding me hard. It's been a while since I've had a woman at my mercy, on her knees while I thrust into her throat. I thought they weren't worth the hassle, but now I'm wondering if I've been cockblocking myself on purpose. Then my eyes trail down to the cast on my leg, and suddenly I remember why.

CANDY

"With my eyes fluttered closed, I ride the shower head while flicking my thumb over my nipples. This isn't my first rodeo. Not the first time I've had an audience either. If my mom taught me anything, it's not to be ashamed of my body. And to have a contraceptive implant at all times.

I'm so lost to the sensations driving my body towards a sweet release, I flinch when a pair of hands land on my hips. My eyes fly open, seeing a tall blonde before me. Jack smirks, a rare sighting of his dimples giving me serious Jasper vibes. The likeness is freaky, too bad it's only skin deep. Easing the shower head out of my hand, he turns off the faucet and places it back into the holder. Wearing only a pair of boxers, his body ripples beneath my touch when I can't resist brushing my fingers over his abs.

"I believe you started something in the bar," Jack mumbles. His green eyes sparkle, his head lowering for our mouths to almost meet. "I think it's best we see it through." His hand wraps around my throat and I grip onto his arm, using his strength to wrap my legs around his waist. He slams me into the wall, grinding his rigid cock against my centre. I groan openly, biting down on my lower lip.

Releasing my neck in favour of gripping my hair, Jack tilts my head up and plunges his tongue into my mouth. He tries to dominate me, forcing my tongue to battle with his whilst grinding against me. My chest heaves against his, my nails digging into his shoulders. Sucking my tongue into his mouth, Jack kisses me with a starved passion. His mouth moves downwards, biting along the length of my jaw before we're moving.

Carrying me out of the shower, he dumps me on the side and shifts me into a kneeling position. Bracing myself over the sink, I find Spade's piercing blue eyes penetrating mine. The conflict in his features increases as I lean closer, softly placing my lips on his. He doesn't move but I continue to kiss him anyway, trailing his jaw and neck to his shoulders.

"It's about time you made my boy feel better, don't you agree?" Jack chuckles, a hard spank cracking against my ass. I gasp into Spade's neck, my hand already reaching for his pants. You don't have to tell me twice, not with a specimen like Spade beneath me. If he hadn't been wearing a mask that night, I doubt I'd have actually shot him but it seems the outcome will be the same. He only shifts to ease his pants down, his cock springing free.

My eyes bulge at the sheer girth of him. Did these guys form a group based on the size of their dicks?! A thick vein trails his length, my hand unable to close around his shaft. I lower my head at the same time Jack tilts my ass upwards, his fingers driving into me as I take Spade into my mouth. I groan around his dick, causing him to clasp my head and moan as well. These poor guys have seriously been denied for too long, I'm doing them a service here. No one this hot should be so pent-up. It's a crime actually and this is probably the most selfless thing I've ever done.

Taking him deep into my throat, Spade holds my head down to grind into me before releasing. I slowly lick my way back up his rigid length before repeating the process over and over. Each time he grunts and jerks in a little further, looking for that sweet spot.

No gag reflex here honey, I could do this all day. Meanwhile, Jack has added a third digit into me, my walls gripping him tightly. His thumb presses against my clit deliciously and I ride his hand shamelessly.

Pulling out of me, Jack spanks me again and I jolt that bit further down Spade's cock. He's not going to last much longer and I'm ready to take that burden from him. No judgement here. Grabbing my ass tightly, I feel Jack's tongue flick over my clit before he latches on. I push back into him, savouring his sucks while my eyes roll back in my head. Gripping my hair tightly, Spade takes the opportunity to hold me still and thrust into me from below. I take his massive length, my mouth stretched over his shaft as the first taste of precum hits the back of my throat.

Shaking out of his hold, I grip the base of his cock and suck hard. One last swirl of my tongue over his tip and he's cumming on a strangled moan. Hot, glorious cum seeps down my throat, overriding my senses with his taste. His entire body goes rigid beneath me while I let him ride it out, my pussy having a fiesta of her own. Jack alternates between licking me from bud to crack, sucking my clit and plunging his fingers into me at sonic speed. I finally release Spade, moaning loudly as a climax prepares to rip through me. My walls start to flutter when Jack withdraws and tosses me to the tiled floor. I land with a crash, my tender ribs screaming out but my unfilled need takes priority.

"What was it you called us, love?" Jack chuckles. Again, so much like Jasper, it's freaky. Leaning over, he spits on my stomach while holding out an arm to help Spade get to his feet. "Who's the sex-deprived submissive now?" I cock my eyebrow, continuing to smile. Scooping up his saliva, I sit upright and wipe it down Spade's shorts as Malik's voice sounds from the bedroom, asking Jack where he is.

"Still you," I choke out a laugh and slink back into the shower before Malik enters. Switching the water back on, I hear muffled voices and see a pair of dark, murderous eyes glaring at me through the glass. "Jeez, can't a girl have a shower around here in peace?! I thought you'd have more control of your guys Malli-Moo."

I laugh to myself as the three filter out, unhooking the shower head to finish myself off. These guys will learn soon enough withholding sex and using it as a weapon is my speciality. But please do try to beat me at my own game, either way I come out a winner.

MALIK

"Downstairs for a briefing, now. We've got a job." I leave Jack's room with a scowl etched onto my face. I don't even want to know what I just walked in on, with Jack sporting a hard-on in his boxers and Spade looking sated as fuck, and I don't want to know. Banging on Ace's door as I pass, I take the stairs down to the bottom level. Busying myself with organising the back room, I clear off the deck of cards in the centre and flip the table over to show the hard wood side. Neatening up the four chairs so we'll all be facing each other straight on, I remove my suit jacket and hang it over the back of mine.

Watching through the two way mirror, I see the bar beginning to fill up for the night. I bought this place at an auction in my early twenties. A decade later and the heap of wooden and scrap metal is now not only our home, but the front for our lucrative business behind the scenes. All the usual punters know to provide us an alibi if necessary. Those who aren't regulars are fooled by our lookalike night staff, who are compensated extremely well to dress like us, talk like us, wear their hair a certain way and even get matching tattoos. If all else fails, we can trace customers through

Ace's secret cameras and pay them for their silence. It's worked this far.

The elevator pings open and the three men I consider family walk through the door. They regard me with disdain, dropping into their seats heavily as if the weight of the world is on their shoulders. There was a time we would sit up all night playing any card game we could think of, drinking and laughing. They can blame me for the loss of those days if they like. I can take the hit, but the truth is Jasper packed the laughter in his suitcase, along with our savings, and took it with him. I did what I had to in order to keep Jack from sabotaging himself, or following his twin out the door. We're a team, a family, and even miserable, we're better here together than out there alone.

"Ace has found us another job on his hidden servers," I state, turning my back on the mirror. Taking my seat, Ace passes me a file without looking, his gaze fixed in his lap. "It's late notice, we'll have to ride out in an hour, but the pay is good."

"Thought we weren't doing last minute jobs anymore," Spade says from my left. His posture is hunched with his elbows on his knees, his attitude grating on me but I let it go. For now.

"This one is a simple pick up and drop off, courier style. Doesn't need as much briefing as a full on heist." Opening the file, I hand out the paper copies Ace printed as I requested. "The stash is to be collected from an abandoned warehouse upstate. We can take the country roads, cut through Vermont woods. It's a ninety mile round trip so Jack, check the engines are full. Ace will take the drone and be on surveillance, as usual. Spade is to sort firearms."

"What about our female guest?" Spade asks, not even bothering to look at the info sheet.

"She's not a fucking guest," I bite back. But he does have a point, what will we do with her? She can't be trusted in the bar or walking around. Even with the extra security on my floor, if she gets up there, we're screwed. Spade's the obvious choice to stay behind since he can only ride with one of us at the moment, although another pair of eyes is invaluable and he's a perfect shot if need be.

My eyes travel to Jack slouched back on my other side, the bulge in his jeans yet to fully go down. Running a hand down the side of my face, I groan to myself. "Apparently the only one I can trust with her is Ace."

"I wouldn't be so sure about that," Jack mutters, his head rolling to Ace's lap. Looking beneath the table, I see that he's not staring at the floor but secretly watching his phone. I know without looking, only footage from one of the cameras would hold his attention that long.

"Oh, for fuck's sake Ace. You should know better than anyone that women can't be trusted." He looks up at this, clearly keeping an ear on our conversation.

"I never said I trusted her, but I'm as much of a red blooded male as the rest of you." His eyes narrow and look at the other two around the table. We've all grown distant lately but the tension in this room is different now. Spiteful and bitter.

"If you didn't ban us from the necessities, this wouldn't be happening," Jack sits upright, suddenly engaged in the meeting.

"Oh so this is my fault now?" I twist to ask. He hasn't bothered to put on a shirt, just a low slung pair of jeans. I make a point to wear a suit everyday and while I don't order it, I'd hoped the others would take the hint. We're as united as we present ourselves, and well…currently the disjointedness is obvious.

"Yeah it is. You took her bat, you brought her here." I clench my jaw shut, taking a second to collect my thoughts. I admit I went through a rough patch a while ago, you know - when I lost everything I'd been building from the ground up, but I don't want respect to stem from fear. All I want is for these three men to understand how much I've done for them, and how much I need them in my life to keep me balanced.

"I didn't realise I was dealing with the stripper version of Harlequin," I say calmly. "When disabling the enemy, you take their weapon of choice away in case they get back up quicker than expected. You know that. She's no different from any thug we've gone up against before."

"Except she is. Completely different," Jack retorts. I now have Ace's full attention, no doubt waiting for me to lose my shit. It won't get that far.

"What are you even suggesting? Until she spills everything she knows about Jasper, she stays here with one of us watching her like a hawk." I share a nod with Spade and Ace, then turn to face Jack again. I don't know why he's so vocal all of a sudden. He's been stuck to my side for the past few years, craving the closeness he's lost.

"No one's suggesting anything Malik. You order and we obey, remember?" Jack pushes his seat out and leaves without looking back. Heading into the bar, I see him help himself to a drink before heading towards the exit. My lips purse. He knows he's not supposed to go out there when his double is in, it'll confuse people. I used to be able to swap him and Jasper out, which is where the whole idea came from. Two places at the same time, no evidence, no…

Making a few final arrangements, Ace scurries off to change and set up his mini drone. We all wear matching outfits on a job, black cargos with a t-shirt and leather jacket. Our skull masks are slightly different, as are our weapons of choice. I ask Spade to hang back when he rises to his seat with the aid of his crutches.

"You know I hate leaving one of us out of a job. It doesn't feel right when we're not all together to have each other's backs." His blue eyes hold mine as steadily as the day I skidded my bike into the back alley he was trying to flee from and offered him an out. Out of his mom's house, out of his gambling debt, out of his own head mostly. I've never understood why Spade has felt the need to self-sabotage but it's ingrained in him, even now.

"But?" he huffs, bringing a small smile to my lips. I close the distance between us and pat him on the shoulder.

"But at some point, you do have to slow down and let that leg heal. I need you back with us ASAP, please don't let your stubbornness make it longer." Spade smirks, his head leaning forward to rest on mine. At the end of the day, we're all the same here. Lost, misguided, searching for something. Patting his back, I guide Spade slowly towards the elevator and help him inside. "And I need you to stay here to watch over Candy."

"Wait, fucking babysitting duty?!" He shouts as the doors begin to close before he can shuffle forwards.

"Keep your dick in your pants this time!" Chuckling to myself, I take the stairs all the way up to my floor. The elevator doesn't come this high for a reason. No nasty surprises going in or out. Two cameras point at my outer door and a keyboard scans my handprint to grant me access. All of the others are able to enter my floor as well, but they rarely do, if ever. This is my domain. The King's home on top of his empire.

Walking through the dining room I've only used a handful of times, I grab a bottle of water from the fridge. There's a fully equipped kitchen in dark wood, matching the rest of the suite, which I use when I take myself away for a while. More often lately, I can hide up here for days at a time and no one comes looking for me. I sigh, sliding open my balcony door and leaning on the railing. I have a clear view of the sun dipping below the mountains and not much else, just the way I like it.

I'm not a fan of last minute jobs personally. I like time to plan all angles, and have contingencies in place. But I'm not in a position to turn down this sort of payout either, not while I'm still shielding my men from the harsh realities of the world. We're screw ups, plain and simple. And eventually, someone has to pay for our past mistakes before they catch up with us.

CANDY

Piercing blue eyes stare into mine, his lips a breath away. I proposition him with my eyebrows but he's had enough Candy for today. Pulling on the straps tightly, Spade fastens a buckle right beneath my boobs. My tongue hangs out like a dog excited for a trip in the car.

"This is very defiant. I feel like we're breaking ground," I joke with his stoic face. He ignores me, loading up the pocketed harness with ammunition for their road trip. "Am I going to get one of these?" I ask, slipping the gun out of the back of his cargo pants whilst he's busy trying to hook magazines to my ribs. I flick off the safety, closing one eye and aiming at his good leg. I've never made a man of his size flinch before, and it feels damn rewarding.

Snatching the gun from my hand, he curses me out and orders me to finish getting dressed. A matching outfit to the one he's wearing is laid across the bed, clearly much too big but I'll make it work. Swanning across the room in a vest from my backpack and pair of boxers from the dresser, I yank the cargos onto my lower half.

"You could fit a whole circus in here!" I pull the trousers away from my waist like a slimming world billboard. Spade frowns too, his Mohawk tipping to the side in thought. "Just give me my own clothes, I'm more aerodynamic in leather." I didn't think he'd go in so easily but he whips out his phone and within ten seconds, Ace appears with my backpack. I squeal in delight until Spade's hand is clamped over my mouth.

"I hope you know what you're doing," Ace huffs.

"He put me on weapons and babysitting, I'm multitasking." I take my backpack from Ace, nodding vigorously.

"Showing initiative is the best way to get a promotion. I read that in a magazine once, or maybe it was a drug dealer's handbook. Either way, it was at a drug den and I was pretty high, but I definitely read it." Leaning on Spade's bicep, he suddenly moves and I catch myself from face planting the floor. Taking my backpack, I find all of my clothes laundered and folded inside. I smile at Ace before he leaves the room, the corner of his mouth hitching up too.

Dragging my clothes on, I catch sight of myself in the mirror and like what I see. My PVC trousers are high wasted, nestling beneath the ammunition holder on my white vest. I found my leather jacket in the bottom of my pack so I've slung it on, but we'll be having talks about teamwork later. My pink hair is a wild mess of waves, my cheeks flushed and a huge smile on my face. Hello, me. All that's missing is a bubble of gum.

I catch Spade in the reflection checking out my ass. Bending forward, I pretend to be checking out my eyebrows to mess with him some more. These guys can pretend they don't want me, but I see it in their eyes when they think I'm not looking. Mistaking me for a barbie bimbo was their first mistake, thinking I'd be put off by their macho bullshit was their second. I've lived my life around assholes, I know how to handle one as long as they know how to handle mine. Snapping himself out of it, Spade goes back to the weapons cabinet hidden beneath the false top on his dresser.

"How about just a blade then?" I revert back to our earlier conversation. "I need to be able to protect myself."

"I'm not giving you a knife, a gun, or an inflatable golf club.

Nothing. You want to live, don't leave my side. You die, I'm still not that bothered, but I won't be stuck sitting around watching you paint your toenails or some shit."

"Could have been fun though. We could have eaten through Malik's weeks' worth of meal prep in one night." I don't miss the glint of mischief in Spade's eyes, or the way his hand pauses over a dagger before he chooses to ignore me. There is hope yet. Once his duffel bag is loaded with weapons, Spade slings it over his chest and turns to me with something in his hand. A skull bandana.

Gesturing for me to turn around, he pulls my hair up into a ponytail, tying it with a band from his wrist and fixes the mask onto my face. I watch him in the mirror curiously, the moment seeming to hold more than I can comprehend before it's gone. Picking up his crutches, he whacks me in the back of the legs to get moving. I can't say going on a drug run with a cripple is the weirdest thing I've ever done, but it's certainly up there.

Jack is sitting on his Ducati, taking a drag from the joint hanging out of his mouth when we finally make it outside. His eyes travel the length of my body, the hatred he's trying to fake battling with his appreciation. Closing the gap between us, I take the smoke from his mouth and pull my mask down and take a toke myself. It hits me in the back of the throat, coaxing a rush of adrenaline to fill me before the calm sets in. Tilting Jack's head up, I transfer the smoke from my mouth into his before popping the joint back in between his lips and replacing the bandana over my nose.

Ace is next to venture outside, holding a grey contraption with four propellers in his hand. This must be the drone I overhead them whispering about in the hallway. The body is slimmer than I expected with a circular lens poking out of the bottom. He pops a hidden storage compartment on his yellow Suzuki Boulevard and carefully slides it inside. I'm about to ask why he has a Suzuki when the rest of the bikes I've seen could eat his for breakfast when a shout cuts me off.

"Oh, fuck no!" Malik steps into view, his strides eating up the gravel. "Absolutely not!" I'm lifting my leg to hop on the back of

Jack's bike when Malik whips me off, tossing me aside. "And you, I thought we agreed you'd stay here and rest," Malik turns to Spade. There's a trace of hurt in his voice but no one else seems to notice.

"I didn't agree to anything, especially not watching over the stray you've dragged in." Ouch. Spade scuffles over to Ace's bike, using his friend's shoulder to support him whilst getting on. Laying the crutches across his lap, he twists to give Malik a questioning look. "You can't afford to leave us behind, I've got the guns and she's got the spare ammo. So are we doing this or what?" This time, I hop on behind Jack without incident. Wrapping my arms around his waist and pressing my cheek into his back, he grabs my wrists and lowers them to his crotch.

"Might as well make it worth my while," he mutters, revving up his engine. Malik stands stationary, his features slack. Without his stern expression in place, I see a glimpse of the man underneath in the dimmed light leaking out from the bar. Merely a man, not a monster of power and control. His eyes land on me, the misery quickly shifting into hatred with a teeth-bared snarl. Jack speeds off, leaving a trail of kicked up dirt behind us while I make good use of my hands.

Pushing the three bikes into an alcove made of low hanging trees, Ace kneels on the ground to set up his drone. We're around a mile from our pick up destination, sticking to the woodland and back roads. Despite being abandoned, Malik flagged us down so the noise of the bikes wasn't heard near the warehouse. He's extra cautious about being caught, it seems. I suppose that's normal and now I don't have someone to bail me out, I probably should be too.

Walking back to the road, Ace finds a gap in the tree's canopy and sets off his flying camera. I pull myself up on a low branch to swing my legs while the guys crowd around his phone, watching intently. Only Spade hangs back, leaning against the same tree with his foot raised off the ground. I can see it's aching by the way he's discreetly rubbing it and trying to find a comfortable position. Once they have eyes on the warehouse, Malik and Jack strap up with guns and take off on foot to collect the package we're here for.

Ace joins us and I edge along the branch to get closer. Wanting a better view of his phone screen, I hook my legs over his shoulders and rest my chin on his head. He doesn't shrug me off which I'll take as an invitation to stay. I'm like that annoying cat no one wanted, but everybody enjoys stroking the good pussy. The screen shows the warehouse approaching, a giant chunk of grey with dimmed lighting hanging above the doors. Ace circles the building, getting a full view of the outside before edging closer.

"There's three possible exits, two doors and one is a closed shutter," Ace states. Hearing a teeny voice reply, I lean to the other side to see he has an earphone in for him to communicate with the boys on the road. "There's no vehicles to be seen, I'll check inside."

The drone approaches a window, hovering outside. A faint light is on inside but the glass is too smeared to get a clear view so Ace tries another one. Floor to ceiling shelves packed full with boxes block our view and I can sense the frustration growing from the man between my legs. Trying yet another, we see a clearing in the middle of the warehouse with a table in the centre. The light hangs directly above, highlighting a small box. It's around the size of a shoebox, causing me to frown but it's the movement in the shadows that catches my attention.

"Huh, that's weird," I point, seeing a figure I vaguely recognise step out with a phone pressed to his ear.

"You're right. It's supposed to be abandoned," Spade suddenly stands upright, hissing at the movement. I lean further in and squint at the screen, confirming my suspicions.

"No, I meant it's weird Cheese's men would be here."

"Who?" Ace twists to ask, our noses bumping inside the masks we're all wearing.

"Robert Leicester. You know...The mob boss that I used to pretend was my dad until he tried to kill me." His face falls, a look of pure horror claiming him.

"It's a trap!" Ace and Spade shout at the same time a gunshot pierces the trees. The dull thud of a bullet hitting the trunk beside Spade's head has us all freezing before jerking into action. Ace chucks me backwards, twisting to catch my falling body beneath the branch. Gripping me tightly, he spins us beneath the thick trunk as another bang tears the night apart. Spade bumps into us a moment later, his chest heaving.

"Yeah, don't worry about me fucker," he growls.

"You shouldn't have come," Ace replies, pulling a semi-automatic out of Spade's backpack. He then digs out a pair of funky goggles from his large cargo pockets and hands one to Spade. Keeping me close in what I hope is a protective move, not using me as a human shield, Ace peers around the trunk and another bullet flies into the tree. Guess they aren't the only ones with night vision goggles. And here's me, using the moonlight breaching the foliage to see a goddamn thing.

Crouching down, I pull the pocket knife from my boot. Swivelling it in my palm, I close my eyes and let my instincts take over. The trouble with only following your eyes is how much your other senses become dulled. Once the sound of blood rushing is trapped in your ears, you're screwed. The ground is littered with twigs and pinecones, making my ears twitch as one is stepped on to my left. Bracing myself to move, I then hear a teeny tiny voice and find the earphone amongst the leaves. Fishing it out and pushing it in my ear, I grin at the panicked voice on the other end until I hear the gunshots on their end as well.

"-cocksucking motherfucker! Answer me!"

"Do you kiss your mother with that mouth?" I smirk. Putting my knife between my teeth, I jump up and latch onto the branch, using Ace's shoulder to boost myself up. He tries to grab my leg but I wriggle out of his grip, climbing out of reach before looking back down.

"You! Where's Ace and Spade?!" Malik screams into my eardrum.

"Dead," I shrug, giving the boys a wink I know they'll see with their fancy goggles.

"We're not fucking dead!" Spade shouts, spoiling my fun. Pouting, I turn my focus to scaling the tree in full stealth mode.

"Okay fine, they're not dead—yet," I whisper. "I was preparing you for the worst just in case." Hidden in the shadows, the branches interlock and I'm able to monkey crawl from one to the other undetected. With a clear view of the forest floor, I count five men shifting forward in a V formation. They reach the treeline of the clearing where we've stashed the bikes, keeping themselves out of sight to the other side. Silently, I lower myself down, removing my boots so as to not make a sound when my feet meet the ground. The darkened figures are too busy sharing hand signals to notice me creeping closely, the one at the back too much of an easy target.

Popping up, I drive my pocket knife into his neck and quickly duck behind his back. Reaching around, I grab his machine gun with one hand and push his finger down on the trigger with the other. His friends drop like sacks of shit, as does he from the various bullets riddling his torso. Pulling my knife from his throat and picking the gun from his fingers, I notice too late there's only four bodies on the ground before me. An arm wraps around me, a hard body plastering itself to my back. On instinct, I plunge my pocket knife into his thigh, which doesn't get much reaction, and the gun sprays a round of bullets as it's pried from my hand.

"I was hoping you would be here, love." It takes me a moment to differentiate the voice from the one who is now speaking in my ear, asking what the fuck is going on. Spinning, Jasper peels a balaclava off his head and smirks down at me. I can't see his dimples but I know they're there, as deep and dreamy as they were that day on the bus.

"We've got to stop meeting like this love," I purr, playing both sides until I can figure out what's going on. Besides, I needed info on him, and who better to give it to me.

"I believe this is mine," Jasper reaches behind me to untie the skull mask and slip it off. I let him since I don't have an attachment to it, even if it did look cool as fuck. Instead of putting it on, he slips it into his pocket and tugs my knife out of his thigh. Tucking the blade away, he pushes it into the waistband of my trousers, his fingers trailing my hip bone. "You should be careful who you bump into in the woods. There's some dangerous people around."

"I'm attracted to danger. It's a fault of mine." I lick my lips, my pulse kicking up a beat. Jack is still shouting into my ear, drawing Jasper's attention as well. Pushing back a tendril of my hair which has escaped my ponytail, he leans down to kiss my neck and speak next to the ear bud.

"I think that's your best attribute, love. I do hope my brother is keeping you company, but remember that this is also mine," Jasper grabs my pussy roughly through my trousers and rubs his palm against my clit. I gasp, heat pooling against his hand. Ace brakes through the trees, raising his gun to shoot the man drawing his thumb off my lips. Diving in the way, I give Jasper the moment's distraction he needs to blend in with the shadows and disappear. I don't know why I did it and it was a long shot that Ace wouldn't just shoot me anyway, but like I said...instincts.

Shoving me aside, Ace takes off, shooting wildly into the dark until his clip is empty. I stay where I am, unable to recognise his face contorted with anger as he jogs back, the usual passiveness a distant memory. He hastily grabs another ammo magazine but it's useless. Jasper's laughter can be heard from the road, the tell-tale roar of a Ducati engine splitting the night in half. Ace and I share a look of 'oh shit' before racing into the clearing, finding Spade slumped against the tree trunk and Jack's bike missing.

"You let him get away!" Ace suddenly grabs me by the jacket, hoisting me upwards. Throwing me into the nearest tree, he storms forward to pick me up once again. Wrapping his hand around my throat, he smashes my skull into the trunk, his grip iron-tight. I kick out, struggling against the fog of confusion in my mind. Why was Jasper here, why did I defend him and how is the cutie with sad eyes so freakishly strong? Batting my legs away, Ace delivers two punches full-force to my stomach. "Who's fucking side are you on?!"

"Ace!" It's Malik shouting into my ear this time so I pick the ear bud out and press it against his. There's spots of gold flashing in front of my vision, my eyelids fluttering shut. My lungs are screaming but not a sound leaves my lips. In the next moment, I'm falling and I crash into the ground, choking in a breath. I lie there, waiting for the next blow but it doesn't come. Prying my eyes open, I see a bulky shadow walking away, leaving me alone in the dark. In the corner of my blurry vision, a bright pink figure is squeaking towards me. I smile weakly, watching Angus snuggle into my side.

"You came," I whisper, my throat feeling rough.

"Of course I did. I always turn up when you're truly desperate and not tough enough to handle shit on your own." I curl around him, holding back a sob. Big girls don't cry, especially this one. But Angus' words ring true which means in this instance, I'm not tough enough and that shit cuts deep.

ACE

Skidding my bike into a lay by, I kick on the stand and hop off. Spade shouts at me for jarring his leg but that's the least of my problems right now. Ripping the bandana off my face, I bend over and heave. My stomach is twisted in knots and my heart is trying to go into cardiac arrest because I'm utterly disgusted with myself. I did the one thing I promised to never do again - I hurt a woman. Everyone's walking on eggshells around Malik, waiting for his anger relapse but it was me they should have been worried about.

I hear the Dyna pull up behind me, Malik and Jack jumping off so I break into a run. I don't want anyone near me right now. Leaping over a railing, I dash up a grassy incline and skid down the other side. Fields greet me, spanning as far as the eye can see. Without waiting for someone to catch up, I take off and don't look back. My arms pump, my thighs burn, but I refuse to stop. Even when the streams of tears leak from my eyes, the wind pushes them back to pool in my ears. They only make me hate myself more.

My mother's voice appears in my head, the spot where her nails would dig into my shoulder beginning to burn. *Pathetic. Useless. A waste of space.* I tried to please her, ever since I can remember but it wasn't enough. By helping out, I was in the way. Hiding in my bed made me lazy.

I could have taken the taunts and I'd come to accept her constant rejection, but it was the isolation that pushed me over the edge. Sealed inside a seemingly pleasant house with a hateful old woman who never told me she loved me. I was homeschooled and without any friends, only allowed out to run errands and even then, I was timed. Take too long and it was a beating with her cane, telling me how I was as useless as my father. No wonder he left, but a hatred festered inside that he didn't take me with him.

I was afraid, starved, desperate. That's what I keep telling myself. That there was no other way. I lasted fifteen long years before I snapped, as did her neck in my grasp but that wasn't the worst of it. I could have lived with that. It was years later when a leggy blonde barged into me in the street, cursing me out for being a waste of oxygen, smacking me with her handbag and I was back in that house all over again. That's the night Malik found me, with blood on my shaky hands and tears streaking down my face. She could have had a family, a husband, children. She might have just been having a bad day, a rough week, a crappy year. Don't we all? Now thanks to me, she'll never have one again and I struggle every day to come to terms with that.

A farmhouse comes into view, no lights on inside and the overgrown weeds claiming the porch. I follow the moon's beacon, letting it lead me straight up to the front door. Bracing myself on the wood, I knock loudly and make sure there's no response before shoving my weight against the door, permitting my own entry. Slamming it closed behind me, I bellow loudly and slam my fist into a dining table. It cracks beneath the force, splintering across the wood floor. I then take my frustration out on any piece of furniture I can find, wrecking the neglected house.

The old box TV goes through the window on a strangled yell, my boots leaving holes in the walls. Tipping over a sideboard, a hammer drops onto the ground and that seals the fate of each rotting kitchen cabinet. Rats scurry out of their hiding spaces and I let them leave, I know how it feels to be trapped. The thought of the life draining from the old woman's glassy eyes makes my gut twist, crippling me in half until I drop the hammer. I rest my forehead on the wood, squeezing either side and screaming until my throat is raw. Nothing helps. Nothing works.

I used to turn on myself in times like this, but Spade and I made a pact not to resort to hurting ourselves anymore. If I cave, he'll do twice as much to himself just to prove a point and that'll be another notch on my conscience. But I can't get the image of Candy out of my head. How I scared her, how helpless she looked. I broke her immortal confidence. I saw it in her eyes just before she started blacking out. At least when I turned on my mum, she'd deserved it. Candy didn't. That middle-aged woman didn't. I took a life and the blood on my hands can't be washed away.

I slump against the wall, having nothing else to break. My chest is still too tight to inhale properly and lacerations cover my palms. I throw my fist into the floorboards, busting my knuckles open. Spade can't use that against me, it was a repercussion of what needed to be done. I needed to vent and dispel the anger that came from nowhere.

I was already punishing myself before we left the bar, watching the re-run of Candy with Spade and Jack on my phone. It was a complete invasion of privacy as I was watching her shower like a pervert before Spade even entered, but then I couldn't force myself to stop. But then I saw her with Jasper, of all people. She's running circles around us, but with him, she was putty in his hands. Literally.

Engines roar a short distance anyway, growing louder until they are right outside. I hang my head in bloody palms, not wanting anyone to see me like this. I keep away from people for a reason. Because my mom was right. I'm a pathetic lowlife, not worthy of a loving family. Regardless, the door opens and the heavy fall of boots manoeuvres a way to me through the chaos. I risk a glance up to see who it is, surprised to find Jack there. Of all the guys, he's the most likely to bow out and let the rest of us handle situations like this. Kicking some broken wood aside, he clears a spot to slide down beside me.

"I'm jealous too, ya know." I frown, eyeing his downcast expression. Jack's the most confident of us all, if he's feeling the strain then there's no hope for me. "I could hear it all through the mic. She didn't even try to resist him." There's more hurt in his tone than I expected and I suppose it has something to do with Jasper being his twin. We used to joke they were literally clones of the same person, but Jack would never steal from and abandon us. His sense of loyalty is too strong.

"Why would she? He hasn't given her a reason to," I mutter. It's not like Jasper beat her up, locked her in a basement, stole her belongings and deprived her of an orgasm. The exact opposite of that last one. I look at Jack out of the corner of my eye, wondering what it is that's really grating on him. Does he want Candy or is he annoyed Jasper took away something else that could have been his? What about me and Spade? There's such a fine line between being intrigued and in-over-our-heads, I don't know which side I'm on. "Question is, what do we do now? She is clearly no good for us but we can't just leave her out in the woods. She's miles from civilization." I leave out the part where we're a bike down and she probably wouldn't want to be in a hundred yards of me anymore.

"Fucking leave her," Jack growls. He looks up at me with newfound determination pinching his eyebrows together. "She wants Jasper, let her go find him. Malik planned on ditching her anyway so the job's done. Let's go home."

Pushing himself upright, Jack offers me his hand and I clasp it to stand. Throwing his arm around my shoulders, we walk out of the farm house together. Malik is on the front of my Suzuki with Spade's head leaning on his back. He's still riding his concussion thanks to the butt of Jasper's gun. No one says a word, leaving me my dignity by ignoring the obvious. I'm weak, petty and I've just blown our chances at getting Jasper.

CANDY

Ooh, yeah. Mmmm, that feels good. I rouse from my slumber to something wet dripping into my cleavage. Nails scour my skin, some kinky bastard wanting to have some fun. I blink rapidly, trying to clear my blurred vision. The coolness of the air washes over me and the trees rustle overhead, reminding me of where I am. Looking down, I startle the raccoon dragging his nose over my chest. I'm not even mad, leaning to nuzzle my face in his fur.

"Well hey there, little one." The raccoon jolts and bites my cheek, making me cry out and punch him away. Feisty rabid shitbag. Patting my cheek, I don't think he's broken the skin so I drag myself up and rest against the tree. The start of a new day has begun, giving the woods a completely different feel. Gone are the shadows and bodies from last night, although the remaining blood stains have caught the attention of my rapist raccoon. Greenery hangs overhead, filled with wildlife and purple flowers dotted all over the forest floor. There's tyre tracks in the clearing beside me and no sign of...anyone.

"I'm still here," Angus fills the silence. I roll my eyes and smile at him. Whatever he's after, he sure is trying hard to win me over with his sudden consideration of my feelings. I stretch high and wide, cracking my neck before trying to get up. My stomach aches from last night, the images I was hoping I would have forgotten flooding back. If I could choose a superpower, it would be short term memory loss. Nothing can hurt if you can't remember it. Looking around, I weigh up my options.

"Hmmm, what do you think Angus? One mile to an abandoned warehouse where Cheese's men might be lurking or forty odd miles back to collect the Candy Crusher?" I look down at him, sharing a nod to the obvious choice. Warehouse in the hopes of a fight. Then get the Candy Crusher and crush some skulls for that stunt last night. Just when I thought we could all do each other a favour; you hide me, I relieve you. It could have been beautiful.

I find my boots dumped amongst the leaves and tug them on. The road is made of concrete, or at least it once was. It's a wonder how we didn't crash and die in one of these potholes. I meander along the cracks at a chilled pace so Angus can keep up. His tiny feet can only stretch so far, the leathery squeak of his body sounding in my head. A dark cloud is crawling our way, the promise of heavy rain thick in the air. By the time I reach the warehouse, it's already begun spitting.

I pause briefly, trying to piece together what exactly happened here last night. The parking lot isn't in as bad shape as the road, but now it's marred by thick tyre skids and black markings from small explosions. Ace's drone is lying on the ground with a bullet hole straight through the middle, discarded and forgotten about. I know how it feels. Leaving it there, I walk to the closest door and try to pry it open with my fingernails. After a little jiggle, it pops open and I sneak inside.

The small windows surrounding the top of the building let the light in, allowing me to wander through the shelving units to see there's no one here. That's disappointing. The box that was in the centre has been taken and there's more blood spray. My gut twists, wondering if Malik and Jack made it out okay. But then I remember they all left me for dead (again) and that I don't give a fuck.

Rounding back towards the door, one of the boxes high above catches my eyes. Hold up, what kind of warehouse is this?!

Finding a mobile, metal staircase, I wheel it over to the shelves and jog up it. Tearing the tape with my teeth, I rip the box open and stare at the sea of dildos in front of me. They're all packaged in plastic, and all hot pink. Suddenly the cogs in my brain start working.

"Oh Angus, I feel a plan coming on."

"Is it a reckless one?" he asks, his gruff voice laced with excitement and I give him a wink. Reckless is my middle name. Just joking, it's Jacky. Dragging the box down the steps and into the centre of the room, I start to explore properly. Picking random shelves each time, I keep searching, digging and pulling items out until there's a stack of boxes before me. Sweat is dripping down the back of my vest but my grin is huge. This is going to be epic.

Doing one last sweep, I then spot what looks like a hand poking out from a top shelf. My head tells me to leave it but my feet are already moving, curiosity taking over. Using the metal stairs, I hesitate a few steps from the top. What if it's one of the guys, even Jasper? Am I ready to have that mental image stuck inside my brain? I've seen dead bodies a lot, but most of them have been complete strangers. Swallowing, I leap over all three steps at once and come face to face with the hand's body.

A female face stares back at me, her lips painted red and fixed into an 'O' shape. She doesn't have any hair, but she does have a cracking set of tits and the smoothest skin I've ever seen. Poking her arm, her silicone limbs wobble slightly and laughter erupts from my mouth. She's perfect. Hoisting her over my shoulder, I have to hold the handrail to keep my balance under the heavy weight. At one point, she tries to collapse to the side and I jerk to grab her, my hand disappearing up her asshole. Throwing her on the pile, Angus joins my side and raises an eyebrow.

"How are you going to transport all this stuff?" I frown then, looking side to side. There's a panel on the wall beside the shutters and after pressing all of the buttons, I figure out how to open them.

The parking lot to the first is empty but I won't be deterred. Walking around the back of the warehouse, I find a white van with 'Dann Winters' printed across the side, in between a set of saucy, red lips. I've heard of this company; it's like a knock-off of Ann Summers, but dirtier and specialises in fetish supplies. Today must be my lucky day.

"Thank you Gummy Bear Jesus," I put my palms together and bow towards the sky. With my pocket knife still uncomfortably tucked into my waistband, I manage to hotwire the engine in no time. Angus is no help loading the van once I've brought it around, but he sits up front and keeps me company as I head towards the nearest town. I haven't felt this good in...I don't know when. I'm revitalized, the scheme filling my head making me giddy to get started. I just need to pick up a few more items and then those boys won't know what hit them. Leave me for dead? I'll be their personal poltergeist and worst nightmare rolled into one.

JACK

"Hey Ace, have you seen my left Converse? I can only find this one," I wiggle my foot at him but he doesn't respond. Ever since we got back from that shithole farmhouse four days ago, he's been hunched over his computer. He says that's something going on with the electrical pulses but I reckon he's just using that as an excuse to be left alone. Malik's also been MIA, pulling one of his disappearing acts upstairs so it's just Spade and I keeping the bar running and each other entertained. I've got to say, despite how fucking insane and annoying she was, this place seems too quiet without Candy. Which is nuts because she was only here for a day. The longest damn day in existence.

The delivery van blares his horn, telling me he's not-so-patiently waiting for some assistance. Taking the elevator downstairs with one bloody shoe on, I find Spade is already at the back door chatting to him.

"Come on Pretty Boy, the man's got to deliver to other bars as well."

"Aw, you think I'm pretty, Spade," I kiss his cheek and ruffle his mohawk on the way past. The driver doesn't offer to help, too invested in talking to the cripple who's suddenly taking his required rest too literally. I know he can't feel that shit but I'm running around like everyone's lap dog. Making sure Ace eats, bollocking the bar staff who don't turn up for their shift, *washing*. Do I look like a maid?!

Unpacking the boxes of gin first, I leave them in a stack by the basement door to take down after this fat, balding cunt has moved along to his next stop. Maybe then I can convince Spade to do something menial like count out last night's takings. Moving onto the wine, I grab a crate and carry it to the kitchen side. Heading back towards the door yet again, I still and slowly turn to look at the boxes of gin.

"Hey, Fatzo. Wasn't there seven boxes of gin?" Spade halts his conversation, counting the six in front of me while the driver mumbles about losing the receipt.

"Pretty sure you only carried in six," Spade says unhelpfully. My right eye twitches as I stare at him, imagining how I'd love to stick my thumb right in his bullet wound and twist about now. I admit, I'm especially cranky this morning. I haven't been sleeping as of late, not even with my avo-cuddle gel mask. I'm fucking knackered, but as soon as I lie in bed, thoughts start swirling around my mind. Then when I do fall asleep, it's some bullshit like Candy stomping over me to get to Jasper, his cocky smirk mocking me awake.

Next to come out are the huge wooden barrels, some of which I have to heave up the back step. My muscles are pulsing and a layer of sweat covers my forehead. Finishing the delivery on auto-pilot, I pay the man and send him away so I can get back to business. There's a lot for one person to do before we open for trading, and as irritable as I am, I'm thankful for the distraction.

First is cleaning the bar before I stock it and put whatever we don't need in the basement. A few of the barrels have already been moved and I add chastising Spade for over exerting himself to my list of things to do. Then I move onto wiping down the tables and chairs before heading back to make Ace some lunch. The next time I see Malik, I'm telling him to make the cleaning service come daily, not weekly for fuck's sake. It's not like we don't have the money.

Finishing Ace's sandwich, I head into the bar to grab him some salted peanuts. The window cleaners have pulled up beyond the revolving door, unloading their massive ladder from the top of the truck. I shake my head at myself, not realising they were supposed to be here today. Returning not even a minute later, I see the empty plate sitting on the counter with only a few crumbs on it. Making a fist and lifting it high, I just about reign myself back in before I smash the plate with my bare hand.

"I swear the fucking god Spade!" I shout progressively louder with each word. I'm not dicking about here in one fucking shoe making sandwiches for everyone. Grabbing a handful of the bar nuts, I eat them myself purely as a distraction. Exhaling deeply, I steel myself and get all the shit back out to aggressively make another one. This time I take it straight up in the elevator, putting it under Ace's nose.

"I'm not-"

"Eat it." I order, my patience about to blow. "Eat. That. Fucking. Sandwich before I shove it so far up your arse, you'll taste it anyway." Nodding stiffly, Ace takes the plate from me and I kick off my shoe, flopping back on his bed. His mattress sucks me in, inviting me to close my eyes just for a moment. "Hey Ace," I mumble with my face against the pillow. "Can I take a nap here? And if I start talking in my sleep, slap me real hard. Okay?"

"Okay," Ace shrugs without looking. I start to curse him out in my head but the sleep calls for me and I give in. The next thing I know, Spade is shaking me awake and moaning about the bar opening in a minute. I jerk upright with a string of drool hanging from my mouth. Rubbing my face, I get to my feet and follow Spade's slow arse out of the room with Ace not having moved. Heading back into the elevator, I start to sway when I bump into Spade's shoulder and jolt.

"Hey man, are you alright? I'm worried-" Spade's voice is cut off by the elevator grinding to a halt. The lights turn off, leaving us with just the red flashing button on the control panel. I have to look away, my head still fuzzy from my nap. At first we just stood there, unsure of what to do. Taking the initiative, I step forward to press the speaker button.

"Er….Ace? Are you there buddy?" There's no response. Stepping back, I tap my thumb on my chin in thought. "You know what, I'm not even mad. Let someone else take over with the bar for a while. I'm just gonna sit right here," I lower myself to the floor, leaning against the wall. Spade looks at me like I've lost my mind and I'd be inclined to agree. Just then the elevator shudders, the light coming on and it starts moving again. Ahh, fuck.

My legs feel even heavier now I have to pull myself up and drag my sorry ass into the back room. Even Spade is moving faster than me on his crutches. The table is all set up for a game of cards, although I don't remember doing that. I guess Spade did, but he's nuts if he thinks we'll be able to convince both Malik and Ace to join us. He should have only dealt for two. Footsteps pounding on the staircase draw my attention to the door beside me as it flies open, a furious looking Malik glaring at us.

"What the fuck just happened?" I look between the three of us, swaying slightly as the dizziness continues to live in my brain. It was just an elevator glitch, jeez. Ace then appears and I fake a heart attack, holding onto Spade for support. No one cares – my Oscar winning performance is not even worthy of an eye roll.

"I told you! Something is jamming the electrical currents and it's messing with my security systems." He looks at me accusingly as if I haven't been the only one keeping him alive while he's been moping. Opening my mouth to argue, my eyes narrow on something through the two-way bar mirror. You've got to be kidding me.

"Not something you asshat, someone." I point between the group, turning everyone's focus to the pink haired chick lounging on one of our sofas. I'm not surprised she's still alive. She's like a cockroach, she'll outlive us all. But to come back here takes some balls, after what Ace did and Malik is about to do. Malik's already out the door and I shove Ace through when he tries to bolt. Spade takes up the rear, blocking his exit and seemingly on my side for a change.

With Malik in front, we march towards Candy as a unit. Clearly she didn't get the message she's not welcome here and she won't be able to sweet talk her way out of this one. There's a lingering scent of alcohol in the air and the lights flicker as we round the sofa, giving her the sense of drama she surely wanted. Her hand is laying across the wooden bat on her lap, her red lips fixed in a circular shape. My eyebrow hitches, watching Malik rip the bright pink wig off the sex doll. He fists it tightly, throwing it across the room.

Following its flight path, I now notice the sheen of liquid covering the bar. Racing over, the sticky liquid drips over the edge and onto my jeans as I risk a look over the other side. Smashed bottles of gin cover the floor, the shards of glass making it impossible to get back there on bare feet. I can see from here though, the gap between the cashier till and the bar. She's fucked us over. Royally.

"Find her!" Malik orders and I don't need to be told twice. Striding to the door to head out back, I smash the pin into the keypad but the door doesn't budge. Trying again with force, the keypad remains red and I turn to Ace.

"Little help here?!" Ace runs a hand over his chaotic, brown hair and sits on the opposite sofa with a sigh.

"What's the use? This is the least we deserve." I scrunch my fist, not having the patience for his down-in-the-dumps bullshit. I figured Malik would straighten him out but instead our leader crouches down to talk to him quietly while Spade makes his hobbled way over to me. The divide between the four of us is obvious, there's those who will do what it takes and those with their baggage holding them back. Hammering my fist on the door, I give it a kick before storming out the front.

Vehicles are beginning to pull into the lot, a few of the regulars giving me a wave. I ignore them, counting the bikes we have left are still there before stalking around back. The only reason people come this far out for a drink is to say they did, like being permitted entry into a high-end club. It's all about appearances. The back door is still wedged open from this morning's delivery. I cross the lower level, smacking the inner release button to open the bar door from inside, where Spade is waiting.

"Are we in this together or not?" I call out. Malik's head whips around, and after a beat he nods. Leaving Ace, he joins us with the temple in his head pulsing, leading the way. Approaching the elevator, there's a Queen of Hearts playing card stuck to the doors. No words need to be said. This little girl is playing a big man's game, but we make the rules here. She can run but there's no place she can hide where we won't find her.

Spade opts for the basement so Malik and I take the stairs. I miss my footing on one, coming down hard on my shin. A bout of dizziness hits me like a freight train, Malik's voice fading in and out as he tries to help me up. Using the railing, I make it to my feet and pull myself the rest of the way, finally clearing the fog. I've gone days without sleep before but I've never nearly fainted because of it. Malik's dark eyes give me a hard stare, his sharp jaw remaining clenched so I shove him away.

Starting on a side each, we scour every inch of the second floor. I find a bundle of left shoes collected and dumped in a pile on the gym floor. Huge pink splodges coat the mirrored wall and continue to be seen down the hallway. The tin of cash has been taken from Spade's wardrobe and her backpack is gone from Jasper's old room.

Crashing into my room, I freeze at the sight before me. My circular bed is still swinging, meaning she was just here, but it's the mound of sex toys covering my mattress that has my focus. Hot pink vibrators, massive dildos, butt plugs, restraints. Everything I could imagine for a hell of a good night if I wasn't fuming and the closest willing female didn't make me want to strangle the life out of her. My eyes drift to the white wall behind, the word 'Submissive' sprayed in black. The paint is dripping towards the tiled floor, pooling in the grooves in one place. This. Means. War.

"Jack!" Malik calls and I stagger back, following the sound of his voice to Ace's room. His computer screens are flashing, codes and words I don't understand popping up at me. I don't know where to look but Malik zeros in on the monitor furthest right, shouting and smacking the side of it. 'System override,' flashes with two surveillance camera screens underneath. A playing card has been stuck to each, one with the King of clubs and the other the Jack of diamonds, both with lines drawn across their necks. I tilt my head, unable to hold onto the thoughts racing around in my mind. That is oddly personal for someone we barely know.

"She's in my fucking suite. We're fucked Jack. It's over." Malik slumps over the desk, the true weight on his shoulders evident for the first time since I've known him. Malik doesn't give up, he certainly doesn't let a few taunts get him down. I place my hand between his shoulder blades, the powdered blue shirt on his desk rising and falling heavily.

"Why, what do you keep up there?" I'm scared to ask.

"Everything."

CANDY

The day before

A teenage waitress places the strawberry milkshake with whipped cream and extra sprinkles on my table. I smile widely at her, grabbing a napkin to spit out my gum. Placing it in her hand, she looks horrified but I return my focus to my list. My plans are almost ready and I can't wait to put them into action. This is exciting, planning my own job and seeing it through. I should do this more often, like a sex-crazed, unhinged, female version of Robin Hood putting the bullies back in their place. I could start my own mob, where everyone has fuchsia hair and demented tattoos and praises me as their queen.

"Sounds more like a cult," Angus states from across the booth. I shrug one shoulder, picking up my fluffy pen to keep writing. We've been staying above this diner because the owner thinks I'm going to suck him off in payment. Everything I order adds another sexual favour, and even though the grilled cheeses are to die for, he'll have to catch me first. I'm not against using sex as payments, but greasy fry cooks aren't my niche and if anything, I'm helping him to learn a valuable lesson. Always get payments upfront.

Working my way through the list, I tick off the ideas I've prepared for and make a list at the bottom for anything that's left to get. A few more boxes of hair dye and I should be good to go. Individually, they're silly little pranks, but collectively, I'm going to rain down on Malik and his guys. I want to see that vein in his head burst and fuck them all so hard, they'll be screaming my name. Smiling to myself, I take the striped straw in my mouth as a figure moves into my peripheral vision.

"This seat taken, love?" My thighs clench on instinct, the voice which has featured in my very wet dreams now coiling around me. If I'm honest, which I always am with myself, that same voice has featured both of its owners, along with piercing blue eyes and a mohawk, a chiselled torso beneath a sharp suit and longing, chocolate eyes. Even after Ace lost his shit and took it out on me, there's a misery deep down I dream about soothing whilst sitting on his face. No one can be mad about eating pussy.

Jasper drops into the seat opposite, squishing Angus. His dimple on one side makes me squeeze my lips tightly shut before I do something stupid, like lunge across my milkshake to tongue the shit out of it.

"You seriously need to get laid," Angus' mumbled voice echoes in my head. Ignoring him, I tap the fluffy pen on my cheek and wait for Jasper to state his business. I'm a busy woman these days.

"Figured I should thank you for giving me an out in the woods the other night," he grins. I feel a blush rising, my motives still unclear even to myself so I hide within the curtain of my hair. Angus mutters about him thanking me by giving us a ride back, but I learnt a long time ago not to depend on anyone. I take care of myself.

"Don't mention it. Like, ever again."

"Alright," he chuckles. "Why don't you let me buy you a drink then?"

"I'm all good here." Taking the straw in my mouth, I suck my strawberry milkshake until my cheeks hollow out. I can do rough sex in storage compartments, I understand basic urges and I enjoy a cat and mouse game. But dating? That shit baffles me. The need to show off and impress someone in the hopes they keep you around long enough to make your life feel fulfilled. Then you get stuck in a routine, following the expected milestones until you have a screaming kid on each hip and wonder where it all went wrong. No. Thank. You. And I refuse to believe fucking the same person day in, day out doesn't become boring after the first...week.

"What's a guy gotta do to get your attention?" Jasper leans forward, genuinely curious. His blonde hair looks yellow in his light, his green eyes a little too focused on me. I swallow thickly, my dreams too vivid in my head. Don't say drop your pants, don't say drop your pants.

"Drop your pants." Angus pops up in the corner of my vision to facepalm himself. *What?* I shrug at him. The bad guys are so much more fun and easily expendable because they're generally assholes. Jasper's smile is dazzling, all white teeth and rugged jaw. He's almost too handsome to look at.

"Anytime, anywhere love." Not needing more of an invitation, I take the straw out of my milkshake and start to down it. Jasper slides my notepad across the table while I'm licking every last drop of cream from around the glass. "What's this?" Wiping my face clean, I ease on my leather jacket and pull my hair out of the collar.

"A revenge list." He continues to read, laughing to himself as he goes. I bet he got to rubbing chilli on the inside of Jack's eyemask, that one tickled me too.

"And what are you getting revenge for?"

"Well, firstly, your old crew muscled in on my heist and stole my bat. After that, I pretty much asked for what I got until Ace beat me up and they all left me for dead in the woods. But mostly, I'm bored and I have nothing else going on so...they're kinda stuck with me for now.'"

"Ace put his hands on you?" Jasper's demeanour suddenly changes. The sharp edge to his eyes and straightened posture is a mirror image of Jack sitting before me. His lips are tight, his hold on the notepad making his knuckles turn white. It's strangely hot, more so because I'm imagining those knuckles dragging over my nipples.

"Hands, fists, tree trunk. It's all the same. Don't get your panties in a twist about it, I've dealt with worse." Hopping out of the booth, I hold my hand out for my pad. Jasper slowly closes it, taking my hand in his and linking our fingers instead.

"Come with me, I'm going to help you get the revenge you deserve."

Pulling up outside a blue shutter, Jasper puts my sex van in drive. He was adamant he wanted to drive and I'm not very good at it anyway. It's everyone else's fault if they get in my blind spot because I don't check those. The clue is in the name - blind spot. I wouldn't have been able to navigate this maze of units anyway. Leaving the key I had cut yesterday in the ignition, he gestures for me to hop out and follow.

His back muscles ripple in the fitted orange workout top he's wearing, the nylon clinging to every ridge in his body. On the bottom half, grey sweatpants hang low and I don't comment about the Converse he's wearing, just like his twin. Pushing the shutter up, he switches on a light and Jack's Ducati greets me on the other side.

"Hey beautiful," I coo, stroking her glossy red fuel tank. Jasper closes us inside, turning to respond when he realises I wasn't talking to him. Trailing my fingers along the leather seat, I shift my attention to the rest of the unit. From the looks of things, Jasper is currently living here. A leather futon sits beside a mini fridge, with a kettle and portable stove balanced on top. His belongings are neatly stacked in boxes and there's a metal safe tucked at the back. A chunky lens camera sits on a shelving unit nearby, leading me to the mass of images stuck on the wall.

There's individual photos of Malik, Jack, Spade and Ace, with post-it notes all around. Jack's has the most. In the centre, a large map of the city and its outskirts is covered in marker pen, from 'sightings' to jobs the guys have done. Stalker much? Before I can read too much, I then notice an image that strikes a little too close to home, making my hackles rise.

"You are working for Cheese then," I point to the photo of him leaving his mansion.

"We currently share a common interest, that's all." I don't have time to ask what it is, Jasper spinning me and claiming my mouth with his. All thoughts grind to a halt, this secretive man becoming addictive to me. He tastes like apples again, my tongue diving in to devour him.

Lifting me up, Jasper carries me across the space and lowers me onto his futon. His chest presses against mine, our laboured breathing joins as we start tearing at clothes. Pulling on the new jumpsuit I lifted from a high-end store, he wiggles it down my body like a snake shedding its skin. Helping me with his t-shirt, he's all hard muscle and defined lines underneath, making my mouth water. I grab a handful of his silky hair, dragging him back down onto me. His dick is already rock hard, nudging against my centre to get closer. Kissing me deeply, Jasper palms my breasts roughly and then flips me over.

His crotch stays pushed against my ass as I hear him scuffle about in one of his boxes. Next thing, he leans his weight over me to wind a thick rope around my wrists. Kinky. Tying them tight, his fingers trail the length of my spine to the pink G-string. I can feel my wetness growing as my patience wanes, the need to feel Jasper fully seated inside me riding me hard. Placing kisses on each of my ass cheeks, he dips lower to lick the outside of the flimsy piece of fabric barring my pussy from him.

"Fuck, you do taste as sweet as I thought you would," he groans. I'm arched and ready for more, nearly begging. Leaning back over me once more, Jasper tilts my head to the side and holds me in place to drag his tongue across mine. I can taste myself, sucking his tongue into my mouth. Pushing my hair out of the way, Jasper sighs against my face.

"This is going to be hard for you to understand, but I'm not the bad guy here."

"Shame. They're my favourite flavour." He chuckles deeply, softly kissing the side of my neck.

"Remember that, love," he mutters. A sharp sting pierces my neck, making me jerk aside. His hand holding me in place is iron-clad, his body settling on top of me. I writhe, but it's useless, the weight of his muscles threatening to crush my backbone. Struggling to inhale, I feel the rush of dizziness claim me and instantly know I'm screwed. And not in the way I was hoping.

SPADE

Shuffling down the basement steps, I brace myself on my crutches before turning on the light. My thigh is starting to flex a little more without a stab of pain shooting from me but it'll still take much longer to heal than I have patience for. I think I hate this more than the bullet that got stuck in my rib cage and had to be pried out by Ace and a shitload of vodka, both in the wound and in shot form.

Checking the stacks of delivery boxes, there's nothing out of the ordinary so I turn to leave. A creak makes me halt, my head turning slowly to find the source. Everything is still, eerie even. I move my crutches slowly so as to not make a sound, rounding the basement towards the chest freezer at the back. A muffle catches my ear and I spin, narrowing my eyes on a wooden crate balanced on its side on a bottom shelf. Suddenly it moves, rocking back and forth. Going too far, it drops to the floor and smashes open like a cracked egg, a bound and gagged pink imp falling out.

For a moment, I can only stare at her. She's practically naked, in just a hot pink thong and some kind of tape strapped around her chest. Rope around her wrists and ankles have her writhing around, her wide eyes trying to make sense of where she is.

Spotting me, she then screams against the rope tied tightly around her face and cutting into her mouth. All the anger I felt in entering this basement vanishes the moment I clock onto the sheer panic in her brown eyes.

Lowering myself down with my leg outstretched, I untie the tight knot at the back of her head. I accidently pull her hair but she gasps as it's released and I shift to work on her hands. The second they are free, Candy throws her arms around me and buries her face in my neck. When I don't react, she shuffles closer with her ankles still bound and drags herself onto my good thigh. Pulling her feet towards my crotch, I wrap my arms around her petite body to untie the rope and then leave them there, partially hugging her.

After a little while, she inhales deeply and loosens her grip on me. My head has unintentionally lowered to rest on hers, my senses tuned in to everywhere her skin touches mine. Gently shifting her upright, I pull my t-shirt off and ease it over her head. Her eyelashes are wet but I didn't feel a single sob pass through her body. Protectiveness pulses through me for the girl I should hate. In the short time I've known her, I've come to learn Candy isn't rattled by anything, which is what is really worrying me.

"Candy, what happened to you?"

"He took me to his locker and drugged me," she replies in a low voice.

"Who—Leicester?" I ask, stroking the side of her face to encourage her to look at me.

"No. Jasper." My eyes widen and I try to shoot upright, forgetting my leg can't handle it. Candy catches me, pulling us both to our feet and hands me my crutches. I move to leave but Candy steps in front of me. "Spade." She rests her hands on my chest and stares up at me, her eyes are large and covered in a sheen of tears. "What happened here..." her gaze moves towards the crushed barrel and I take her hands in mine.

"No one needs to know. I'm going to protect you from now on." I hadn't planned on those exact words but they're out there now and doing anything else would make a liar. I vowed not to be an asshole like my mom's boyfriends, so lying can't be an attribute I become comfortable with. Neither can standing by while the man who screwed us over continues to hurt others.

"Why are you being so nice to me? I shot you, remember?" I raise an eyebrow. As if I could have forgotten.

"I really hope I'm not wrong, but I reckon if half the people in your life treated you with decency, you wouldn't have to live in self-defence mode all the time. So the fault is with the rest of the world and correcting it has to start somewhere, right?" My words surprise and confuse her, and I wish I could spend longer exploring why I suddenly give a shit about someone I barely know. But with Jasper fucking around in our affairs yet again, there's no time. "Come on."

Limping up the steps, Candy looks between the playing card on the elevator and the state of the bar from the mirror, cursing loudly.

"He did my plan to perfection. I don't know whether to be impressed or furious that I missed it." I smile despite mine, her usual brashness breaking through.

"Hold onto the fury Crazy Girl, you're gonna need it." Spotting Ace's sorry ass still hunched on the sofa opposite the sex doll, I bang on the window and whistle loudly. "Ace, get back here. I need you." I know he wouldn't be able to resist that last bit. Shooting upright, he crossed the floor and stepped through the door, his eyes immediately landing on Candy. Surprise turns into anger and then sorrow, a whole orchestra of emotions filtering across his eyes. Stepping in front of her, I level him with a hard stare. "It's not what you think. We need to find the others. Now."

Grunting, Ace takes my right side to help me hop up the stairwell while Candy carries my crutches behind. Fuck taking the elevator again. Ace's gaze keeps slipping about over my shoulder, the tension in his stance making it hard to use him for support. He's the one I'm least worried about, it's Jack and Malik I'm going to have a hard time shielding her from. Why did I have to settle on her, out of all the women in the world, to take under my protection?

Reaching the top floor, I take my crutches back and find the pair standing in front of Ace's computer screens. Pushing Candy back to wait in the hallway, I step into the doorway and Jack looks back at me.

"It's not good news lads. She's in Malik's suite, uncovering who knows what since he won't tell me." Jack throws an evil glare at the side of Malik's face, not that he notices. He's hunched over, his hands gripping the edge of Ace's desk.

"It's way worse than that, I'm afraid." Spinning on me, I take the brunt of Malik and Jack's hard stares while Ace taps my shoulder. I shoo him off, needing to handle this properly if we don't want extra blood on our hands. "If there's someone upstairs, it's not Candy." Ace taps me again and I flick my head around to shout at him, but find Candy's gone instead. Looking either side, I then see her exit Jack's room with her bat in hand and re-enter the stairwell. Shit.

Ace shoves his way into his room, taking a seat and aggressively types on the keyboard. I quickly fill the others in on what happened in the basement and as much as I know. The monitors stop flashing, several camera screens coming back online. A group of customers have gathered out front, peering inside to wonder why we aren't opening up. Other than the usual vehicles, there's only the white delivery van from this morning waiting near the dirt road leading away from here, the driver still sitting behind the wheel.

"What the fuck is he still doing here?" I point out.

"I'm on it," Jack says, grabbing a pair of odd right shoes from beside Ace's bed and racing out the room. Malik remains silent, watching Ace work his magic until all cameras are back up and running. Spotting Candy's shadow beneath the playing cards blocking out the view of Malik's front door, Ace brings up several windows of code, working through them all for a buzzer to sound on the floor above us.

"Tell me you did not just permit her entry to the one place I was trying to keep her from," Malik says in a dangerously low voice. Ace spins in his chair, leaning back and folding his arms.

"Jasper's in there anyway. Let them take each other out." I frown at Ace's carefree attitude, not knowing what's going on in that mind of his. Maybe he's finally surpassed feeling sorry for himself and gone straight to not giving a shit about what's happening around him. Maybe seeing Candy had something to do with it. Malik storms out, never being one to let someone else fight his battles for him.

"Should we go after him?" I ask out loud, knowing I'm not going to be of any use in this state. Not that a leg cast would stop me from trying. Ace turns back around, keeping an eye on the screens and muttering about Malik being stupid enough to get involved. I lower myself onto the bed, not taking my eyes off Ace. He needs to sort his shit out for good, but it's not my place to tell him that and this isn't the time. Chaos is raining down around us, and I get the feeling this is only the beginning.

CANDY

Scraping the bat along the walls, I watch for any shift of movement around me. The dining room is the first room I enter, an impressive yet unused mahogany table splayed before me. A divider made of black wood columns allows me to see into the kitchen, the bar presenting a place someone would hide. I don't expect Jasper to be hiding, but I slowly make my way around to check anyway. The cabinets around me are curved into a semi-circle, facing a balcony beyond an open, sliding glass door. Veering left, I find an equally expensive living area but no blonde, British sex symbol who likes to play with Valium.

I came to last night in the back of the van, already tied and seriously pissed off. Jasper camped out there too, filling the vehicle with the scent of weed without offering me a single toke. As if my situation didn't call for it. He offered me some of his MacDonald's fries which I kicked back in his face, screaming around the gag to let me go. If only he'd told me the thought process behind his plan, there's a chance I would have been raiding this suite myself. It's not like I was on a side and I had my own vendetta. One he's now turned on himself.

Crossing back on myself, I go in search of the bedroom instead. I find it, easing the door open to look at Malik's room. Triple the size of any I've ever seen, naturally. The door bumps without hitting the wall, giving away Jasper's position and me the advantage. Stepping inside and raising my bat, my hand is hovering over the handle when a hand clamps over my mouth. I know better than to scream, twisting back to see Malik shaking his head at me. His other hand rises with his finger primed on the trigger of his semi-automatic and I smirk beneath his hand.

Edging out of his way, I stay in a geared up position with the Candy Crusher in my hands. Malik braces himself, speeding around the door with his pistol at the ready. A hand flashes out, knocking his arm upwards for the gunshot to ring out and the bullet nestling somewhere in the ceiling. Jasper throws himself into Malik, taking them both to the ground. I dive forward next, smacking Jasper across the shoulders with my bat. Take that, *love*.

His leg sweeps out, taking me down while the boys fight for possession of the gun. Another shot sounds, this one close enough to make my ears ring. Grabbing whatever body I can, I yank myself closer and tug at the backpack on Jasper's back. Hey, that's my backpack! Tearing at the handle, I dislodge it while Malik punches at Jasper's face from underneath. Jasper manages to wrestle the gun out of Malik's grip, emptying the remaining bullets into the wall. I have no idea why we are still alive but I won't be deterred. The bag's strap then snaps, sending me flying back into the corner of the wall. Pain bursts through the back of my head, but it's the scattering sound that grabs the guy's attention.

A USB stick is sitting between the three of us. Jasper lunges for it, marking its importance to him so I reach for my bat and try to smash it. The men both scream 'No!', Malik dragging himself up Jasper's back to get there first. My head is swimming, warping my vision so I swing my leg out and kick the USB beneath a cabinet. Shoving Malik off, Jasper pries the bat from my hand and swings wildly. Catching Malik on the temple, he then shoves him into me before rushing towards the cabinet. Claiming his prize, Jasper pockets it and tries to run. Using my stomach to push himself off, Malik launches himself across the room.

Rugby tackling Jasper into the next room, I scurry on my hands and knees to join them. At this point, it doesn't feel like I'm needed in this fight but I'm invested now. The two of them are rolling around on the dining room floor, throwing fists into ribs and elbows into faces. Jasper gets the upper hand, the blood from his busted lip dripping down on Malik's shirt. Diving on top, I tighten my arm around Jasper's neck. He chokes, diving aside to wedge me between him and the wall. I tighten my legs around his waist, holding him in place for my free hand to explore.

Malik takes the opportunity to punch Jasper's face yet again, the beautiful harness becoming more marred with marks. Sitting forward, he smashes me into the wall again and agony slices through my back. Releasing him, I heave out a choked breath, digging my hand into my sticky tape bra. My movements are sluggish now, the men swinging their fists and hoping one of them lands. Crawling forward, Jasper shoves Malik back as I'm right behind him. Malik tumbles on top of me, my arms collapsing under his weight.

Scrambling to get off me, Malik shoves my head into the tiles in the process. Jasper runs the length of the suite, stepping onto the balcony before vaulting himself over the side. My heart jumps into my throat, a mix of emotions colliding in my chest. Pushing myself up, I catch up with Malik, taking the hit of the railing hard in my stomach as I look over.

The biggest ladder I've ever seen is falling away from the balcony, making the people loitering around the parking lot scream and scramble. The ladder crashes into various cars and by that point, the window cleaning truck is skidding away down the dirt track, followed by a delivery van. Jack leaps out from behind some bushes, shouting and cursing as he takes off after his twin but it's useless. He'll never catch him on foot.

Holding onto the railing, I lean back and sigh. Well, that could have gone better. It sure as shit could have gone worse, but better is always preferred. Malik is already back inside, slamming his fist into a wall. I wander after him, soothing my hand over his bicep. He flinches away, scowling at me.

"How could you let this happen?" The question is directed towards me but I feel like it was more aimed at himself. Clawing at his hand, he mutters about being screwed and drops onto his cream sofa. I skip after him, getting a real look at the place Malik has made his domain. An electric fireplace is attached to the wall beneath a huge, mounted TV. The windows span the entire right side of the room, thick black curtains hanging on either side. Avoiding the coffee table and shaggy, cream rug in the centre, I move to stand in front of the mopey man slouching on the cushion.

"Come on, it's not so bad." He ignores me so I straddle him, and he's in such a mood, he doesn't shove me aside this time. Taking his face in my hands, I finally get to stroke my thumbs over his trimmed facial hair like I've been wanting to since I first saw it. His tanned skin is soft, cared for intensely by expensive moisturisers no doubt. When his eyes finally meet mine, there's a touch of vulnerability in their dark depths.

"You have no idea what was on that USB. We're all going to jail. There's no use trying to run from it."

"Oh," I breathe. "Sounds like you're really screwed. If only someone could do something to ease your mind," I roll my hips over his. Still in Spade's t-shirt, my G-string lets me feel everything from Malik's zipper to the bulge underneath.

"Do I look like I'm in the mood?" Malik growls, twisting his head out of my grip. I don't want to point out how he's hardening beneath me and as I sense he's about to chuck me to the floor, I push my hand into my sticky tape bra.

"Does this put you in the mood?" I pick out the USB I lifted from Jasper's pocket during all the scrambling. His expression doesn't give anything away, that controlled look fixed into place, but his body can't hide the way his thighs tighten and his back straightens. Licking his bottom lip, Malik smooths down his blood-smeared lilac shirt and fixes his cuff. I sense the moment he's about to lunge and I beat him to it, holding it out of his reach but my chest is now in his face. Win. "Na ah, not so fast."

"I'm done with your games. Give me the USB. Now," Malik growls. I cock my eyebrow at him. His leader bullshit might work on the others but it does absolutely nothing for me. Relenting, he sits back on a sigh, his hands landing casually on my bare thighs. "Fine. Name your price. Ten K? Twenty?"

"Money means nothing to me. I've now joined your vendetta against Jasper, but there's two things I need to remain on Team Malli-Moo." The vein pops in his temple, his lips pursing at the nickname. Putting my finger to my lips, I have a very brief thought about what I could use this stick as leverage for, but there's only two things that really matter to me. "Sex and drugs, and by drugs I mean an unlimited supply of pink bubble-gum." There's a beat of Malik staring at me, hunting for the catch. No catch here, I'm easily pleased as long as I'm cumming and chewing. Dropping his hands away, he looks into the distance.

"My men aren't allowed to have sex here, and I abide by the same rules. They can take women wherever they like in the city but not in our house. It causes issues and divides us, as you've proven since the moment you dropped into my bar."

"You're the big boss man, allow it," I shrug. Leaning forward, I brush my lips over his on the way to whisper in his ear. "And no one said it had to be divided."

MALIK

I stare into the brown doe eyes looking right back at me. There's a rare moment where she doesn't open her mouth, allowing me to see beyond the smirk she usually has fixed in place.

Becoming an orphan, whether by birth or a cruel twist of fate, is something Candy and I have in common. I almost envy her for not really knowing her parents or seeming to care about reconnecting with her mom, but the thought of not knowing mine stirs a visceral pain inside I've spent years suppressing. I refuse to let myself go down that path, instead relying on my rules to keep me surviving from day to day. Rules that say I need to pay off all my debts, in any shape or form, to feel free and not to let others fight my battles.

Candy muzzled in on my fight with Jasper, somewhat unhelpfully but she still did. I don't know why. But now I have a new debt to pay. I narrow my eyes, trying to find the ulterior motive in her face. It can't be as simple as sex and bubble-gum. I sit here with her slowly rolling her hips over my crotch, stuck on the notion that money doesn't rule her. She has no ambitions, no aspirations. She simply lives for each moment, and I envy her for it.

On the flip side, those same qualities are what brought her here to irritate the life out of me. I'm at my limit with Candy and her smart ass. The way she's turning everything I've built upside down and has my men running after their own tails. The wheels in my mind start turning, merging her request with ways to teach her a lesson and get back the one thing I need in life. Control.

"You wanna play, Crazy Girl?" I ask, having heard the others call her that. It fits impeccably well. "Let's play." Her eyes crinkle in the corners and she bites her lip, reminding me there's a fine line between cute and crazy. She thinks she can handle us all, she has another thought coming. It's time she learned there's consequences for trying to fuck with the big dogs. Flipping her off me, I leave her in a heap on the sofa and stalk over to my intercom system.

"Everyone up here, now." I demand, and in no time, my men appear at my side. Matching pissed-off expressions greet me, all three of them feeling the effects of Jasper doing us over, again. The longer I look at them, the more I decide this is for the best. We all need to blow off steam, together.

"Jack," I bark and he steps forward, his green eyes full of resentment. "Grab a range of the sex toys decorating your room, and for fuck's sake, wash them all." Ignoring the way he freezes and gapes at me, I turn my neck to look at the others. "You two. Move Candy somewhere she'll be more *un*comfortable. We're all blowing off steam tonight."

"Well it's about time," Candy smirks. Skipping over to join us, I grab her wrist when she tries to reach for my dick.

"Nobody gave you permission to touch me." I say in a cold voice, and a shiver runs down her spine. Her tongue licks a slow path over her lips, trying to get a rise from any one of us. At the jerk of my chin, Ace and Spade each grab one of her arms and haul her away from me. Jack suddenly takes off at a sprint, grinning ear to ear as if waiting for confirmation this is really happening. For this once, I'll let Candy have everything she's asking her. She will soon realise not to ask again.

Following the way the men dragged her, I find Candy has willingly stripped off and is plucking at her nipples beside my pool table. Ace and Spade slink off and soon return with a roll of duct tape each.

"We couldn't find any rope, boss. But this should work," Spade cocks an eyebrow. Perfect. The burn will last long after we rip the stuff off of her.

"Do it," I command, and Candy jumps up and down on her toes, clapping with excitement. I turn my back on them and adjust my cock in my pants, ignoring the sound of the tape being ripped from the roll. I yank the knot from my tie, leaving it dangling open around my throat.

"You boys are so naughty," Candy laughs. The tinkling of her voice makes my stomach roll, but whether it's from nausea or desire I couldn't tell you. I'll decide when she's screaming my name. Turning, I watch Ace lift her hips and dump her heavily on the table, wrenching her arms back to tape a star pattern over her wrists. It's going to ruin the table. But watching the way her pale lithe body is pulled taught and tight across the surface is a price worth paying to see her squirm.

Spade takes her feet, slapping several layers of tape up her calves to ensure her continued compliance. Not that there's any chance of her trying to get away. I've never met a bitch as freaky as Candy, even in the clubs I used to frequent before the novelty wore off. Nothing holds my attention for long. Jack skids into the room, face red and panting, holding a bag of toys in his hands. His face breaks out into a cruel smile that would make my skin crawl if I were in Candy's position. Her though, it's probably a turn on.

"One toy each," I tell them, and Jack drops the bag onto the table next to Candy's hip.

"If I can make a suggestion," Candy starts, stretching her neck to watch as my men pick their weapon of choice and discard the other sex toys she brought with her.

"You can't," I interrupt, remaining at an angle where she can't see me clearly, but close enough that I'll be able to catch all the action. She arches her neck backwards, trying to bring me into her line of sight.

"You boys make out like you're all rough and tough. But from where I'm looking, there's four of you, one of me, and you still couldn't handle me without me being tied down." Candy flexes her hips, wiggling and strutting as much as she's able with her hands duct taped to the table. I close the distance between me and the table, Jack immediately moving out of my way. I slap her sharply on her cunt, and she mewls at the contact.

"Do it again," she grunts through a smile, and I bring my hand down, just stopping an inch from her clit.

"Fucking tease," she winks, her lips remaining curled upwards. I want to cup her face in my hand and squeeze until she's unable to smirk at me again. She'd be so much fun to play with if I let my inner beast loose, except a girl like this would probably stick around until I fell asleep and cut off my balls. Pulling my tie from around my shoulders, I walk to the top of the table and wrap it around her eyes, latching it tightly behind her head.

"What? Don't wanna go full Dom and plug my mouth?"

"No," I say calmly. "I want to hear you scream. It's time you learned to be careful what you wish for, Candy." I step away from the table and cross my arms over my chest. The guys are waiting at the other end, their chests rising and falling heavily and their dicks barely restrained in their pants.

"Make her come," I order. "Don't stop until I tell you to." All at once, they're on her. Even Ace. I watch him closely, not letting myself become fully infatuated by Candy's gasps and moans. Ace has a very specific trigger, brought on by women who condescend him - another reason the guys can't parade sluts around or why he can't work the bar without me nearby. We keep Ace behind the scenes, but where Candy's concerned, it's all new territory.

Jack has gone straight for her breasts, giving them each a squeeze before clipping a set of nipple clamps to her. Candy squirms at the contact, biting down on her lip. I lean over to pull her lip back out, letting her noises fill my game room.

The sound of the duct tape ripping from the roll catches my attention, and my eyes flick to Spade. He tapes a battery-operated vibrating wand to her inner thigh and switches it on. Its blue light flashes, the strength of its vibrations audible from where I stand. Using his fingers to spread her pussy, Spade centres the vibrator directly over her clit and stands back for a better view.

Candy squeals in delight, her voice high and tight and quaking from the assault on her body. I swallow thickly, being affected as much as the others who have stopped to simply watch her. She's a thing of beauty, writhing and screaming. Flushed and cursing. I feel her pleasure all the way to the tip of my dick, the bite of my zipper giving me little relief.

Ace steps in then, ripping the tape from her left leg. He spreads her thighs at an awkward angle, dropping her leg over the side of the pool table and holding it there with his thighs. Rounding the table, I join Spade for a clear view into the valley between her thighs, and the moisture already dripping from her pussy.

In another time and place, it would be my face between her legs and me pinning her down as I thrust my tongue into her holes. As I sucked on her slit and made her keen underneath me. It's been a while since the notion took me and now I can't stop the images from invading my mind. Taking a step back, I refuse to be tempted. Partially for my men's sake, as this is for them, but mostly because I don't want to give her the satisfaction of knowing she got to me.

Jack removes the vibrator pulsing over her clit and tosses Ace a bottle of lube. He catches it deftly in one hand and pops the lid with his thumb. Pouring an obscene amount over a vibrant purple butt plug, and without any warning or preparation, Ace then shoves it into her ass. Candy groans from deep in her belly, her head jerking side to side on the ruined felt of the table. Her hips grind as Ace holds it in place, her greedy ass taking it all.

"More," she begs through clenched teeth, and my boys are only too happy to oblige her. Ignoring my one toy rule, Jack pulls a bright pink Rabbit from the black duffel bag and flips it upside down before spreading her hole wide and ramming the dildo inside. He flicks on the switch, and it's vibrating ears start a punishing rhythm against the butt plug, sending a second set of alternating vibrations coursing up her spine.

There are several ways to make a woman fall apart. You can take your pleasure from each other; hard, fast and dirty. Or you can tease her, ease her through gentle caresses and obscenely sweet pleasure. This is not that. The first orgasm is ripped from her body, and it is breath-taking to behold. Her back arches up from the table. Her skin is patchy and pink from the assault on her senses. Her muscles fire at random intervals, until you can't tell if she's coming or having a seizure.

Still, she moans "More."

All three of my boys look at me, and I give them a silent nod. Ace twists on the table, leaning over her pinned leg to reach into the bag. Like a well-oiled machine, Spade moves forward to pull the plug from her ass and Ace grabs a big black monstrosity of a dildo from the bag of tricks.

Jack, who's always been a tit man, is back at Candy's breasts, pulling and flicking at her rosy tipped nipples. She has no idea how much it's going to burn when the blood rushes back into those things. I don't turn my back this time when I adjust my cock in my pants. I'm not the only one straining with a raging boner. As a team they slick the dildo with copious amounts of lube, then Spade spreads her butt cheeks, as Ace eases the rubber into her ass.

Her moan is guttural, and her body writhes at the onslaught, as my boys start thrusting the dual cocks in and out of her matching holes. They set a brutal pace, one pulling out as the other rams back home. Sweat is coating her body, and the toes on her right foot are curled into the felt of the pool table. There's a constant stream of curses slipping from her mouth until I can't make out the words as her voice rises in pitch and her arms begin to tug on her restraints.

When Candy comes again, she keens in an earth-shattering wail. It's fucking glorious. It's a full-bodied experience, as she shudders and peaks. Spade leans down to drop sloppy kisses up and down her stomach and hip, not that I blame the bastard for a minute. She deserves kisses, for the show she's performing.

Her skin is raked with goose bumps, her pink hair tousled and wild like my perfect sexual minx. My tie has slipped from around her eyes and is across her forehead, but her lids are squeezed tight with the fever rushing through her nervous system leaving her panting and gasping on my table.

"Okay, okay!" she pants. Begs. Pleads. She squirms on the table, trying to get away. The muscles in her arms are bulging as she tries to pull herself free. But there's no place for her to go. She's mine until I say so. My boys look to me for instruction. I hold up my finger. One more.

They never slow their roll. I jerk out my arm so my cuff rises above my watch and I zero in on the second hand evenly ticking beneath the glass. I don't watch the woman slowly deteriorating on my pool table and the succulent way she falls apart. This round, it's all for them, as I time how long it takes her to fall apart once more. How reactive her body is, how wild she can really be. Twenty. Twenty-one. Twenty-five seconds pass and she's crying out to the heavens.

"Malik!" she screams, and I shudder at the sound of my name being ripped from her lips. My body seizes up, my eyes flicking up despite myself. The scene before me has a groan locked in my throat, the way my men taunt and tease her into submission. Her voice is raw as the pleasure is drawn from her body unrelentingly. Whether Candy realises it or not, she just gave me what I need. She bent to my will, gave me the power over her. And as soon as the feeling starts to dwell with the lessening of her screams, I immediately want to do it again.

I tilt my chin up and run my fingers across my throat, signally that's enough. My men start turning off her toys, one by one. Jack pulls the nipple clamps off, and Candy hisses at the pain it causes, before slipping on a beatific smile. They drop the toys haphazardly back into the duffle bag, but don't unstrap her from the table. Her body has gone soft as chocolate melted in the summer sun and my tongue waters for a taste. Candy opens her eyes, her gaze is dazed and unfocused.

"That was fucking amazing," she sighs. The boys look at each other, and I can't read their expressions. I decide I don't want to. If her brand of crazy turns them on, I don't want to know about it. Ordering Ace to untie her, I pull Spade and Jack aside for a quiet word. They eye me suspiciously but concede, understanding this is what needs to be done for the good of us all. Nodding, the pair leave, sliding the wooden panels closed behind them.

"Not so fast," I catch Candy by the shoulders as she tries to stumble past me. Her brown eyes flick upwards and I look away, hunting for Ace lingering by the pool table. "There's a rift here that needs to be fixed. Tonight. I'll remain in the room but you need to vent whatever it is you're holding against her before it's too late."

Seeing the panic flare within him, I raise my hand to hold his argument at bay. My word is law in this house and Ace knows without my rules, he'd be sitting in a prison cell right now. Candy's shown me an out, a way to bring us all together like we once were but I need all my men on board. Turning Candy, I push her in Ace's direction.

"You say stop and I'll make sure he does. This is purely sexual, Ace won't physically hurt you now or ever again. Understood?" I direct my last question to the brown, puppy-dog eyes pleading with me to stop this. To send her away. I shake my head slowly, moving back to lean against the window.

Gazing out towards the mountains, it's not long before Candy's convinced him to do as I say. I peek over every so often to check on them, at least that's what I tell myself. Ace grips the sides of her head, thrusting his dick into her ferociously so I can hear his dick hitting the back of her throat. I'd be inclined to step in if there wasn't a blissed-out pleasure on her face or her hand working between her legs. Turning away, I grip the windowsill and work on controlling my breathing. One thing is for sure after tonight. Candy is going to be the death of me.

CANDY

Rousing to the smell of bacon, my stomach instantly grumbles. It's still dark all around, but I feel like I've been asleep for longer than the average little white chapel wedding lasts. Sitting upright, my mouth feels claggy and my hair's a mess, but my body feels goooood. There's an ache between my thighs that I wish I could bottle and save for a rainy day. I don't need to be fucked to have a good fucking, which last night proved tenfold. A shirt is buttoned over my chest, the cuffs hanging way past my hands.

Rising, I pass by Angus' judgemental stare from the armchair and go in search of food. The blackout curtains aren't drawn in here, my eyes sealing shut at the brightness that assaults me. Feeling my way to the kitchen island, I squint to find a stool and carefully lower myself onto it.

A plate is dumped in front of me with a loud clang, next comes a coffee hastily shoved across the island with a scrape so the liquid spills. Blinking my eyes open, before me is not who or what I was expecting. I'm in Malik's suite and Malik's shirt, but there's no Malik to be seen. Instead Ace is washing up with his back to me, wearing the same t-shirt and sweatpants as last night. Rolling the sleeves up to my elbows, I pick at a piece of bacon and chew on it while watching him throw the frying pan on the drying rack and turn to face me.

"Usually people are calmer after being sated," I wonder out loud. It was mildly amusing watching Ace try to make me gag while he fucked my mouth. Even though my thirst was fully quenched for the night, I've found that pretending to still want more is the best way to infuriate a man. Makes them work just that little bit harder when they think they have nothing else to give. Ace pummelled into me until his monstrous load pumped into the back of my throat. He needed it for sure and I was only happy to do him that service.

"You think you're indestructible but everyone has a breaking point. You seem to have the shortcut to mine and one of these days, you're not going to like what you find." I sip my coffee and dig into the breakfast he presented me with, shaking the fork at him.

"If you haven't noticed yet, I can take care of myself. You can keep pushing me all you like, I'm attracted to the damaged ones anyway. On that note, where is Malik?"

"He had an errand to run. You can't be trusted alone in his suite but he insisted I let you rest and made you food. I followed his orders, now get out." When he starts to round the island, I grab a sausage and the mug, slipping away before he catches me. Pausing to look back in the doorway, I lick the length of my sausage before stuffing it all in my mouth. Chuckling down the stairs, I head towards my new, bland room in hunt for a change of clothes when Jack steps into my way.

"Did you have a well-satiated sleep?" he cocks an eyebrow. I open my mouth to tease him with a 'I've had better,' but he doesn't give me a chance. "I've been tasked with cleaning the mess Jasper made, but since these were your plans, I've decided you're doing it instead." He throws a long paint roller at me, which strikes my arm and drops to the floor. I stare at it for a second.

"No thanks." Disappearing into my room, I lock the door and finish my coffee. Setting down the mug, I dive into the dresser looking for something to wear. A pair of gym shorts and baggy top will do, pulling them on and yanking the collar down over one of my shoulders. Opening the bathroom door, I flinch at finding Jack there, the roller back in his hand.

"Cleaning. Now. Start with my room," he points through the bathroom. I don't know where he slept because the swinging bed is still full of sex toys, the spray paint on the wall behind making me laugh.

"We could always make use of some of those sex toys instead?" I flutter my eyelashes. Jack's nostrils flare and his green eyes harden.

"Malik gave strict instruction. It's all or none, and only when he deems it appropriate." Gotta love appropriate, planned sex, I muse to myself. I push past him when he remains in my way, trying to persuade him to get started while I have a quick shower, although he sees straight through me. Quick showers are a crime against humanity. Grumbling, I enter his room and start throwing dildos and butt plugs into the garbage bag by the door. Such a waste. Jack gets to work repainting the white wall while I tell him I preferred it my way. Apparently, Cruella de Vil is more his style and he won't be persuaded to unleash his inner submissive. Even after last night where he proved that's exactly what he is to Malik.

Once finished in his room, we spend the day on the rest of the floor. I scrape the pink hair dye from the gym mirrors and the matching handprints across the bathroom surfaces. Jack sorts out everyone's shoes and puts them back in their rooms. I catch a glimpse of Ace at his computer, trying to slip by to fuck with him some more but Spade catches the back of my collar.

Giving me a stern eye, he pushes me in the direction of his room to straighten up the furniture. Spade wasn't in my original plans as I didn't really know what would get a rise from him, but it seems Jasper had a good old time generally tearing shit up. Jack drops a cleaning caddy in the doorway and disappears downstairs, spouting some bullshit about jobs to do in the bar. Huffing, I get to work while Angus watches from the desk. Spade's room is minimalistic, most of his décor in the form of motorcycle memorabilia. A pair of handlebars stick out of the wall and a tyre has been converted into a footstool for his desk chair. Many of the mini bike ornaments are now smashed over the floor, as are the frames that contained jacket patches, flags, posters, all that shit.

"For the record, none of this was my idea." I turn to see Spade has lowered himself onto his bed to watch me work, his mohawk a little deflated today.

"Oh, I have no doubt this was all Jasper. He never saw the point of collecting mementos. But you trusted the wrong man."

"Story of my life," I mumble, more to myself. Kneeling down in a clear spot, I pick up the pieces of metal that I'll superglue back into the mini version of a vintage BMW bike. As I go, I start to hum a tune. I'm not surprised when it turns into 'Once upon a December' from the movie Anastasia, it always does when I'm concentrating.

Getting lost in a world of my own, I start to sing to Angus the way he likes. Every group home I went to, I always had a copy of the DVD in my backpack and would hide away to watch it on repeat. I imagined I could be that orphan whose grandmother never stopped looking for her and whisked her away for a life filled with riches in Paris. I thought if I learnt the song the pair shared and sang it often enough, some rich old lady would recognise it and take me in. Alas, here I am surrounded by only egotistical dicks.

When I've finished picking up what I can, I place the pieces on the dresser and turn to find Spade is missing. I look around, now hearing the sound of water splashing in his bathroom. The water shuts off, a cloud of steam leaking through the crack in the door. I knock, telling Spade I'm all done when he tells me to come inside. Spread out in a huge bathtub, his mocha skin looks like melted chocolate along the rim. I can't catch the emotion in his eyes from here, my senses distracted by the heat and floral scents wrapping around me.

"Care to join me? First bath I've been able to have since you shot me." Smirking, I close the door and strip off, stepping into the water. It's scolding hot, but I feel like that's not where the warmth seeping into my body is coming from. Leaning back into Spade's solid chest, I gently brush my finger over the lumpy, tender scar on his thigh. Taking my hand in his, Spade brings it up to place a kiss on the back of it. I chew on my bottom lip, now in unfamiliar territory.

I can take sex, simple meaningless sex, any day of the week. It's like a transaction of the bodies where both people (usually) get paid with an orgasm and you move on. Soft kisses and bubble baths however, I'm at a loss. Melting back into Spade's body, I let the steam close in around us as if this moment is hidden, even from me. His head lies on mine but not once does he try to touch me in any other way .

Sentiment isn't something I believe in, but twisting onto my side and snuggling into Spade, I let myself get a little carried away. In my mind, I pretend we're long term lovers who regularly bathe and watch movies together. Maybe there's a puppy scratching at the door and a fugly camper van outside we take for camping weekends. I smile to myself, ignoring the twinge of mourning I have for a life I'll never live. After all, I have a wicked imagination.

CANDY

"Here," Malik passes a credit card over me to Jack in the driver's seat. My eyes light up and Malik grabs my cheeks roughly, twisting me back to face him. "Don't go insane," he warns. I twist out of his grip, giving him a wink. Insane is my middle name. Just joking, it's Deborah. The Tesla beneath me roars to life with a flick of Jack's wrist. I didn't even know they had a hidden garage camouflaged amongst the trees, never mind a 4x4 tucked away inside. I clap my hands excitedly, Angus sitting on my lap. Rolling his eyes, Malik moves to the open window behind.

"Lay low, keep your eyes peeled," he orders Spade. Beside him, Ace is glued to his phone screen, watching the security footage while Malik is out here. Since I told Jack where to find Jasper's locker and he ultimately found it empty, they've all been extra on edge. From now on, at least one of the guys is going to stay back at the bar remaining on high alert at all times. If the guys weren't sick of me stealing their boxers and walking around in baggy vests that make my boobs pop out the arm holes, we wouldn't be leaving at all. Alas, I'm just too sexy and I get to go shopping!

Waving out the window, we set off for town. Jack thinks we're going to the nearest, crappy little town with barely any shops, but I rerouted the sat nav while he was checking the tyres. We're going back to the seaside town that I crawled up on the beach on my hands and knees. Bobbing up and down, a sigh from the back seat dampens my mood. Ace and I are in a weird place right now, so I leave him to brood.

"So there's a few things that have been bugging me," I announce to anyone who would like to answer. No one does, so I spin and direct my questions to Spade through the gap between the headrest and seat. "Why doesn't Malik have a card themed nickname, what's the deal with the card themed nicknames and why do you bother with the bar? If you're going to be criminals, you can do that from a bunker without the added hassle of running a bar." His blue eyes hold my gaze and I turn to give him time to compile his answer.

"None of your fucking business to all of the above," he replies. I can see his smirk in the windscreen mirror. He wants to get a rise out of me, and I'm happy to give it. Unclipping my seatbelt, I throw myself between the seats and land between the thick thighs manspreading in the back. Twisting to Spade, I start to tickle him under the arms. He stares at me like an idiot but I know there will be a sweet spot, I just have to find it. Digging my nails into his neck, lightly scratching his chest, pinching his thighs. I'm about to resign and just go for a good ball tickle when I squeeze his knee and Spade suddenly jerks forward. Aha!

Jumping up on the seat, I squeeze his knees in both hands, the laughter erupting from his mouth spurring me on. Even Jack encourages me, enjoying the guttural sounds leaving Spade that he's probably never heard before. An elbow nudges me in the side, the mood-killer in the car piping up.

"Watch your ass," Ace hisses. Halting my tickles, I look at him over my shoulder.

"Oh, this ass? I'll watch it, watch it twerk in yo' face!" Lifting my butt high in the air, I shake it on Ace's shoulder in these stolen denim shorts they kept for some reason. I reckon Jack has been parading around in them, they do feel looser. Giving it my best booty popping action, Ace tries to shove me away but I end up dropping into his lap.

"Answer my questions Ace, and I won't converse with you the rest of the day." His chocolate brown eyes don't take me seriously so I hold out my pinkie. Accepting it, he pushes me into the middle and stares out of the window.

"He does have a card nickname, Malik means King in Arabic. His parents used to call him that before they were killed in the casino they owned. Left Malik a rich orphan, but it's a family he's always wanted. He just doesn't know how to go about it." Angus' little head pops around the passenger seat, a frown etched in his squishy mouth. Now I have so many more questions but I can't mess with a pinkie swear.

"And the bar?"

"The bar is more of a promise that one day we'll go straight, when we've all sorted our shit out and Malik's paid off whatever he's saving for. We don't ask for details because he won't give them. Now fuck off in the front." Using the seats to pull myself forward, my foot not-so-accidently uses Ace's dick as a crutch to jump back to my seat. Turning onto the first real, tarmacked road, Jack starts muttering about where the sat nav is taking us so I turn up the music. Jenny from the block is playing, letting me distract Jack with my body rolls all the way to the beach.

My abs have had a hell of a workout by the time we pull up, and I'm even impressed with how much I can move whilst belted into a seat. Parking right on the seafront, the sunshine has brought the whole state to the beach. Surfer's wax their boards, children jump on stranger's sandcastles, women top up their tans with a layer of red. Hopping out of the 4x4, I stretch my arms high in the air.

"There's a café just down this street that will give you a view of the entire strip opposite," Jack tells Spade and Ace. "How about you guys watch in comfort whilst I handle this?" His green eyes trail the length of my body.

A flashback to last night springs to mind, a shadowed figure cutting through the adjoining bathroom to crawl in my bed. Through the haze of my sleep, Jack just wrapped his arms around me, muttering something about not being able to sleep. I found the rise and fall of his chest oddly comforting and when he was gone this morning, I thought I'd dreamt it. But the chemistry between us over breakfast had shifted and I've decided it must have happened after all.

Angus tells me I should be worried about how attached these guys are becoming to me, but my motto is to live for the present and not give a fuck about five minutes from now. Whether for the best or worst, things will play out and I'll deal with them when the time comes.

Agreeing, the two walk down the street at a snail's pace while Jack and I cross the road. I don't know where to start, the shop displays are filled with bright colours and floral patterns. They're pretty but I don't really do pretty. My style is more beautiful nightmare crossed with dreamy psycho. I keep walking with Jack just behind, coming to a display of leather and straps. This one. Reaching out, I grab his hand and drag him inside. It's like every emo's fetish in here. Buckles, zips, PVC, edgy cuts, missing panels and best of all, it's all black.

Pushing Jack into a seat by the fitting room, I leave him there and dive into the clothing racks. Oohing and ahhing, a sales assistant approaches me to ask if I need any help.

"Oh yeah, hold these and keep picking stuff out. Don't worry about price, he's paying," I dump the clothes I'd already chosen into her arms and stick my thumb towards Jack. He rolls his eyes, digging out his phone while we continue down the aisles. The sales assistant is exactly my kind of person; blonde dreads, colourful tattoos, hollowed out flesh tunnels in each ear and a piercing between her blue eyes. Her style is awesome too and she manages to find the last pair of her platform boots in my size.

After an hour of trying on every item she gave me and getting Jack's obvious approval with each one, we take the whole lot. I wear a fresh outfit out, proudly displaying the style I've never been able to afford and the best part is, it's actually paid for this time.

The platform boots tie up to my knees, a cute red, pelted mini skirt just covering the thong underneath. I'm wearing a bra for once, a netted black top sitting on top. It has a built in collar, sleeves to the elbow, an open chest and corset style closing over my abdomen. I've decided I want to be buried in this outfit one day and make a point to tell Jack until his free arm winds around my waist. It's an odd sensation, his limb hanging heavily over my ass and my footsteps becoming awkward, but I kinda like it.

"Are we done, love?" I eye Jack suspiciously, his crooked smile not a sight I'm used to seeing on him, but maybe I have something to do with that.

"Not quite." Sidestepping to link my arm in his instead, I lead him across the road to dump the bags he's carrying with Ace and Spade. Holding up my hand when they begin to stand, I drag Jack away until we are out of sight. I can't relax with Ace's eyes staring at me all the time and it's way past time we had some fun. Real fun. A giggle escapes me as we dodge the crowds, my feet scurrying towards the funfair gates in these platform boots. It's even busier than last time, people bumping into us and rushing past, giving me the perfect cover to slip the credit card out of Jack's back pocket.

Leading him into the arcades, Jack's posture begins to relax as we wind through the machines. I tell him I need the bathroom and throw my hip into a coin machine for the ones idly waiting on the edge to drop out and give him something to do. When I'm sure he's not looking, I sneak back on myself towards the technician's box. A middle-aged man with glasses and a try-hard tie is surprisingly accommodating, placing a call for me and handing over the phone when prompted. Thanking him for his time, I fight to keep the skip out of my step when returning to Jack. Malik's going to love what I have in store for him, and by love, I mean he's going to hate it and I get another torturous foreplay session. I can't fucking wait.

Not spotting him at first, I hunt around and find Jack at the back of the arcades. His back fills out his white tee a little better, as if he's been pumping weights lately without me noticing, his stance wide and confident. Rounding his side, I see a pink gummy bear teddy being raised in the metal claw, only to drop at the last moment. "Dammit," he mutters.

"Aw the teddy Angus' are still here," I smile. Jack jumps at the sound of my voice, looking bashful so I put my chin on his shoulder. "Hey, whatever happened to my one? It wasn't in the backpack with all the files Jasper tried to steal and I haven't seen it anywhere else."

"It wasn't?" he asks, eyeing me in the mirror at the back of the grabber machine. I shake my head, winding my arms around his middle. "Oh right, yeah. Well, I was fuming about losing my bike and blamed you, so I had an angry wank and spunked all over it and chucked it in the bin." I'm going to presume whatever he just said is a British thing but I got the jist. He came over Angus 2 because he couldn't handle his own emotions. Pussy. Grinning at him, we simply stand there. Hidden in plain sight, sharing a rare bullshit-free moment. Machines ring out and lights flash all around. A little porky kid tries to shove us out the way but we don't budge. There's something different about him since the night at the pool table, but I can't put my finger on what it is.

In the mirror, a figure in the distance catches both of our attention as he stands still and stares directly at us. Wearing shades and a high collared jacket, he taps his phone screen and lifts it to his ear before disappearing in the crowd. Moment ruined. Jerking into action, Jack is gone and I'm left staring at the teddies below. Noticing there's one more turn left on the dashboard, I twist the janitor's screw twice and grab the pink gummy bear in one, easy swoop. Collecting it from the prize drawer, I hand it to the little girl wandering towards me, her eyes glued to the bear.

"Trust me kid, the bad ones are always worth it in the end," I pat her on the head. Walking in the direction Jack went, I breach the outside and inhale deeply. Mmm, popcorn. Following my nose, I find the truck in no time. Instead of joining the back of the line, I walk on by to the pier railings behind. A kid around eighteen, nineteen years old is there with his friends, a whole tub in his hand. Leaning over the railing to look at the sea, I take a handful and stuff it all in my mouth. He eyes my cleavage, his eyebrows shooting up.

"Oh man, can I get a picture with you for my insta page. I've got 700 follo-" I put my finger over his lips to shush him. Social media baffles me, sharing your fake life whilst crying behind a screen while the person next door does the same.

"Give me the tub of popcorn first." Handing it over, I lean over to peck him on the cheek, his friends all getting the picture on the phones shoved in my face. They thank me and move a few steps down but continue to take photos while I enjoy the popcorn. It doesn't take long for one of the guys to find me. As luck would have it, it's Ace who's demanding what the fuck I'm doing at the side of my face.

"Weird, I'm sure I can hear something. Unfortunately I pinkie swore I wouldn't converse with a certain someone for the rest of the day." Gripping my arms, Ace spins me around, the box of popcorn tipping out of my hand and dropping into the water below. Bastard.

"This is serious Candy. We're all out here trying to protect you, you could at least give a shit." Brushing his hands off me, I flick my pink hair over one shoulder and return to lean on the railing. My beloved popcorn is dispersing and drifting away.

"That's rich coming from you Ace. I figured you'd have the fireworks on standby in the hopes I went missing and didn't return." There's a pause with him just standing there. Stepping close enough for his body heat to transfer into mine, his mouth brushes my ear.

"You have no idea who I am or what I've been through. I push you away to keep you safe, from me. But if you think for a second I'd let Jasper get his grimy hands on you, you clearly haven't been watching closely enough."

ACE

"How much?!" Malik storms out of the Devil's Bedpost before we've even stopped, shaking his phone at us. He didn't seem this pissed when I called to tell him Jasper was in town, just sighed in disappointment. Exiting the vehicle first, Candy leaves the bags for us.

"You said go insane," she shrugs, popping a bubble of gum in Malik's face. He twists to correct her, falling silent at the view her tiny skirt provides before turning on us.

"Women are expensive Malik," Jack pats him on the back. "Especially this one." I busy myself rounding the trunk to grab the bags, wondering just how long Candy is staying for. It seems like something we should all sit down and discuss as a group without her present. Don't get me wrong, the blowjob was phenomenal and she's definitely spicing things up, but I know I'm a ticking time bomb until I next explode. What if it's worse next time? When I'm around her, I feel like a giant holding a piece of glass in my hands. She'll slice me open and give as good as she gets, but ultimately I'll end up shattering her. The quietest and most withdrawn out of the four of us is the more dangerous, and I couldn't hate myself more for it.

Carrying her bags up to Jasper's room and dumping them on the bed, I slink back into mine and close the door. Leaning back, I sigh heavily. The truth is I hate being alone. I had enough of that growing up. But when I'm around people, even my boys, I never feel a part of the conversation. Always on the outside looking in, as if I don't know how to interact. Which is met with looks of worry or pity, and that's even worse than being alone.

Dropping into my computer chair, I pull myself towards the desk and switch on the desktop. The background pops up, making my heart sink like every time but I won't change it. The photo is from the early days, back when we just picked the twins up.

Staring back at me, the five of us are all smiles with the grand opening of The Devil's Bedpost. We had a total of four customers, but it didn't matter. It was our place to belong. Now it's my place to hide from the world. Even Malik's lips are tilted, his arms crossed cockily in the middle. To his left is Spade, using his shoulder as a prop. I'm on the other side with a slanted grin as Jack ruffles my hair, his other arm around Jasper. Or Jester, as he was known as back then.

Malik stripped him of his nickname and right to come back the second he stepped over the property line with our life savings. It wasn't just the cash in the vault Malik trusted him with, it was the entirety of our accounts. Jasper doesn't have a specialised subject like the rest of us, he's the whole package. Tech savvy, utterly charming, trigger happy. Losing him was a blow to our jobs, but it was nothing compared to how much it fractured us. Malik's smile is a distant memory, his rules are as solid as the law. Get on board or get out.

Opening a new window, I connect my phone to the monitor. The moment Jack's name appeared on my screen, I knew something was wrong. Leaving Spade at the cafe, I'd managed to catch a glimpse of Jasper ducking through the crowd coming out of the fairgrounds and better yet, I managed to snap a few pictures. Dragging them into the dark servers I'm a part of, I put an alert out with the timestamp and location attached. Hopefully this gets us a few bites. We've stopped taking on jobs until Jasper has been dealt with, but I can tell Malik is getting twitchy about money. He doesn't tell us anything anymore, although I can only imagine starting from scratch in a world that revolves around bribes wasn't easy.

Minutes drag into an hour with no hits and I grow impatient. Switching to a different screen, I head deeper into the servers, not looking for any in particular. I'm the eyes in the sky that keeps us from ambushes, usually. I run daily coded algorithms to pick up on anything that potentially involves us, including the bar and our birth names. An idea comes to mind and my hands hover over the keyboard, a frown pinching at my eyebrows. Figuring fuck it, I throw Candy Crystal into the mix and sit back while the bar loads.

The first ping through my speakers sets off an avalanche of a hundred more, windows popping up all over the screen. My eyes can't move fast enough, the amount of hits ordered on this girl making my mouth drop. What the fuck have we welcomed in? The most recent has been reposted, a lot, making it hard to pin the original location, but suddenly things begin piecing together in my mind. Printing off a copy, I barely wait for the printer to finish before whipping it out and flying up the stairs to Malik's room.

Pressing my hand on the scanner, I burst in unannounced. Checking every room, he's nowhere to be seen so I help myself to his mini bar. Two double whiskeys down the hatch and my jittering has calmed for the anger to begin setting in. It's dulled and it's nothing Malik can't handle, but a slither of fear still works itself into a band in my chest. Fearing myself is worse than fearing anything else in life. I know who I want to be, how I want to react. But those choices were taken from me during my childhood, the urge to turn in on myself and destroy whatever is left is all I know.

The buzzer on the door sounds as if releasing, Malik freezing as he spots me through the panelled divider. Closing the door softly, he slowly edges forward. Usually I only disturb him unannounced when it's late and I need a fight or there's bad news. Noticing the piece of paper on the side and my lack of primed fists, Malik relaxes slightly. Along with promising Spade I wouldn't self harm, I have a pact to take my anger out on Malik rather than the bar punters I find staggering around outside. Bad for business and all that.

"She has to go," I state. Those four words hang between us, thickening the air. Malik watches me carefully, not saying a word so I shove the paper his way. Remaining on the other side of the island, his eyes flick downwards. A somewhat grainy image of Candy taken from CCTV stares back at him, a large bubble of gum covering her mouth. She's winking straight at the camera like the cocky shit she is, her pink hair like a beacon for anyone who decides to take on the reward for her head. The silence hurts my ears, my hands flexing back and forth the longer it goes on.

"I thought after the other day, you'd be more inclined to keep her around." Malik takes the paper and drops it into his garbage disposal. Rounding the island now, he takes the bottle of whiskey and uses my glass to pour himself a measure. I can only watch, the band in my chest tightening, until it's hard to breathe.

"She's a walking target on our backs," I grind out through my teeth.

"We were five once. Maybe it's time we were again." Malik tips his glass my way, downing it in one.

"Are you fucking kidding me right now?!" I snap. Smacking the glass from his hand, it flies across the room and smashes against his mahogany cabinets. Malik waits a beat before rising to face me.

"It's been a while since we did this Ace. I was starting to think it wasn't going to be a problem anymore."

"She's the fucking problem," I growl. Shoving at his chest, there's a moment where my mind says 'oh shit' before Malik's eyes turn dark. He doesn't usually fight back, so the crack of his fist puncturing my jaw and the force of his kick to my stomach are enough to throw me back into the bar. More bottles crash and shatter beneath me, the slice of heat behind me telling me there's glass in my back.

I'm not sure at what point I lost Malik's faith. I suppose it was when I called Candy a problem, not realising he didn't feel the same way. No one can say I didn't give her the benefit of the doubt, if anything I was the first to see her coming. I let the events play out, presuming Jack would have chased her out like the good errand boy he is and we wouldn't have to see her again. Picking myself up, I hold my hands up in defence.

"What I'm trying to say is, she's the reason Jasper is fucking with us. Clearly Leicester put out the hit and Jasper is after the money. Again."

"Jasper had his shot at Candy, multiple times and he didn't take it." Straightening his shirt cuffs, Malik walks past me to his living area. I follow after, dropping onto the edge of the sofa while he lights the electronic fireplace. "Something's going on but I don't think that's it." I hang my head, hearing the click of his dress shoes walking away on the marble floor. Pulling a drawer out of his metal filing cabinet, Malik picks out a file and returns to throw it on the coffee table in front of me.

Flicking it open, I see a thick stack of papers on Candy. Many of the warrants and transgressions I've seen before, but this search is more intensive than the one I did. It'd take a professional to compile a folder containing everything from her nursery graduation to dentist appointments, shoplifting warnings and noise complaints so quickly. I'd ask why Malik didn't just get me to do it but I'm fully aware how he tries to keep me away from Candy where necessary. Flicking through the papers, I see she hasn't had a single tie with Jasper before the night of the jewellery burglary, hence proving Malik's point.

"So she's staying then?" I ask in disbelief. Malik isn't swayed, especially not by something as disposable as a pussy. I've seen him turn away all the women that throw themselves at him in the bar. In fact, I've never seen him with a woman before the other night. "She's pure trouble, severely unhinged and she-"

"Keeps things interesting? You can't deny you haven't felt the hole in your heart as much since she turned up. Yeah she's everything you've listed, but even when we were trying to shake her loose, she brought us all back together. Something's got to change." I watch Malik's back, noticing how his spine isn't rigid or the side of his jaw isn't clenched.

Mine on the other hand is throbbing like a bitch but I guess I had that coming for misreading the situation. Malik's house, Malik's rules. I've followed blindly up to now, happy to have a direction and people around who understand me. The question is, can I let Candy in long enough to give her the same chance, or will I continue to push her away for her own good?

CANDY

Standing on the dresser, I stretch as high as I can to stick the fluffy fairy lights in the corner as a crutch bangs on the door. I shout for Spade to come in, edging along the dresser with the heart frame I'd been clenching between my thighs.

"Does this look straight to you?" I ask, holding it in place. It's about time someone covered all these screws in the walls and the extra stop on the way back has allowed me to do just that. Jack was only filling up with gas but there was a home décor superstore across the road. Spade wasn't fast enough to catch me, Ace didn't care and the kid's section was an entire floor!

When Spade doesn't respond, I twist back to see him distracted by the view up my skirt instead. "Focus! Does it look better on this screw, or this one?" Moving it back and forth, he rests against the door jam and points to the left one. Hooking it in place, I hop down to appreciate my hard work.

Along the bottom of the bay window, I'd added these cute candy glass stickers I found and some pale pink curtains. I reckon Jasper's bed was a swing like Jack's, although it had been cut down and looked pitiful laying on the floor. I added a net canopy to the hook directly above and filled the circular frame with fluffy pillows. I never had my own room before, always moving between group homes or running away, and the basement really was a shithole like Big Cheese said. Even if I don't end up sticking around too long, knowing I made a place my own will stay with me.

"You know you're meant to put your own photos in the frames before you hang them up, right?" Spade mocks. Twisting my lips, I shrug and move to stand in front of him. When he doesn't wind his arm around me the way I've seen in movies, I pick up his beefy limb and put it around myself.

"I don't have any friends and even if I did, they wouldn't look as happy as the stock pictures." Not liking the way Spade's arm tightens around me in what I'm supposing is pity, I turn and plant a smile on my face. His chest is firm beneath a fitted vest, probably on his way to work out. "Not that I'm complaining, but is there a reason you sought me out or do you just want to be in my company?"

"Oh yeah. There's some woman downstairs for you, something about a ladies' night?" The smile becomes genuine now. Fake it 'til you make it, works every time. Leaning up on my tiptoes, I wind my arms around Spade's corded neck. His eyebrow raises suspiciously over his stunning blue eyes, the contrast against his mocha skin making them seem that much brighter.

"Do me a favour. Keep the rest of the guys busy for a while." Pushing my body weight against his, Spade releases me to grip his crutches and awkwardly step back. Keeping up the pressure, I walk him back all the way to the elevator beside the staircase. Once I've pushed him to lean against the wall, I place my lips against his cheek. "Whatever you do, don't let them come downstairs."

"That's a big favour. It's going to cost you." I giggle. I'd have been disappointed if he'd said anything else.

"I bet it will. How about you stay right here and think about what I can do for you when I get back. Remember, don't let them come down under any circumstances." Backing away, I start to skip down the steps as his voice filters after me.

"Not a problem. Ace is keeping Malik busy and Jack's working on the truck in the garage." My laughter echoes around the stairwell, the image of Jack all sweaty and greasy sticking in my mind for later. Entering the bar, I see a woman peering through the revolving door and wave enthusiastically as I approach. She's a pretty brunette, in her forties I'd say, in a smart pantsuit with a clipboard in hand. After introducing herself, she asks for a breakdown of what I'm envisioning and is soon ordering the truck she brought to head around back to get started.

I pass through the building, propping doors open as I go. I then stand aside, letting the burly men who jump out the truck unload and get to business. Walking around the corner, the woman that is Nina Phipps the event planner ends her phone call and smiles at me.

"Everything is all set, the decoration crew are almost here and the guest list is shaping up to be a sell-out. Is there anything else you need Miss Crystal?" Winding my arm around her, I draw her into the kitchen and point to sit on the stool.

"Please call me Candy, and there is one more thing. Come pop a bottle of champagne to celebrate with me. Tonight I'm going to prove I'm not just a pretty face, I'm a freaking entrepreneur!"

Stepping into the bar, my jaw drops. It's perfect. A rose gold balloon arch frames the doorway and pink buntings are hanging from the high windows. Down one wall, an illusion of bubbles has been created cascading downwards. A DJ booth with large speakers has been set up in front of the patch of wooden floor I've never seen anyone on. The strobe lights are dancing to the beat of Nicki Minaj, getting everyone in the partying mood. Each woman who enters gets a feather boa and the first drink is on the house. That's not the best part though. The best part is the dance machine I've assembled for the night.

Jack reappears through the bar doorway, after he entered the kitchen earlier with smudges of oil on his face I ushered him upstairs to shower with specific instructions to put on a shirt. His hair is gelled back, a white short sleeved shirt pulling tightly around his biceps. I catch his eye from behind the bar, my smile infecting him until his dimples are on full show. Lifting a cocktail glass, I carry it over to him. His eyes devour my corset and fishnet tights with each step, until he notices the dick straw in the drink I give him.

"Go on, be a man and suck it," I tease. Picking the straw out and chucking it over his shoulder, he downs the fruity liquid and yanks me into his body.

"I'll save the sucking for your clit, love." Every time he says that, a flutter rolls straight between my legs. Licking my tongue over his bottom lip, I nudge out of his hold and back away in my new knee-high platforms. Spade hobbles in not long after. I mouth that I owe him along the bar and he pushes his tongue into his cheek suggestively. With a wink, I turn back to the group of women pushed against the bars trying to nab one of my 'Sex on the Beaches.' It's all I know how to make since one of the hired help for the night showed me how.

I spot the two guys winding through the crowd, suspiciously eyeing the hordes of women. Many try to gain their attention, but taking seats at a heightened table, their eyes keep returning to me. They don't need to be on edge tonight, the event planner ran an invite only system to past clients she trusts, and even then everyone was vetted before they were given the location.

Next to be drawn into the bar by the thumping bass are Malik and Ace. It's hard to tell in this light but Ace's jaw looks bruised, his eyes more resigned than usual. He refuses to look at me, unlike Malik who is glaring. Popping my gum, I shake my jazz hands with a 'Ta da', but he doesn't seem impressed. Barging through the other female bartenders, he doesn't stop until his chest bumps mine and his mouth is beside my ear.

"I don't know what the fuck you think you're playing at-"

"Saving your ass," I interrupt. He gives me a hard side eye so I pull him to an alcove at the end of the bar. Tucking myself into the darkened corner, I fist my hands in his shirt and pull him into me. The hard length of his body feels right against my skin, the heat between us powerful enough to start a fire. "The bar's a promise until you have enough money to go straight, right? Well, I'm helping bring in the cash so you can get there quicker." Malik pulls his chest away from me so he can read my face, not that I let him venture too deeply.

"Why do you care if we go straight?" I duck my head into his shoulder. I don't exactly have an answer. I do whatever intrigues me at the time without delving into the reason. But for Malik's sake, because he won't chill out and enjoy himself until he's satisfied, I dig deep to come up with one for him.

"I know what it feels like to not have a home. Or a place to belong. I'm living day to day but you've built something here. I guess I just kinda wanted to feel a part of it before I move on." I don't catch Malik's expression in response, not that I expected it to be anything but the usual stoic look. His lips are on mine, taking me by surprise. I flatten my palms, steadying myself on his chest. The delicateness of his fingers tracing my jaw and rounding my neck are a direct contrast to the way his mouth claims me.

I've kissed a lot of guys before, usually because I want something, but Malik feels different to all those other times. I'm wrapped up in his scent, his arms, the liquor bite on his tongue and the rest of the room falls away. That's new. Like the man behind it, his tongue exudes power, raw and unrestrained. Coiling around mine, coaxing me to press harder into him. A thousand words are passed through the movements of our mouths on one another, and I can't make out a single one of them. Pulling back, Malik kisses me once, twice more before levelling me with a serious gaze.

"I'm not used to people looking out for us," he admits. I can relate to that.

"Yeah well. People are cu-" 'Who runs the world' by Beyonce starts to blare out of the speakers and I gasp in delight. "This is my jam!" Slipping out of Malik's hold, I find a huge crowd of like minded ladies on the dance floor, those who have left their inhibitions in the parking lot. Those who are ready to get wrecked, have the night of their lives and most importantly, throw money at the bartenders.

Finding myself in the centre of the dance floor, the ladies around me close in. Hips bump, arms rise, butts shake and laughter rings out. One wild chick with black hair grinds up against me and I'm here for it. Rolling my hips in time with the beat, she strokes her hand up my fishnet tights and spanks my ass. Through the heads bobbing around, I catch sight of four pairs of eyes from the only men in the room fixed on me. I can't make out their expressions in the passing strobe lights but I can guess. Jack'll be smirking and letting loose, Spade secretly impressed, Ace wishing I'd never been born and Malik…well I'm not sure about Malik but his face will be as expressionless as a rock.

After the next song finishes, I move towards the bar to grab a drink when a figure approaches me. I look up in the mirror, closing in on the blue eyes staring back. She's trying to conceal her face in her waist-long, brown hair but I'd recognise Tanya anywhere. Gone are the floral summer dresses she's failing to seduce Cheese with, in the hopes of him fucking her into a promotion, and instead a black catsuit is stuck to her body. Hey, that's my fucking catsuit!

"You're not welcome here," I sing-song. "If this is your idea of an ambush, I take the pleasure of telling you I hired extra security for tonight. Specialised marksmen you won't see coming."

"It's not an ambush," Tanya says, leaning forward on the bar. "I came to warn you." I turn to purse my fingers at her in a way she's done many times to me. It's the 'you're full of shit' look Tanya's perfected. To be fair, she had plenty of chances to perfect it because most of the stuff I tell her is a lie, just like the marksmen I just mentioned.

"What kind of warning would I possibly take from you?" Tanya reaches for a drink, downing it and sighing.

"I've been exiled from Leicester's gang too. I don't care what you do or don't take from this, but I've got a price on my head now – just like you." Her blue eyes hold mine, no trace of deceit visible. So she's been practising, but I still don't buy it.

"What are you talking about? There's no price on my head." Reaching into her cleavage, she pulls out a folded piece of paper and tosses it at me. I catch it, looking inside to see the order image I recognise all too well. Cheese has given me similar himself, sending me out to prove my loyalty. Is that why she's here, to claim bragging rights? Tanya must notice the way I stiffen around her and she rolls her eyes.

"I have no interest in killing you. Even after what you did to Riley. I'm a dead woman walking anyway, figured I'd take a page out of your book and enjoy whatever time I have left." Hearing that, I realise Tanya and I are in the exact same position. Sitting on the stool beside her, I signal for a tray of cocktails for us to share.

"Riley was a cock though," I lift my glass towards her. Tanya smirks despite herself, clicking her glass on mine.

"A rapist cock. We lost a lot of good women who couldn't handle being around that sleaze. I only lucked out because he was my brother." I choke on my drink, the buzz taking the edge off. I didn't even speak to Tanya before the two of us instantly became enemies and I'm starting to realise she's not as blind to her dead brother's antics as I thought. The beat has me tapping my fingers on the bar, my head bobbing.

"Come on then. What did you get exiled for? Did Cheese finally take you to bed and realise you were a shrivelled-up old nun?" Tanya bumps my shoulder, the playfulness between us is new territory.

"Least I have my decency. What was it you used to say, you're always soggier than a slug?"

"Moister than an oyster, and I stand by it." We cheer again, laughing to ourselves.

"Nah, it wasn't that, but it was about sex. A stupid oversight on my part." When she doesn't continue, I remove the drink from her hand and spin her stool to face me, trapping her between my thighs. "Some guy came by the mansion, the one who's taken on your hit. Tall, blonde, killer dimples, charming. Took me out for drinks to find out info on you and…it just kinda escalated from there." Tanya misses my frown as she looks away, the regret on her face clear.

"Wait—you fucked Jasper?" She nods into the distance. The room starts to spin and I don't think the alcohol has anything to do with it. I tell myself I hate him for taking advantage of me but I can't help the whip of jealousy that lashes through my chest either. Me and feelings don't bode well. I push myself up, needing some space to think but Tanya just keeps on talking.

"I told him everything about you Candy, I would have done anything to keep his attention that little longer. But then he didn't kill you at the warehouse as planned and Leicester blamed me for double crossing him. He's even more paranoid than he used to be, saying I was the one to tip Jasper off about the warehouse."

Backing away, I bump into the women queuing for a drink behind me and spin around. Jack's frown is visible across the room, and my moment's hesitation draws Tanya's attention to him too. She says something I don't hear, my erratic heartbeat pulsing in my ears drowning out the music.

I can't pinpoint why I feel like I'm going to either pass out or heave. It's like my brain is starving of oxygen while my stomach rolls over on itself. Of all the women, after I gave myself to him so freely, why would Jasper go for Tanya. I don't mean to put a bitch down, but ultimately she's a bitch. She sold me out for a taste of his dick, and set him on my trail. Yet here I am, resentment coursing through me. The trouble with craving bad boys is the more they fuck you up inside, the harder you want them.

So even though I have absolutely no right, even though the four men facing me haven't looked at another woman all night, I can't help but embrace this newfound envy. This is why emotions suck, and if I know what's best for myself, I'd cut my losses now. Grab my shit and go. Leave the stress of caring behind.

"No, you won't," Angus pipes up from the stool beside me. I

scrunch my features up at his ability to see straight through me. Nah, I can't do that now. I've started something and I'm invested to keep it for a while longer. Once I've had my fill with the Gambler's Monarchs, I can revert back to my trusty, old ways. The ones that kept me protected from being let down. No feelings, no exclusivity and definitely no fucking jealously.

JACK

Through the crowd, I watch Candy with interest. Women are so complicated. One minute she's laughing and drinking with the brunette beside her and the next, her gaze keeps flicking from me to her with hatred burning in their depths. Not that the brunette is aware, as her eyes are busy studying my face like a museum exhibit from across the room.

Raising a cocktail glass to my mouth, I sip the fruity liquid slowly, my eyes never wavering from Candy's. Beside me, Malik grabs the ice pick from the table and turns to stab the inflatable dick resting against the wall that's been annoying him all night.

"It might be her night but this is still my bar," he growls. A waitress places a tray of shots on our table, yet another offering from the thirsty women at the bar. I reckon our bar being full of women would be Malik's worst nightmare, and a look to my right supports my theory. His thumb is tapping on the table, his eyes unable to focus on one spot. I was surprised he didn't instantly shut it down, whatever Candy said to him hidden in the corner must have been one hell of an argument.

"You wanted change," Ace grumbles back, taking a shot of whiskey directly from the bottle. I don't know what's going on between them, not that I care. Candy turns to reach behind the bar, the black thong in her hole-ridden tights calling to me. I stand without thinking about it, Ace's sneer meeting my ears. "Have fun chasing her tail, errand boy."

He's clearly been drinking a while, the bottle clasped in his hand almost empty. I hover, not wanting to prove Ace right but Candy standing upright with her bat now in her hand makes the decision for me. Screams have filled the bar area by the time I get there, the brunette staggering back with wide eyes and holding her shoulder. I burst into the middle, the brunette's arms winding around me from behind. I try to remove her vice-like grip but Candy sees red, swinging the bat down on the girl's fingers. The wood scrapes my abs as I suck right in, grabbing the end of it. Like a rope, I tug Candy towards me via her beloved Candy Crusher until she's flush against my body.

"Let me go," she struggles but I refuse. "That bitch thinks she can get her claws into you, she's got a concussion coming her way!" Wait, this is about me? Not the others, just me? I hold her tightly by the forearms, trying to find the words to say but there are none. I can't deny the surge of satisfaction that rises within, or the smirk taking place on my lips. This chick is wild, untamed, spontaneous and all I've been able to think about lately. I'm not planning to claim ownership of her but I must have done something right if she's this determined to keep me for herself.

"Take your bitch outside where she belongs!" The brunette shoves at my back.

"It's not who you think! It's just Jack!" Candy's words halt my actions, piercing my thoughts. Just Jack? I thought Candy was jealous but apparently 'Just Jack' isn't worth her time. My grip tightens, my nostrils flaring. Tossing Candy aside into a group of women who've stopped to watch, I turn and grab the brunette by the hips. Lifting her with ease, I dump her on the bar and sink my tongue into her mouth. She tastes like fruit and ash, making me wonder if that's how I taste too? My dick shrivels at the feel of her sloppy tongue flailing against mine like a dead fish but I grind into her anyway. If Candy wants to know jealousy, I'll give it to her.

Not able to continue, I pull back and hold the brunette in place when she tries to follow my mouth. Her hand cups my cheek, her eyes dazed. I lean towards her ear to tell her I never want to see her face in my bar again and then shove myself away from her. By the time I turn back around, Candy is gone. The crowd is still there, watching me closely and a few hands brush my arm, asking for a turn. Ramming past, I make my way to my stool at the back.

"You handled that fantastically," Ace tips his bottle in my direction. Snatching it out of his hand, I down whatever's left just to get the taste of the brunette out of my mouth. Shoving it back in Ace's face, his sluggish reactions miss the bottle and it smashes into his mouth, his teeth slicing into his own lip. Jackass.

Candy suddenly reappears, her bright pink hair marking her trail all the way to the DJ booth. They share a smile, her hands stroking his arms as she moves into his personal space. He places his headset over her ears, getting too handsy whilst showing her how to spin the decks. Her laughter filters through the microphone on the headset, blending into the beat pulsing through the speakers. I bite down on my tongue, my fingers curling around the edge of the stool. She's screwing with me. Beating me at my own game.

"This is for that special someone," she sniggers. 'Jessie's Girl' starts to play through the speakers, with Candy saying Jasper every time Rick Springfield says Jessie. The guys at the table all burst out laughing, and admittedly, I fight against the smirk building inside as well. She's a feisty one, that's for sure. Even for the guys sitting around me like old times, it's impossible to spend a single moment in Candy's presence and not start to become addicted. Somehow they manage to hide it much better than me, but that girl is all of our twisted fantasies rolled into one.

After showing her the ropes with his body plastered to her back, the DJ exits the booth and makes a beeline for the men's toilets. Ace sniggers as I push up out of my seat and I stick my middle up behind me. I don't care what any of them think. Whether I'm pissed off or not, there's no way I'm going to let Candy dangle a carrot in front of me like that and not expect me to bite back.

Entering the bathrooms, there's no one else except the DJ standing at one of the urinals. He's a young lad, early twenties with scraggly black hair and a fake designer jacket. I bet he thought all of his birthdays came rolled into one when a girl like Candy showed him attention, but I'm here to rid him of any hopes that he'll be taking her home tonight. Giving him the chance to button up his jeans, I hang back until he's washed his hands before I step out of my hiding space. He jumps like a little bitch before I grab onto his jacket, throwing him into the closet wall with my teeth bared. All the colour drains from his face, his eyes wide enough to bulge.

"How about we make a deal?" I snarl and the DJ nods wildly without even waiting to hear it. Snatching his hand between us, I wrench his fingers back until he screams. "You keep your hands off Candy, and I'll let you keep them. I'm sure you'd struggle to keep your business alive with a pair of stubs spinning the decks. Not to mention all those knobs and buttons." I don't actually know anything about DJ'ing but I yank his fingers even further for effect. The guy's screams are lost to the sound of music as someone bumps into the door, surrounding us with Candy's latest joke with me being the punchline—Mr Brightside by the Killers.

Pushing away from the man that distinctly smells like piss despite just emptying his bladder, I stalk outside and duck into a corner to watch what happens next. It's not long before he emerges, his eyes flicking around anxiously. Spotting me, I salute him and cross my arms with a smirk. He then hurries to the booth, shooing Candy out with exaggerated movements for my benefit. I swoop in as she staggers down the steps, catching her in my arms when she trips. She tries to push away from me but I refuse to let her determination settle into my features. We're even now.

"No more games. Dance with me," I order, pulling her onto the dance floor. We find a spot in the centre and I spin her around, holding her against my front. Candy looks back with a raised eyebrow, her hand in my hair pulling my head down.

"I'm guessing you had something to do with that," she says into my ear, dragging my hair back to look at the DJ still eyeing me nervously. I don't answer, preferring to kiss her neck. Her ass presses into me, my dick pulsing as it grows. Licking a path from her neck to her jaw line, I tilt her head back to capture her lips with mine. Driving my tongue inside, I can't help to look up and make sure the DJ is watching, like a dog claiming his territory. She opens up for me, her tongue lashing across mine with just as much vigour and my hands roam her corset.

Releasing her, I merely stand and watch the curves of her body riding the rhythm of the music. She lights up the dancefloor as if she's the only one on it. Capturing the attention of my brothers and a few of the women around us, I grip her sides and hoist her back into me. I want her to feel every ridge of my muscles and every inch of my cock to remind her what she's got here. At the same time, I fail to block out the little voice in the back of my head that says we're not enough for her.

With each song that ends, another woman tries to muscle in and turn my head, asking for their turn. I shrug each one off, not releasing Candy until the DJ shakily calls for the last song of the night. The slow tempo of a soppy Ed Sheeran song starts to play and I turn Candy in my arms, only to have her snatched aside. Spade is there, propped up on his crutches with one arm around Candy and a warning in his eyes. I raise my hands in defeat, stepping in behind her.

Unlike when I saw her with the DJ, I don't feel anything at Spade draping himself over her body. I slide my hands around her hips and sway to her rhythm. The word 'whore' catches my ear and I bolt upright, but Candy slaps her hand over mine to hold me in place. For the entire three minutes, we remain clamped together, swaying as a unit. The dance floor empties so only us and a few female couples are left. Malik and Ace watch us closely through the dark as the strobe lights soften, their movements slowed. Each inhale draws Candy's deeper into my lungs, the press of her hand over mine branding her onto me.

Suddenly, the song ends, the lights turn on and our bubble is broken. Spade places a kiss on her cheek before moving away but I hold her in place.

"No more jealousy, got it?" I say into her ear. She looks back at me, her expression unreadable.

"I can't promise that. I get all of you but all you get is me. Exclusivity leads to boredom." I smirk, stealing a kiss from her lips as everyone starts to file out.

"Are you bored, Crazy Girl?" She doesn't meet me with the playfulness I was expecting. Giving me a solemn look, she pulls out of my hold and puts a small distance between us.

"I'm not, but you will be soon. I'll keep my gum and bat close for the day it happens and then I'll be on my way." I frown as she leaves, my fingers twitching to reach out and drag her back. No doubt I won't be able to sleep again and I'll slip into her bed later, savouring the feel of her pressed against my body without the others present. I play it cool for now, Malik slapping me on the back whilst leading the others towards the side door.

"Don't forget to lock up when you've cleaned up," he calls and I snap out of my thoughts to notice the chaos of spilled drinks, fallen decorations and a quivering DJ all around me. Ahh fuck.

CANDY

Banging on the bar door downstairs wakes me with a start. The pounding of a headache instantly rushes through my skull, the wave of nausea from too many Sex on the Beach's last night rolling through me. A heavy limb is pinning me down, the scent of morning breath making me retch. Shoving Jack, I kick his shin to make him stir.

"Something's happening. Grab a mint and get downstairs." I grab the sweatpants he left on the floor, dragging them on underneath the vest I slept in. Poking my head out of the door, I see Malik striding down the hallway, pounding his fist on each door he passes. Jack rushes out of his room in his boxers, his hair a mess and a mouthful of pink gum between his teeth. Motherf-

"Police! Open up!" We hear hollered from the bar doors. Spade appears out of Ace's room, a groggy eyed Ace following after. What the fuck happened there, Angus and I wonder together. Malik breaks into a stride, taking the stairs with an almost naked Jack and scowling Ace on his tail. I hang back to take the elevator with Spade, staring at him with my eyebrows raised until he caves.

"He sleepwalks when he's drunk, that's all." Spade pushes the elevator button, sealing us inside. I move in front of him, barring his exit when the doors reopen with my hip cocked and arms crossed. "It's the truth! And since he's pissed at you for existing right now, I slept propped against his door so you're fucking welcome." Pushing me aside with his crutch, he follows the sound of commotion to the back room behind the bar. I'm right behind, even though he tries to nudge me to stay back. Halting in front of the two-way mirror, I nudge by to stand beside him and watch from behind the safety of the glass.

"-tip off about some stolen property," a fat man with a suit is saying. I've quickly adjusted to seeing Malik's fine shirts and tight fitting slacks. So much so, this detective or whatever his badge says gives me an all-round greasy feeling in his cheap limp suit jacket. Malik, however, is giving me all the sharply cut vibes of his pressed trousers and rigid collar, even at this time in the morning. I watch his back flex as he straightens and holds his head high, his men flanking on either side.

"Everything in this building belongs to me," Malik replies sternly. I share a look with Spade, wondering if I'm now included in that statement. I should feel trapped and panicked, but the warmth spreading through me suggests quite the opposite. I belong somewhere.

"Well this warrant gives us the right to check," the detective sneers. A swarm of policemen spill through the revolving doors, stopping behind the greasy suit with a challenge fixed in their eyes. They're hoping for a fight. Jack begins to scratch the back of his head then, catching our attention. He starts to move his fingers then, jerking his wrist and making weird symbols.

"Ahh, shit," Spade curses beside me. I frown, looking at him while some rookie calls Jack out on whatever he's doing in the mirror.

"What is it? What's happening?"

"Jack didn't give over Leicester's diamonds like he was supposed to. There was a drop site. Leicester must have tipped off the police."

"No way, Cheese doesn't use the cops. He handles shit his own way. But Tanya on the other hand…" My eyes darken, a frustrated huff like that of a bull. One swing of a bat and she runs to the police? Pussy. "What can I do?"

"You need to hide them. I won't make it there in time. Listen to me carefully Candy. Jack has a false base in his wardrobe, you'll need to pry it up and get the diamonds. Then take them to Ace's room. There's a safe room hidden inside his bathroom but your hand won't work on the scanner. Just hide out until one of us is able to get up there and let you slip in." I stutter as the detective orders the guys to wait outside during their search. I'm sure finding me with a bagful of stolen diamonds would give Captain Knobstick back at my usual arresting station the hard on of his life. I can't be implicated in any activity which gives that man's moustache a stiffy. I'd happily die first. Spade grips my chin, regaining my attention.

"Go beautiful, we'll come through." We share a nod and without wasting any more time, I'm gone. I hear the kitchen door burst open and the heavy pounding of boots hitting the tiled floor as I shoot up the stairs. Spade's voice follows me, cursing for the hands to get off him so he can use his crutches to leave. My heart jumps into my throat while a thousand ways this could go wrong plays out before me.

Skidding into Jack's room, I drop to my knees in front of the open wardrobe. This 'false' bottom seems pretty stuck to me, my fingernails all cracking as I try to pry it open. I scramble amongst the shoes and shit he's dumped there, my hand clasping around a shoehorn. Wedging it in between the two planks of wood, I almost snap the shoehorn when the bottom finally lifts about half an inch upwards. That's all I need to wriggle my hand inside, the grainy sack of priceless gems just beneath the surface.

Hugging the bag close to my body, I snap the wood back into place as the static of a radio reaches my ears. My stomach flips, drops and crashes into my anal cavity as the bedroom door begins to open. Angus screams at me, snapping me back into action. I fly into the bathroom, slipping into my room unseen as the junior police officer checks over Jack's side. He seems to be the only one so far, some try-hard wanting to find the diamond stash before someone else does.

Peeking into the hallway, I see the coast is clear but more heavy footfalls are on their way up the stairs, accompanied by the odd bark. Bolting into Ace's room, I silently close the door to give myself a moment to think. Where the fuck is a tall girl with fuchsia hair supposed to hide?! What if the boys don't pull through and I get my face eaten off by an attack dog?

Stuffing the diamond bag into the gigantic pockets of Jack's sweatpants, I set my sights on Ace's wardrobe. I reckon it was the same type as Jack's before he painted it black. Wedging myself into a gap beside the chunky piece of furniture, I push back so I can walk up the wall. Shimmying higher, a smile graces my lips until I get to the top and suddenly realise I don't know how I'm going to flip around. The stomps halt outside the door, the handle jiggling.

Crossing my arms over my face, I cling onto the wooden edge and flip myself around as quietly as I can. Dragging myself into the top of the wardrobe, my feet just tuck in before the door is thrown open. A cough lodges in my throat as the dust I've disturbed starts to settle. I swallow hard, trying to clear it but it starts to tickle more. Bodies march inside and Ace's computer chair is thrown to the ground and I seize my chance, coughing into my shoulder. There's a still pause afterwards, my heart not daring to beat. Shit. Shit. Shit. How can someone be blessed with no gag reflex but the first sign of dust, I might as well walk myself into the big house?! That's bullshit.

"Get the fuck away from my stuff!" Ace roars, flying into the room like a torpedo. Grunts follow with the sounds of struggling. Angus just barely convinces me not to look, against my better judgement.

"Sir!" A strangled shout comes. "You need to leave the premises while we conduct our search!" Others come for back up, a team of skidding boots dragging Ace out of the room. I take my chance for a shot at getting into the bathroom, hoping Ace managed to get his hand on whatever scanner he needed to. After a brief glance to check the coast is clear, I drop down and slip into the en-suite. Nothing seems to be out of the ordinary. Well, if you discount that the toilet seat is down and the bathtub is weirdly clean for a man.

"We're bringing the dogs in now," a voice shouts from the hallway. Ducking behind the door, I claw a hand into my hair, fisting it tightly in an effort to latch onto an idea. It usually works in dire situations and if not, Angus will soon have something to say about it. Dropping into the bathtub, I plaster myself to the base as if I'm invisible. Ace's voice booms through the door, jolting me upright.

"You can do your search, but I'm not leaving this goddamn room! There's tech in here worth more than all of your lives put together and I won't let you screw it up." When he doesn't appear around the door, I grow nervous and decide I need to move. Peering out of the window, I see the overhang of the porch below. There's an unnecessary amount of police vans filling the car park, a few of the regular customers queuing down the dirt track behind a strip of yellow tape.

Pushing the window open, I don't have the time to lower myself gently. Instead, I throw my legs over the ledge and drop down with all the subtlety as a period in white denim shorts. One of my hands is still prying onto the window's ledge with a tight grip, allowing me to find my footing before softly pushing the window back closed. The bark of a dog inside sets off a chill working its way through my bones. I'm never usually so rattled, but then again, I don't usually have anything to lose. Or live for. I'm not naïve to think my stay here is any more than a vacation, but the least I'd like is to stay long enough to break through Ace's 'I'll-hate-you-before-you-have-a-reason-to-hate-me-bullshit'.

An officer in the car park walks into view, a phone pressed to his ear. I lie flat and cram myself against the wall, squeezing my eyes tightly shut. If I can't see him, he can't see me.

"You're an idiot," Angus deadpans. I squint to see him balancing on the porch's edge on one foot.

"Thank you," I whisper back. Clattering from above makes me curious and I slowly sit upright to get a better view. The officer down below has his back turned so I rise up until I can see Captain Greaseball himself hunting through the bathroom cabinets. Ace catches my eye from the doorway, sternly nodding for me to duck down. Soon after the dogs pass through and I brace for another look. Aw, they're so fluffy and cute, yet deadly and vicious. Like me.

"Are you done in here yet? I need to take my morning piss," Ace says louder than necessary. The captain starts to argue but the thunderous expression on Ace's face takes care of that.

"Be quick," Greaseball grumbles, dragging his feet out of the room. Ace steps inside then, slamming the door closed and shoving the window open fast enough to nearly smack me in the face. "Hurry up Emo Barbie," he hisses down at me. Starting to hoist myself up, he grabs me roughly under the arms and drags me the rest of the way. Dumping me back in the tub, I watch Ace turn towards the toilet and pull down the front of his gym shorts.

"Get out of here already. I can't go with you watching." Pointing his thumb over his shoulder, I now see the thin break in the tiles where he's popped open the safe room door. The Captain bangs on the locked door, shouting that's long enough. Hopping out of the tub, I slip in behind Ace and reach around to grab his marshmallow of a dick.

"No need to be nervous around me Babycakes, not after the performance you put into fucking my throat in Malik's suite." I dodge the shoulder that's thrown back in my direction, as well as his bark to move my ass. Entering the panic room, my laughter suddenly dies. The door is closed, presumably by Ace, sealing me and Angus inside. I'm too busy trying to convince my eyebrows to descend from my hairline to worry about how long I might be locked in here for. This isn't just a safe room, this is an evil genius lair/bomb shelter/apocalypse sanctuary all in one.

The layout curves and spirals downwards with alcoves set back from each series of steps. Each one is distinguishable, either by the sets of bunk beds, small kitchenette or shelving units floor to ceiling to hold the water and food supply. I can see the glint of screens further down by the motion-sensored lights which have now fully turned on. The walls are grey stone like the steps, not a splash of colour in sight.. Either they made this place in a rush or their interior decorator needs firing.

I'm rooted in place, trying to figure out how I haven't noticed any of the levels from walking the hallways. Impatience claws at me to get a closer look and I'm finally able to shift one foot in front of the other. I now understand why the entrance is connected to Ace's room, given the masses of screens, monitors and wires laid out before me. Rat's paradise I reckon. Approaching the screen, I hit the keyboard's space bar and suddenly, every screen lights up before me. Met with surveillance from every angle of the bar, inside and out, my eyes flick rapidly to find my boys. Wait, no…not *my* boys. The boys. THE boys.

Jack and Spade are lounging by the motorbikes outside, passing a cigarette between themselves. The bar is utter chaos, a swarm of uniformed officers tearing through every inch of the place and not bothering to pick up after themselves afterwards. The kitchen is already destroyed, the stairwells a conveyor belt of cops. Up and down, back and forth. I pick one out with rounded specs and play a game of Where's Wally with myself. He manages to evade me by ducking down to mess about with his shoe before reappearing, making me scoot in closer to not lose him again. Tricky fucker.

My eyes snag on a sharp suit with pale blue making its way up the top staircase. Malik's strides are long, measured. He leads the conga line following him all the way to his scanner and stands aside to permit them access to his suite.

"Huh." I muse out loud, dropping into the seat. The diamonds crunch in my pocket so I take them out and Chuck them onto the desk.

"What?! Fucking spit it out already!" Angus scolds me when I don't elaborate.

"Just seems weird the hum-drum Malik made over Jasper being

in his suite, yet has no problem with the police going up there." I kick my feet up and thread my fingers over my stomach - where Angus has made himself comfortable as well.

"Maybe he destroyed whatever was on that flash drive by now."

"Mmmm," I twist my lips. "If it wasn't important enough to save on a flash drive and hide in the first place, I doubt he'd have done it. Malik is hiding something big, the question is where is he hiding it now?"

"What do you care?" Angus scoffs, turning his black furrowed eyebrows on me. "We live for the now and fuck the rest of it. Secrets and gangs hold no interest to us."

"Maybe this gang does….hold interest to me, I mean. I haven't decided about their secrets yet." I look away, watching the screen where Malik is posted against the wall. He fixes his cuff, straightens his tie and stares directly at the camera. My eyes widen, a sense of foreboding pricking from my scalp to the back of my neck. He can't see me…right? I hunt around for a camera of my own, slowly sitting up straighter. Malik's head tilts to the side and it's then I realise he's listening in to the conversation in his suite. His shoulders are slightly raised, his stance wide. At first glance, he looks composed but I'm becoming familiar with his cues. He's on edge.

Relaxing again, my thoughts turn to Jasper. How does he fit into all of this? A moment filters through my mind, one that has filled my dreams but I didn't spend much time thinking about it until now. Jasper's breath on my neck, his words swirling around the shell of my ear. 'I'm not the bad guy here.' Why would he waste his time lying if he was planning on drugging me anyway? And why would he care what I thought of him? Naturally, tying me up isn't typically how one would prove their lack of asshole-ness.

"I can hear the cogs turning in your mind from here," Angus deadpans. I shove him off my lap, standing to pace instead.

"Get out my fucking head then." He mutters something back about living there but my thoughts have moved on. Suddenly, things don't seem as carefree and easy as before. I was meant to screw around with them, then screw them in general before cutting my losses. But now I'm invested, in Malik, in his dynamic with the guys he claims to own, even in Jasper. My brain takes this opportunity, whilst sealed into a mad-max bunker with a stash of stolen diamonds, to re-evaluate everything I thought I knew. Once again.

SPADE

"I still can't get my head around what the fuck you thought you were playing at." My voice is muffled through my skull mask, not to mention drowned out by the roar of my Kawasaki beneath us, but Jack knows what I said. I've been repeating it all day since the cops left. Now night has fallen and we're on our way to fix his stupid mistake. Jabbing him in the side, just cause I felt like it, he glances back over his shoulder with a grunt.

"It just slipped my mind, alright?! We've all been distracted since the night we picked up the diamonds." That's the understatement of the century. Even before Candy fell into our laps, we had the issue of scrubbing every speck of my blood from the jewellers, whilst I was still pissing out blood. I drove my damn self to the hospital in the end, bored of waiting for the others. Luckily, gunshots were always coming in that part of town and the police were so overwhelmed, I managed to slip in, get stitched up and discharge myself by the time Malik turned up.

Refocusing on the road ahead, the headlights fall upon a set of thick, iron gates with the mansion looming behind. After being permitted entry, our cocky bravado's die along with the bike's engine. A figure looms in the doorway, his silhouette hunched with the support of a cane. The man I'm guessing is Leicester turns away, leaving the door open behind him. Jack helps me upright and steadies me on my crutches, his eyes lingering on mine for a long moment. I shove him away, not wanting his sentimental bullshit to psych me out. This is a simple drop off, nothing more. Yet it's already the opposite of what I was expecting, which is what's unnerving me the most. No armed guards or forceful entourage. There's just….no one around.

Making our way inside, my crutches ring out on the marble flooring. There's a wide staircase in front of us, rooms off to either side and not a sound to be heard.

"Just drop them on that table and let's get out of here," I nudge Jack. The diamonds are in his bag because it's his damn mess to sort out. I'm not the errand boy, I'm not touching that shit. My speciality is my marksmanship, which is the only reason Malik insisted the most injured one out of the four of us had to tag along.

"It's not that simple," Jack replies cryptically, striding onwards as if he knows where he's going. I stare after him before sighing and beginning to follow. It's even more difficult to walk with this leg cast when there's a shotgun strapped to my other thigh. I don't care who can see it tied over my cargo pants, it's a clear warning not to fuck with me. The two pistols in the back of my waistband are the real threats.

With every room I pass through, trepidation expands in my chest until I have the feeling I might throw up. The living area, the kitchen, the billiard room; they're all completely empty. I can't even spot any cameras around, the silence pressing down from me all around. I know to listen to my instincts, but Jack's nowhere to be seen and I'm not leaving without him. Not that I can ride my bike like this even if I wanted to.

Pausing at the pool table, thoughts of the other night come rushing back. How the roughness of the felt reddened Candy's creamy skin. How she arched upwards, moaning and begging for more. How we all came together for the first time in years with one singular goal in mind—pleasure her. Worship her. Own her. Shaking my head clear of how much of a rush I am to get back and urge Malik to let us do it again, I move onwards with hurried steps this time.

Finding myself at an open patio door, I pick up on the low hum of voices and stick my head out. Leicester is sitting heavily on a wicker sofa, the bag of diamonds and a pistol sitting on the cream cushion beside him. Jack's standing opposite on the other side of a glass table, his arms crossed and stance wide. I look all around before stepping out, the orange glow of patio lights causing too many shadows for my liking. Noticing me, Jack drops his arms and nods for me to join him, but the pool catches my attention.

The closer I limp, the more my eyes widen. The rippling surface is illuminated from underneath, the darkened water barely visible around the amount of bodies floating face down. A shudder rolls through me, my hand reaching for a pistol when the distinguishable click of another makes me freeze. I slowly turn my head to the side, looking down a barrel with my blonde-haired comrade hovering his finger over the trigger.

"What the fuck are you doing, Jack?"

"I didn't want to do this, Spud. I tried to leave you out of it but your loyalty is your downfall." My gut drops. The realization that only one man has ever called me Spud makes my shoulders sag as if my limbs are suddenly too heavy to hold upright.

"Jasper. You shady fuck." I glare at him, ignoring the gun so he can look me straight in the eyes when he pulls that trigger. Let him remember how he killed one of his former brothers, former best friends. Let him see how I refused to cower or beg for my life. I won't make deals or double cross my team, that's his forte. Leicester stands in the background, creeping forward with his cane.

"Don't you want to know why? Or how?" Jasper smirks. I do, I really do. But denying him the satisfaction is the only card I still hold.

"Nope." Bracing myself on the crutches, I stand tall and wait for my execution. The hardest part isn't accepting my fate, it's resisting the urge to scour the bodies in the water for one that looks like Jack. No doubt he's there and I'll be joining him soon enough. Joining Jasper's side, Leicester also stands to watch me, the silence dragging on. My fingers twitch, my patience wearing thin. If he doesn't make a move, I will.

In one swift motion, I duck and smack my forearm into Jasper's, knocking his shot wide. The sound pierces my ear drums but I have my gun out and in between Leicester's eyes before Jasper manages to recover. His green eyes falter a millimetre, barely visible in the dimmed lighting but I saw it. This time, a smirk grows on my face. Jasper can act like he's invincible, but all he's done is trade one leader for another. He still yearns for that authority as much as the rest of us.

"Is Jack in there?" I nudge my chin towards the pool without taking my eyes off my target. The old man whose sagging skin and dead eyes are begging me to put him out of his misery. I didn't expect him to be the one to answer, since Jasper seemed to be in charge of this shitshow, yet his gravelly voice carries a hint of boredom.

"Not yet. His life is in your hands, for now." I fight a roll of my eyes but at least my heart can ease off palpitating for now. This is all a game, an ironed out scheme which gives me all the info I need right now. They were never going to kill me because they needed me. I don't give a shit about why, and I won't be sticking around long enough to find out.

"Is this still about whatever was on that flash drive?" I scoff, keeping my gun aimed at Leicester's forehead.

"I never needed the flash drive, I needed Jack. It was the perfect distraction while one of my men drugged and dumped him in the delivery van, then stripped him of his clothes for me to quickly change in a fucking bush. The switch was so smooth, none of you suspected a thing," Jasper grins, so proud of himself. I knew since he outed himself, he's been dying to tell me all about his genius plans. I fake a yawn, causing Jasper's smirk to drop and his jaw is tight, just like Jack's usually is. "Besides, I already know everything Malik thinks he's kept locked up tight. Aren't you curious why he was hellbent on getting it back?"

I don't allow myself to contemplate the answer, done with talking. Taking my finger off the trigger, I whack Leicester across the face. The old man stumbles and falls, blood pissing out onto the ground as Jasper dives for my ribs. I somehow manage to stay on my feet with the crutch supports hooked around my elbows, shoving my weight back into Jasper. He grabs my wrist and twists, the gun clattering across the ground.

"Don't make me do this Spady," Jasper almost begs. "If you'd just hear me out, everything would make sen-" I punch him in the mouth. I don't want to hear his bullshit now, not after the years he could have walked back and I'd have given him my time. Not after the way he used Candy, tying her up and shoving her into a barrel for fuck's sake. And for what? Just to screw with us all some more and kidnap his own twin? No, I'm done listening and the time for understanding is a distant memory.

Jasper takes my moment's pause as contemplation, stepping forward so I throw my forehead into his face. Not relenting, I lean on one crutch to swing punch after punch whilst he's still recovering from the last. Nudging him further back, I then use both crutches to hold me up whilst kicking my good leg upwards, booting Jasper's sternum hard. He stumbles, reaching out for something to grab onto as he falls backwards, straight into the pool of blood. I don't hang around to see the bodies bar his way as he tries to resurface, spinning to get the fuck out of here.

Learning from all those stupid movies I've wasted hours watching with Ace, I take the time to slide the patio door shut and lock it. A hand reaches up high, slapping on the poolside. I flick the switch beside me, flicking off the outside lights and smiling to myself. Drown in blood in the dark, fuckface.

Trying to remember my way back through the mansion, I pause

by the pool table for the memories to flood back. It only just dawns on me that it was Jasper with us that night. We were all too distracted by Candy's juicy pussy to realise, and he got to have his fill of her. Again. My hands tighten around the grips of my crutches, my breathing heavy. Get Jack back first, then I'll add this as another reason on the long list of why Jasper needs to be dealt with. Permanently.

I hear clattering inside a room to my left, the door slightly ajar and a faint light on inside. I draw my second pistol, using one crutch to hobble forwards while the other is dragged along by the crook of my elbow. I swear after this, I'm refusing to leave my bed until I'm fully healed. I'm all for staying active but I'm thoroughly sick of these shitty sticks holding me back. The front door is visible across the lounge, my legs working as fast as they can when a body collides with mine.

Being thrown over the sofa and dropping onto the hard flooring, my second gun disappears from my hand once more. I reach down, trying to unstrap the shotgun from my right thigh but I'm flipped over before I manage it. A boot stomps on my hand and then flies into my gut. Jasper bends to lift my torso and punch me in the jaw, keeping my jacket crushed in his fist. His body, hair and clothes are stained red with drying blood so I spit a mouthful of my own at him just for decoration.

Something sticking into my ass reminds me of the gift Candy gave me on the way out earlier, along with a sweet kiss I could still feel the warmth for most of the way here. Digging out the small pocket knife, I lash out and slash Jasper's cheek with the blade.

"Kiss goodbye to being identical," I chuckle. On an outraged cry, Jasper drives his knee into my wounded thigh and shoves all of his weight on me. It's my turn to cry out, my strangled scream cut short by another punch to the face. My head falls to the side, my mind spinning as Jasper continues his assault. The blows blur into each other, the pain melting into an overall agony I can't escape.

I retreat to a dark part of my psyche to keep myself from passing out, focusing on trying to work out what the odds are one of the corpses in the pool had hepatitis to pass onto Jasper through the cut in his face. Black spots appear in front of my vision, my body now limp. Jasper's hand suddenly releases me and I drop back, my head smashing on the floor.

Grunts and a struggle meet my ears right before the coffee table beside me shatters. Chunks of glass, from tiny shards to thick rocks, rain down on me and slice my skin. I roll onto my side, trying to shake the glass out of my eyes before I try to open them. Despite the swelling which is already setting in, I make out two figures on the other side of the room. Dressed all in black with his hood up, the newbie is battering the shit out of a red-coated Jasper. I can't tell where the pool blood begins and Jasper's ends, but there's a healthy splattering coating the floor from both.

Rolling myself over, I start to drag myself across the marble, desperately trying to make my way to the front door. I'm not sentimental in any way, but I currently have a sickly sweet girl waiting back at the bar for me and I'll be damned if I'm going to lie around here to bleed out before I've had her the way I want. A small voice in the back of my head tells me that once I've sheathed my cock to the hilt inside her tight pussy, I'll be hooked. And I'm okay with that.

A glint of metal catches my eye just before I reach the lobby, the call of my pistol ringing in my ears. I divert off course, closing my hand around it as I'm pulled onto my back. Flicking off the safety, I raise the pistol directly at the man looming over me. My instincts scream all at once, jolting me off target just in time for the bullet to sail past the pair of puppy dog brown eyes staring back at me.

"Spade, Spade! It's me!" My mouth is slack, my hand shaking around the gun as I grab onto Ace's forearm. He drags me up and for a moment, we just stand there chest to chest, blowing out a shaky breath. That was a damn close one. Ace props me against a wall before fetching my crutches, my eyes falling on Jasper's limp frame.

"Is he…" I begin to ask but then the body stirs on a groan. Ace strides over to kick Jasper in the face and knock him out for a while longer before returning to me.

"Don't judge me, but I still just…couldn't kill him," Ace hangs his head as if that's a bad thing. Not wanting to take another life isn't a bad thing, in the real world it's considered *normal*. There's too much history here, it blinds us to the truth and if I'm being honest, I doubt I could have killed him either.

The shuffling heading our way with the tell-tale click of a cane, however, can get fucked. I unstrap the shotgun from my leg, cocking it just in time for Leicester to round the corner and for me to blow his brains all over the wall. His body and what's left of his head drops instantly, hitting the floor with a thud. I had no real issue with Leicester, we've run jobs for him in the past. But there's a pool full of bodies outside and at least a few of them must be leaving behind a grieving family. I know what it's like to lose a dad at a tender age and have him replaced with asshole boyfriends for years after, it fucking sucks.

"Oh by the way, what the fuck around you doing here Ace? I had it all under control." I limp towards the main door, struggling to see through squinted eyes and my bad leg is throbbing like a cunt.

"Yeah, I could see that," he chuckles and slaps me hard on the back. "Actually it was Candy who came to me, said she didn't feel right about the way Jack was acting. We looked over some surveillance and I had to agree so I followed you out here. She was trying to convince Malik to let her take his bike when I left."

"Candy came to you? Wow," I muse.

"I haven't been that bad," Ace nudges my shoulder. I raise my eyebrow at him as I pass through the main door, not buying that bullshit for a second. "Fine, maybe I was at first but she seemed genuinely worried about you and Jack, which is all I am too. She also gave me a mental layout for the mansion and a way to get in unseen."

Smirking to myself because those two have finally seemed to sort their shit out and I only had to almost die for it to happen, I spot Ace's bike is sitting next to mine and I sigh. We can't leave one for when the cops inevitably show up, but mine's going to be a bitch to ride home. But when I do get back, I'm totally having that Crazy Girl tend to my wounds, kissing them better one by one and no one is going to say otherwise.

CANDY

"I really hope you're right about this," Malik says from over my shoulder. His level tone doesn't hide the threat behind his words. There's nothing Malik can do that scares me, but secretly, I'm also silently praying to the gummy bear gods that I'm right about this. When I sent Ace away earlier this evening, the vein in Malik's temple nearly exploded. Turns out he doesn't like others ordering his men around. Who knew? But then I told him about my hunch and I figure the notion of being deceived was enough to assuage him. For now.

Hopping off the front of Malik's Dyna, I leave him to switch off the engine while I assess the outside of the locker. The blue shutter stares back at me, causing bile to rise in my throat at the thought of the injection in my neck. Despite the gargoyle-style characters inked onto my arms and chest, I'm not great with needles. Although, it's when I have blood taken that really makes me lash out at the nearest doctor or crackhead looking to sell my blood for their next hit. That's my fucking blood, get your own.

I pull my lock picking kit out of my back pocket when Malik strides past with a wrench. Smashing through the bulky padlock, it hits the floor with a thud just before the wrench joins it. I can't help but stare as Malik heaves the shutter upwards, his back flexing in a black t-shirt. Something about seeing him out of a fitted shirt and tight slacks has my libido sitting up and paying attention. It's like seeing a unicorn squeezing into a spandex onesie for the first time, odd yet strangely hot.

Peering inside the shutter, I grab the light string and yank hard to illuminate heaps of Jasper's boxed shit. Everything is still and quiet, but it's all here. Not packed up and vanished like Jack supposedly said. In fact, it looks the exact same. The stalker wall displaying the map and photos draws Malik's attention but I didn't come here for info. I came for a certain blonde twin I'm not seeing.

"Shit," I curse myself. I circle the locker just in case, peering around the back of the shelving units as if Jack might be stuffed behind there. I won't contemplate any other situation than finding him alive. I'm still struggling to come to terms with who had his arms wrapped around me on the dance floor and who's been holding me in bed each night. A fucking psychopath, that's who. Coming from me, that's quite a feat too. I thought Jack and I had come so far, yet we're back at square one and the twisting in my gut doesn't want to acknowledge that.

Malik pulls out his phone, taking photos of the wall before taking more around the locker. Inch by inch. I get out of the way, stepping outside to inhale deeply. It's starting to rain, a dusting of rain pattering across my nose. I yank up the cotton hood of my cropped denim jacket and tug the cuffs down over my hands. Angus appears on Malik's bike, covering his own nose with his chubby little paws. We share a nod in agreement. The lighter the rain, the more deadly it is. You fail to realise it's even on your skin until it soaks in, gives you the flu and then you die. Dead. From a drizzle.

Leaving Malik when he starts rifling through boxes, I walk the length of the lockers, turn into the next row and do it again. My thoughts are crashing into the forefront of my mind, giving me a headache while my limbs are growing restless. So instead, I focus on the crunch of my Doc Martens on the aged road, kicking aside crumbled rock until I reach the end of the next row. Voices catch my attention and I suddenly look up, a siren blaring in my head to lunge out of the way.

"Wooo, wooo, woooo!" Angus screams at the top of his croaky, gruff voice.

"Stop that you little shit!" I hiss at him, peaking around the corner of the wall I'm plastered to. Beside a large, white van, there's a fat, bald man that seems to trigger something in me. I can't quite place him, but he's arguing with the lot owner in front of the main office block. Keeping my hood pulled tight, I remain in the background, walking casually across the parking lot to the other side of the van.

"—missed his payment for the fourth time. Either empty out his shit today, or I'll throw all of it in the skip."

"There's no need for that," the bald guy says from the other side of the cab. I use the van's handle to hoist myself up onto its heightened step and watch him through the windows. He approaches the other, a hench fucker that looks ready to break some legs. "I've got your back payment right here, although we have enough to cover the next six months. My employer has been a bit tied up, that's all." He hands the owner a thick envelope and turns back without waiting for an answer.

I hop down, scooting around the side of the van as I hear the driver's door open. I get ready to dart off whilst in the wing mirror blind spots when I hear it then. A low noise from inside the van, soon drowned out by the rumble of the engine. Heat blasts against my legs from the exhaust, a thick puff of smoke following. I cough and waft my hand in front of my face, that ashy smell expanding in my lungs as I struggle to breathe. Then I remember.

I remember the crack of the exhaust as it struggles to start, the disgusting taste of burnt oil clogging the back of my throat. The rattle of the van's lock as I came to from being tranquilized, spying the blonde man in the driver's seat through cracked eyelids. This is the van Jasper had me inside, which means that tiny muffle could be exactly what I've been looking for. The van begins to roll forward and I jump onto the back ledge, which is barely big enough for me to fully tiptoe on. There's a metal latch on each side of the closed doors, ones I grab around the outside of and cling on as we pick up speed.

Luckily, the driver abides by the slow speed limit until he reaches the main gate of the lot. Even so, my head smashes into the back when he stops and I'm forced to jump back as I lose my grip. I hear the driver call for someone in the guard's booth to let him out and without wasting any time, I grab my lockpick kit and get to work. Moving the picks as quickly as I can, the engine covers the noise of me jingling the back desperately until the right door pops open.

I yank it, losing my grip on my picks as the van begins to move once again with my foot dragging on the ground behind. I manage to drag myself inside, the door closing itself on his next sharp stop at the junction and I duck down to avoid his rear view mirror. There's a small window between the back of the van and the cab so keeping low will keep me out of sight, for now. Army crawling across the floor, I head for the only object in the back. A heap of restrained limbs and a mess of dark golden hair in the faint light. Moving up into Jack's personal space, I pull my phone out and shoot Malik and Ace a text to track me.

Ignoring the string of angry, cursing emojis Malik sends back, I shove my phone away and turn my full attention to Jack. Jesus fucking Christ, make that – what used to be Jack. His face is a darkened mess of blood and welts, his shoulder popped at a funny angle. Using the pocketknife in my boot, I cut him free from the rope on his ankles, knees, wrists and elbows. He must have given hell to have earnt so many restraints. I brush the hair back from his face, the usually silky locks sticky and matted.

"Hey," I whisper in his ear. His body judders every time the van does, his slack posture making me think he's passed out until his head shifts upwards slightly. He forces an eye open to stare at me lifelessly. I brave a smile, an unfamiliar ache scoring through my chest. I want to pull him into my arms and hold him as much as I want to scream and burn the whole fucking world down. The need to fight, damage and destroy riles me because I know I can't undo what he's been through, but I can at least soothe his wounds. Kiss away his pain. Aid his recovery the way he and his gang have recovered a lost part of me.

"Candy," he mutters. I lie on my side, nudging as close as I dare and taking his hands in mine. I brush them lightly over my cheek, feeling the thick residue that's left there from his split knuckles. He gave them hell for sure, and I wouldn't expect anything less. These men are warriors, plain and simple. They can hide behind their bikes and leather jackets, their secluded bar and mutual nicknames, but they have all overcome their pasts. They survived and found each other, then found me. Well, technically, I stalked them, but they saw through the sarcastic bullshit and *found* the person inside I've always secretly wanted to be.

"Yes, Jack?" I breathe when he doesn't continue, gently placing my nose on the end of his. I place a soft kiss on his broken fingers, cradling them in my palms.

"Your…"

"Yeah, that's it. I'm here. I've got you now." A weak smile pulls at my lips at the bittersweet moment, marred by the bruises and swelling on his face. At least he's here now and I won't be letting go anytime soon. I've leeched on, at least until I get to see Jasper crawling through a pool of his own blood to beg me for mercy. He may confuse the hell out of me, but he's gone too far this time. Jack sputters and draws my attention back to his now fully open green eyes.

"Your….fault," he croaks, drawing his hands away from me. I simply stare at him and the considerable amount of effort it takes him to roll onto his back so he doesn't have to look at me. A familiar numbness washes over me, Angus wriggling closer to hold my face in his tiny, squishy hands. I've been rejected before, by every foster parent who failed to fix me and even some guys who couldn't handle my persistent sex drive, but this is different. This is like a knife just plunged through my soul and cut an opening for the demons to escape through. They invade every part of my body, shutting me down limb by limb, organ by organ until I'm just lying and staring.

It doesn't matter how much Jack does or doesn't know, he blames me. Not Jasper, not even Malik. Me. The van slams to a stop, throwing me into Jack's side and he hisses in pain. The windscreen shatters, a spray of bullets abruptly ending the driver's strangled cries. Looks like Malik found us, but I no longer care about returning safely. Instead, as the rear doors are yanked open, I merely push to my feet and leave. Malik grabs my upper arms to halt me, his eyes searching my face until Jack groans and thankfully distracts him. Releasing me, Malik is jumping into the van and I begin to walk. And walk. And walk with heavy feet and an empty mind.

"We've been here before," Angus pipes up, trying to sound chipper from over my shoulder. "Time to move on, find somewhere to start new. Ohh, how about camping out at the back of a bowling alley and screwing with people's strikes? We could cement the pins to the floor after hours." I purse my lips, kicking a rogue stone on the road.

"I don't think it'll work this time, Angus. I don't really feel like…anything." My steps slow to a stop, my gaze being pulled from the long road ahead to the pair struggling behind me. I can't pull away from the way I thought I felt and the truth that's glaring back at me. I never stopped being that nuisance no one wanted, I just fell into Jasper's trap like all the others. Turning away from Jack's pained cry as Malik tries to heave him onto the Harley, I find Angus standing in front of me now with his chubby arms crossed and black eyebrows tighter than usual.

"Candy Martha Jacky Deborah Crystal," he glowers. Uh oh, I've been fully named. "What the fuck are you waiting for? Annoy those motherfuckers until they learn to love you like I do. Living with you might be a pain in the ass, but living without you is worse." A slow smile spreads across my face, a fresh burst of confidence running through me. That little, anus-coloured turd is right, I'm fucking adorable. Irresistible some might say. Okay, that's just what I'd say but I've made an impression on these guys and that means half the leg work is done.

"Hey guys, wait up!"

MALIK

"Come on then, get on with it," Spade scowls at me from across the poker table. I continue to shuffle the deck in my hands, sparing him a brief glance. Everyone has gathered, including Jack even though I ordered him to rest. He lost his shit upon hearing Ace didn't finish off Jasper, his knuckles splitting open again when he punched the table. There's a blood mark in the felt, not that I seem to care. A stain like that would have set me off once upon a time, but I've worked hard on quelling my anger. After all, there's currently plenty of other issues I should reserve my frustrations for.

"What's the rush? You always fold first anyway." I tease Spade, beginning to deal cards out to each of my men, and Candy. She's the only one who has changed since getting back, her hair pulled up into a messy bun and a large wad of pink gum sandwiched between her teeth. A tiny scrap of material bands around her chest, displaying her cleavage and the abs disappearing into high-waisted PVC trousers. She's favoured a chair beside Ace, pushed right into his side while he tries to ignore her.

"You know that's not what I meant," Spade pulls my attention back towards his blood-stained face. He and Jack have that in common. "Get on with your ranting about how we should have done and known better. How we should have seen the signs, how we dropped the ball and Jack paid the price." I raise my eyebrow, watching Spade glance at his cards and toss them aside to fold with a tut.

"Seems like you've covered that one so how about we skip it and just play some cards?" All eyes turn to me now, Candy's head tilting to the side like a curious puppy. Blowing a large bubble, she pops it to break through the tension surrounding us.

I'm sure they were all prepared for an outburst but I'm more concerned with our welfare at the moment. Not to mention how Jasper had me fooled too. For the briefest moment since he left, we were all getting on like old times and I think I turned a blind eye to what my instincts were trying to tell me in favour of that. Now we're back to being a fractured unit and I refuse to let that remain.

Opening a hidden drawer beneath the table, I hand out stacks of poker chips, sliding a pile to Candy last. She bops up and down in her seat, visibly vibrating with excitement. It baffles me how nothing seems to faze her. I thought I saw the hint of doubt in her eyes outside the van but I must have imagined it – this girl is impenetrable. Spontaneous, wild, impulsive. Candy does what makes her happy and nothing else, which I'm more than a little jealous about.

Even after the drama she's brought with her, I still wholly believe she's the answer to fixing us. It's probably because she's the exact opposite to me, and as much as I have tried to build us a home and a family, I'm ultimately the one who's fucked it all.

Everyone deals with loss in their own ways - I rely on my routines. Like this debriefing, for instance, sitting around this table before we disperse to our separate zones of the building. All of our briefings, debates and decisions happen here. We deal with our issues over poker, and this time is no different. I relate to the games due to their set rules and sense of order. You have to think three moves ahead at all times and never let yourself become rattled.

Checking my cards, I place them back down with my hands pressed on top. Jack starts the round with his bet, blinking through the dried blood on his eyelashes. Through his squint and the dirt caked on his face, I don't miss the way he's glaring at Candy across the table. Whether she notices or not, she doesn't show it. Instead, she not-so-sneakily asks Ace what she should do with a ten and Queen of the same suit. I fight to hide a smirk, enjoying how obvious she is to everyone around her. Ace doesn't seem that bothered either, reaching over to take two of her chips and throw them into the centre.

Dealing the cards into the centre, she continues to lean on Ace for help and popping her gum while we all watch her more than the game. Fascination, hunger and the bitter undertone of disgust coming from my right churn all around the table, all focused on her. Not giving a shit, as usual, Candy goes all in and we're all forced to match it, sealing this game to a swift and blunt fate. Flipping over the last card in the middle, I fix my practised stoic expression back into place to cover the fact I have a straight flush in my hands.

"I raise."

"With what? We're all out," Jack turns his head to spit on the floor. I don't react, giving Jack that one and only pass due to his recent trauma. Sitting back, I thread my fingers together calmly and meet the excitable pair of brown doe eyes staring back at me.

"I raise a night with Candy, to myself."

"You're on," Spade suddenly sits upright and grabs for his discarded cards. I'm unable to withhold the smirk that plagues me this time, the stretched feeling unfamiliar on my face. A moment passes, everyone eyeing each other to gauge their reactions. It's clear Jack wants to challenge me for such a night, even if he's avoiding her gaze at all costs. It might even be for the best that the two of them hash out their demons, but it's not in my nature to forfeit. I have to win, at all costs.

"We get to do whatever we want with her? For the whole night? Alone?" Ace asks, his eyes brightening as he looks down, his gaze trying to devour her. There's a slight clench to his jaw so I click my fingers in front of his face to regain his attention.

"As long as you have Candy's consent," I nod to her. She slowly licks her top lip and throws a wink at Ace, who announces he's also in.

"Fine," Jack grits out. His tracksuit is torn and stinks like hell, the quick scrub he did on his face revealing just how many cuts he has. From what I've been told, both Jasper and Jack came out of tonight with scars, making them not so identical anymore. It's a shame really, like the official end of their bond. In theory, that happened years ago but now we all have the visual reminders of how low Jasper stooped, and for what? Some information he thinks I'm hiding. If only that man knew what I've done for him, he wouldn't be so hellbent on destroying what I've built here.

I lean forward, displaying my straight flush of clubs proudly. Cocking an eyebrow at Candy's wide eyes, I go to pull on my cuffs until I remember I'm wearing a t-shirt. I was working out in the gym when I saw Ace rush out, then found Candy swinging around in his computer chair with full access to his surveillance system. My first instinct was to strip her down and take her right there, until she told me exactly why she was bossing my men around. The force of it took me aback, and then she single handedly found Jack, enticing me to both thank and ruin her even more. Jasper clearly still needs dealing with, but not tonight. Tonight is mine.

Spade holds out for as long as he's able, revealing his bluff with a grunt. He'd hoped his high card might have beaten at least one of us, but both Ace and Jack have pairs. Not enough to beat me though, which is good. I won't be forced to break any limbs tonight to get what I want. And I want her. Standing with a smug smile, I start to collect up the cards when Candy clears her throat.

"Not so fast, Sunshine." Grabbing the cards from my hand, Candy lays them down face up again to present her own hand. A royal fucking flush. I stare at the cards, a brief flare to my nostrils betraying my confusion. "Oh, I'm sorry. You didn't think I also wouldn't play for a night with myself, did you? The next time you decide to play for a party with my pussy, you'd better check I don't have a vibrator on standby upstairs." I don't miss the way she winks at Ace again, the smile he tries to hide or the cards he magically produces from beneath the table. Fucking cheats.

Candy turns, more cards from the draw tucked into the back of her waistband. Swaying her hips, taunting me, she makes her way towards the stairs and I see red. I don't like cheats, I can't stand losing and I won't be denied. Stalking after her, I wrap an arm around her waist and hoist her off the steps, ignoring the responding squeals.

"Participation is by invite only!" Candy shouts as I drag her through to the kitchen. Continuing out the back door, none of the incoming punters pay me any mind as I throw Candy over my shoulder and spank her sharply. Her cry is more of a moan, making me bite down on my lip. This girl does things to me I can't comprehend, but I plan on exploring it before I do anything else. Wrenching the door of the garage open, I shove our way inside and plant Candy on the hood of Jack's truck.

"You weren't complaining when I made the deal. I won, fair and square. You're mine tonight. All mine."

"What happened to all or none?" she smirks at me, mocking me.

"I need this, for me. My men will understand and if not, they'll still do as I say. You know why? Because I'm the fucking boss." I yank Candy back by the ponytail, forcing her to look at me. Her tongue clacks as she chews her gum, until I stick my finger and thumb into her mouth and snatch it out. Tossing her gum over my shoulder, I silence her argument by crashing my lips against hers. My tongue delves into her mouth, tasting the hints of cherry bubblegum and a flavour that's all Candy. She moans into my mouth, digging her fingers into my hair and pulling it roughly.

"I like it when you're arrogant," she winks when I finally pull away.

"Does your mouth ever stop moving?" I ask her, already tugging at her top.

"Only when you give it something better to do," she sasses

back. Challenge accepted. I trail my lips down her throat, my fingers searching for the fucking cinch keeping that scrap of fabric around her breasts. With a flick of my wrist and a tug of my arm, her top is on the floor. Her breasts fit perfectly in my hands, her tits like ripe berries in my mouth.

"I thought you were supposed to be filling my mouth, not yours," she smarts. I ignore her completely. I want to taste her, to fill her, and I won't let her ruin what I've won. I've been dreaming about having her to myself since we tied her to the pool table.

Reaching behind me, I pull my shirt over my head, then shove it into her mouth. Her eyes light up in pleasure and she laughs through the fabric between her teeth. My cock is already aching, and I rub my dick through my pants to try to ease the throb. I need to be inside her.

"Up," I smack her hip, and she plants her hands and feet on the hood of the truck to lift her ass high into the air. I work the too tight pants over her hips, peeling them off her legs. There's a triangle of hot pink lace convering her pussy, and I rip it from her body, dropping it to the floor with the rest of her clothes. Using my hands to spread her thighs, I bury my face between her legs. Her pussy tastes like heaven. Sweet and tangy, just like her name implies. Her back collapses against the truck and I lift her knees over my shoulders, using my thumbs to spread her labia.

"Fuuuuck," she hisses and I smile against her clit. I thrust my tongue into her core, feeling the inside of her walls clench around me before I lick a strip between her folds. Her bud is already swollen, and I suck her clit between my lips, flicking it with my tongue. She arches up against me, digging her fingers into my hair and tugging on the strands. I plunge my fingers into her pussy, driving her to madness.

"Is that all you got?" she asks on a gasp, and I look up as my shirt goes flying across the room. I slap her pussy with one hand while yanking on my fly with the other.

"I'm going to fuck you so hard, Crazy Girl, you're going to be feeling me all week."

"Don't threaten me with a good time," she laughs, twitching like a fish on the hood of the truck as I slap her pretty pink pussy again. I free my cock from my pants, leaving everything else in place, then slide her from the hood and down the front of my body. Her sex glides down my abdomen, leaving a trail of her slick in her wake. I'm going to make her lick up every last drop.

She links her legs around my hips and it feels so good to be wrapped around a woman again. Her pussy is dripping all over my cock as I fill my palms with her ass to help grind her clit up and down my length. I spread her cheeks with my hands and dip my fingers into her slit, coating my digits in her pussy juice and circle them around her asshole.

"Stop teasing me you fuck," she mumbles through clenched teeth. Maybe now she knows what I feel like, watching her prance all over my place like she owns the joint, pushing her way into my life and my family. Driving me fucking insane until I need to fuck her up against Jacks truck before I lose my damn mind.

I line her entrance up with my cock, and shove her down my length. Her moan, as I fill her tight quim with my massive cock, sets my blood on fire. It's primal and deep, and I echo her moan in response. She doesn't need any time to acclimate to my size. Instead, she starts to ride me like I'm a bull at the rodeo. Her hands are on my shoulders as she thrusts up and down on my dick. Her skin is flush, her eyes wild, and the feel of her walls milking my length makes me growl against her chest.

I latch onto her throat and feel the vibrations of her pleasure pass through my lips. She's mewling, whimpering with need, and fuck, it just does her for me. I wrap my hand into her ponytail, arching her back and thrusting her breasts into my face. Her nipples are so pink and hard, I could spend the rest of the night alternating between pinching them with my fingers and tugging on them with my teeth.

Candy is a mess against me. I slam her pussy down my cock, revelling the way she sighs with every thrust and grunts at the moment of impact. She drags her nails across my back, causing me to hiss and shudder at the sting of it. I already know I'll be marked by her, and I find I don't fucking care. In fact, the thought sends a blinding spark of need shooting up my spine.

Her body starts to tremble and I help her ride me. Her breathing turns to gasps, her eyes roll into the back of her head. I use my grip on her ponytail and bring her mouth to mine to shove my tongue between her lips. She screams into my mouth when she comes, calling to my most primal need. To claim, protect and own. I take a moment to pull back and just watch the nymph who has crashed into my life. I didn't realise what was missing until she filled the empty void, doing for my men what I never could.

Her orgasm is fucking glorious. Chest heaving, guttural moaning, legs clenched around my waist. Pink tendrils of hair have come loose, falling around her flushed face in gentle waves. Her entire being radiates pleasure, her muscles shaking from the weight of it. I go still inside her to better appreciate this vision of Candy coming undone around me. When she isn't back talking or giving me sass, when she's simply…herself. This could become addictive, really fucking fast.

"Do you know why I avoid women, Crazy Girl?" I fill the silence when both my chest and cock are pulsing to explode. Candy shakes her head, her eyes still dazed and chest flushed. "Women are weak. Too reliant on men like me to protect them, but you don't need protecting. You've been fighting to live another day for far too long. I think that's why you slipped right on by my defences and forced me to care, even though I didn't want to."

"You…" Candy breathes, coming back from her reprieve to focus on my words. "Care about me?" I tuck a lock of hair behind her ear, thrust into her hard to drive my point directly into her core.

"Yeah I do, Candy. I really do."

CANDY

Closing the tongs around the stack of crispy bacon in the frying pan, I layer them over the buttered rolls and turn off the hob. Squeezing a long line of sauce along the length of them, Spade and Malik enter the kitchen, drawn in by the smell.

"Damn, that must have been one good fuck to turn you all domesticated. This almost makes my blue balls worth it." Spade reaches out to grab one of my bacon rolls and I snap his hand with the hot, metal tongs.

"Domesticated is the worst insult I'd ever heard. The only 'D' words that relate to me are dick-filled and dominatrix." Grabbing a silver tray like the ones they use in the bar, I load up my rolls and blow a bubble of gum in Malik's direction before leaving. He can put his sharp, grey suit back on but nothing can hide how the dynamic has changed between us. There's less annoyance in the air and more acceptance that I'll be doing what the fuck I like and he'll allow it. Because he cares about me. The notion is still foreign to me, and it hasn't fully set in yet.

Climbing the stairs with the tray in my hand, I half-skip along the hallway and glance into Ace's room. He's nowhere to be seen, a clang from the gym telling me where he's hiding out. I pause by my room, cutting through the bathroom to lock the door from the inside. Then I exit and take the long way around to Jack's room.

"Room service!" I call, knocking twice and permitting myself entry. The room is dark, the black-out curtains still drawn and a lump nestled in the swinging bed. Kicking the door closed, I grab the TV remote on my way towards Jack's sleeping form. I almost dropped the tray while jumping backwards into his bed, causing it to swing wildly. Ignoring his slurred protests, I snuggle closer and switch on Netflix. There's too many damn options to choose from but I heard some girls at a store talking about Supernatural once so I settle on that.

"Fifteen seasons?! Jesus titty-fucking Christ, looks like we aren't moving for the next two weeks." Jack jerks upright at my voice, seeming to have thought one of the guys had come to bother him in bed. Kinky. He tries to shove me out, knocking the tray until the smell hits him. "Careful, asshole. I had to pry these out of Spade's grabby paws."

"You can stay until the food runs out," Jack growls, settling back on the pillows. I bite my lip from offering to be his snack, Angus telling me it's not the right time. I have to agree, for once. I don't want Jack's face between my legs until it's less messed-up and distracting.

Jack takes a roll, despite me at no point offering to share my breakfast, and slumps back. Out of the corner of my eye, I can make out the dark bruises covering his legs in the TV's shine. The sheet covers his crotch, hiding if he's wearing boxers or not. Me, on the other hand, I definitely am wearing boxers under a loose vest. I'm not sure who's; I just pulled them off a pile of folded laundry on my way back inside last night, heading straight for the shower. Let's just say I was covered in more than just spilt oil when Malik bent me over a workbench.

"Why are you even here?" Jack asks, even though I'm *clearly* trying to watch the TV to understand which one's Sam and Dean and why the hotter one is acting so shady. I give Jack a glance, finding his eyes not on the screen but solely on me beneath tense eyebrows.

"My room doesn't have surround sound," I shrug. It still feels weird to claim ownership of a room that was only given to me whilst Malik thought I had info for him, but I've decided to keep it. Dare I say, I kinda fit in amongst the misfits and outcasts. My fake friends in the framed stock photos agree the room and I are a good fit too.

"No, not here in my room. Here, with us. Don't you have anywhere else to go, anyone else to annoy?" I let the question pass by, too interested in the show to think about it too hard. Besides, if you don't get the pilot episode, there's no hope for catching up later on.

"Malik wants me around." The words slip off my tongue between chewing, a warmth spreading through my chest. Jack pulls himself up straighter now, nudging me to get yet another roll and mutter something about not seeing the appeal. "That's Malik's whole vocation, right? Taking in strays and giving them a master to look up to. I'm just like you, I have a past and nowhere else to belong, so what does it fucking matter why I'm here? Why are you here?!"

A thick silence follows, my offhanded comment holding more meaning than intended. I admit I am curious as to the twin's past and why I'm being used as a pawn in Jasper's games, but I also wouldn't pry. Even if it killed me to know, it's not my business. Finishing the rest of the food, I toss the tray aside and awkwardly edge backwards. Angus is across the room, judging me like the little prick he is, but Jack doesn't seem to notice. Soon, we're shoulder to shoulder, watching Netflix and chilling like the most casual fuckers in the world.

"Jasper and I were sent to boarding school in the US," Jack sighs as the rolling credits end and a new episode begins. "Our parents were filthy rich, too rich to know what to do with and certainly too impatient for us to finish school. They travelled constantly, so much that we never knew where they were half the time. It didn't matter, we had each other and together, Jasper and I ruled the school." There's a sadness in his eyes despite his smile, his fingers fidgeting with the cover. "So when the news came that our parents had died in a helicopter crash, it wasn't even a big deal. A new day started and everything was the same, right up until we graduated."

I know all about absent parents so his nonchalant attitude doesn't seem strange to me. People make a choice to be in their kids' lives and if they decide to choose themselves, that's on them. Ultimately, our only duty is to look out for number one. I shift slightly, wanting to know more but I don't probe. I estimate there's around three minutes before Jack shuts me out completely and starts blaming me for everything again.

"It's all downhill from there. We were left a shit-ton of money, which we blew through. Fucked our way from Vegas to New York and back again, attracting the wrong kind of attention from a cartel who had their eyes on a bunch of virgins we ruined within the space of a night. They hunted us wherever we ran. Blood was spilled, rarely ours since we learnt marksmanship in our fancy archery and fencing classes at boarding school. Funny what sticks and what you forget," Jack's eyes side to mine.

I stare back, not able to have much input from my community high school experience. Talk about a place for aspirations to go and die. Daily fights, underage sex in the toilets, the janitor sold meth to teens in his basement. I'm still in contact with him in fact, he's a pretty cool dude for someone with no teeth and a hollowed out face. I always joked that if I did pick an unlucky bastard to marry me, Janitor Tom could walk me down the aisle since he's the most constant older man I've known.

Silence hangs between us and I suddenly realise why I was intent on coming here this morning. Even after Malik wore out every bone in my body, I didn't sleep last night. Instead I found myself lying in a half-dozed state, waiting for the bathroom door to open. Then, as soon as I truly woke up, Angus was there to lecture me on what I'm doing with my life and I forgot all about it. Until now.

Snuggling downwards, I rest my head over Jack's chest and hear the hint of a rattling sound inside as he slowly wheezes in and out. It's fucking with my head that I spent a week growing comfortable with this man, or at least a man with this face, only to bring him back and for it all to mean nothing. I can't seem to separate what I thought I knew with how dependent I quickly became. Not just Jack but all of the guys are like a drug addiction, except there's no physical side effects that will make me break the habit.

"You can't depend on people," Angus snarls from somewhere beneath the swing. "People are assholes." And as if he heard that too, Jack rests his chin on top of mine and proves Angus right.

"This changes nothing. I still hate you."

"I know," I reply quietly, the sweet reprieve of sleep finally pulling me into her grasp.

CANDY

Every day that passes, I expect Jasper to bulldoze the door down via wrecking ball while he mechanically laughs behind the controls, but he doesn't. Days turn into weeks and slowly a routine becomes apparent. Ace and Malik mostly stay in their rooms, Jack has thrown himself back into running errands in the bar and Spade is hogging the gym, on a mission to be back to peak physical health. Not the best routine, and one I try to shake up as often as possible.

"Where the fuck is today's delivery?!" Jack growls, slamming his fists on the bar above my head. My leg swings back and forth, hanging over the edge while my body is stretched out along the wood. I hang around Jack because he's the most active, and also because it's hilarious how hard he's been trying to ignore me. I sneak in at night to sleep beside him, I push my stool too close, even eat off his plate. Yet Jack seems to think if he doesn't look at or talk to me, I'm not really there. Sometimes I like to see just how far I can push it.

"It'll get here when it gets here," I yawn and stretch. My fingertips knock a glass over and Jack curses, clearing the bar before I ruin his past hour of cleaning. Dude is so OCD when it comes to the bar; he notices every time I twist the bottle labels around or rearrange the glasses into random order instead of sorted by height.

Walking past, I lash my hand out to grab Jack's belt and yank him to a stop. Pulling myself upright, I drag my tongue over the hard clench of his jaw and all the way up the side of his face. Standing stock still until I release him, he then walks away without saying a word.

"Oh come on! Pay attention to me already!" I whine like a desperate bitch. The dog kind, not the controlling, whoring kind. Today. The sound of a van pulling up distracts Jack from his mission to leave, his boots eating up the wood floor to the revolving, glass door.

"What the fuck is that?!" he yells, deciding to talk to me now. I swing my legs over the other side of the bar, spotting the lilac van with a cartoon unicorn logo on the side. His tail hangs heavily between his legs in the shape of a cock as he covers his nipples with glittery hooves.

"What do you think it is? Your delivery is here." I hop down on bare feet, still in my mini pyjama shorts and a fitted vest. Jack can't help but eye my breasts with each step I take, my nipples rubbing against the cotton. The back door opens behind me, more footfalls joining us. "Did you know The Ejaculating Unicorn do every type of alcoholic drink in pastel colours and glitterfied?!"

"What's that got to do with us?" Ace mutters, crossing his arms and bumping against my back. I *think* that's his version of an affectionate greeting. I wink at him over my shoulder, seeing both he and Spade are dressed all in black. Malik is in between the two in a dark suit, a striped tie nestled into the collar at his neck. The faintest twitch of his lips is like being rewarded with a full on grin in Malik terms.

"Well, I wanted to try each one, so I took it upon myself to edit your usual delivery. You now stock Unicorn Cum, of every kind! Isn't that awesome?!" I grin widely, waving to the woman driver as she jumps out of the cab. Jack loses his shit, turning to yell at Malik for giving me access to his credit card information. It's not completely Malik's fault; I only needed to see his card once to make up a rhyme and remember the numbers off by heart.

"Doesn't matter now," Malik's stern voice cuts Jack off mid-sentence. "I've called the staff in early, we have business to attend to." With that, the three men surge forward, cutting through Jack and I. Spade dumps a pile of folded clothes into my arms, telling me to change and meet them outside. His mouth lingers by my ear, the brush of his lips killing any argument I might have given about being told what to do.

"What's going on? Is it Jasper?" I ask, failing to hide the excitement in my voice. Hopefully no one noticed, but the way all four men just stilled, their backs stiffening says they totally did. Shit. Why the fuck would my go-to feeling about Jasper still be excitement, after everything?! Angus nods at me from his lounged position on a nearby sofa and I know what he's gonna say. Because I like the bad boys too much.

"I'm just eager to get out of here and give him what he's owed," I play off, smashing my fist into my own palm. The boys grumble and stalk away, leaving me alone to ponder my thoughts. Yeah, that's all it is - I want to show him just how a Crazy Girl like me reacts to being tricked yet again. He toyed with me, dangling his hotness like a charming, dimpled carrot with a six pack on a string for me to blindly follow. For that, I want payback in blood, wringing an apology from his lips and then I'll fuck his face. Wait, no, that's not right. Absolutely not. Well…maybe…if he offers.

Quickly dressing in the long sleeved top, skinny black jeans and boots Spade gave me, I pause to assess myself. Every inch of me neck down is covered up and clad in black like a fucking nun. That will never do. Finding my trusty pocket knife in the sole of my boot, I slash the jeans in strips from the pockets to the knees, exposing my thighs underneath. Then, wriggling my arms through the neck hole of the top, I hike up the material over my stomach and use the sleeves to tie a bow at the back in a makeshift boob tube. Angus gives me an appreciative nod before I head out, passing the delivery van. A broad woman with hefty muscles smiles at me from the rear, yanking out cases of glittery gin for the bar staff to bring on their way in.

The guys are resting against the three motorbikes they have left, eyeing me hungrily in my DIY outfit as I approach. None of them openly offer me their back seat so I stride towards Ace, edging myself between his firm chest and the Boulevard's handlebars. His thick arms band around me to push the key in the ignition and rev the throttle. The bike purrs beneath my legs, making me arch my back and push my ass into Ace's crotch.

Sitting back, his fingers thread into my hair, pulling the pink strands back and securing it with a hair tie. I tilt my head to the side, hoping he'll kiss my neck when he shoves a biker helmet over my head instead. I growl, reaching up to take it off but he won't let me. Me wearing a helmet is like a dog wearing a cone, it's unnatural and annoying as fuck. The sounds around me become muffled but I can feel the rumble of Ace's chuckle when he reaches around me again, his chest pressing against my back. He skids the bike out then, my hands flying forward to hold on too. Malik has already left, leading the way towards the dirt track, expecting to be followed.

The journey takes longer than I expected, alternating between country back roads and various towns. I reckon we've headed into another state by now, and the end still isn't anywhere to be seen. On the freeway, Jack weaves Spade's bike between cars, trying to get ahead of us. Spade sits a little too casually on the back, loosely holding onto Jack's middle with one arm. We entered into a silent race a while back, Spade and I swapping raised middle fingers and throat slitting hand gestures.

Ace handles his bike the way I'd want him to handle me. With powerful finesse and smooth control. He glides over the tarmac like butter. Not to mention the hardened cock I can feel pushed against the curve of my ass and the way his thumb is stroking the rubber throttle captures too much of my attention. I bite down on my lip inside the helmet, suddenly feeling hot despite the cool air brushing over my exposed skin.

Leaning far left, we continue to follow Malik up ahead as he takes the next exit and temporarily disappears down a ramp. The road curves back on itself beneath a bridge, a tall building in the distance coming into view. We fly towards it, the sheen of the glass getting brighter as we near. The tint of the visa before my eyes darkens the pale stone exterior and the brightened lights beaming out from inside. The three bikes pull into the designated parking lot, halting beside one another.

"Anyone want to fill me in?" I ask, yanking the helmet off my head. My hair is plastered to my forehead by a layer of sweat and I can tell without looking in the rear-view mirrors that my face is as flushed pink as my hair. No one answers me, the guys dismounting in their black cargos and boots. Everyone except Malik is dressed for one of their jobs, which is why I've been expecting to pull up somewhere miles away and prepare myself for a long stake out. Not to drive right up to the front door.

A man pushes the glass door open from inside, approaching Malik with a wide smile and firm handshake.

"Malik, it's good to see you again. Everything is ready if you'd like to head inside." He's a tall man, easily over 6 ft to be eye level with Ace and Spade, with that whole silver fox thing going on. His full beard and combed back hair are practically shining, the creases bordering his eyes speaking of a life well lived. I appreciate his suit as I begin to follow the others, dipping my hand when the man addresses me.

"You must be Candy," he smiles knowingly. I stop to glance up at him, one eyebrow lifting. 'Robert', as the ID card on his lanyard states, takes a leisurely look at me, the glint in his blue eyes seeming to like my personalised outfit almost as much as I do. "I understand now why Malik was so specific in his requirements."

"How delightfully cryptic," I drawl sarcastically and continue to make my way inside. Once inside, without the sun's reflection in the glasses front blocking my view, I look over the vast showroom splayed out before me. Bikes of all makes, the most expensive ones I might add, cover the gleaming white floor. Everything looks so shiny, I have to wonder if they have live-in cleaners or just a herd of cows they let in each night to lick the place spotless. Staff in shirts and ties, even the women, must smell their next commission as they flock to Jack who is bounding through the bikes. Like a kid in a candy store, all the strain floods from his face and he finally looks like the easy going guy I know if lurking underneath.

"This is it? We're all dressed up and on the defence for Jack to pick out a new bike?" I ask. The three faces that turn back to me are closed off, unreadable, and my eyebrows pull together.

"That's not why we're here," Malik states evenly. The silver fox who opened the door passes, gesturing for us to follow him to a side door. Malik whistles loudly, beckoning Jack like a dog and dragging him away from the crowd of gold diggers he's attracted. I hang back, allowing his Royal Reluctantness to obey Malik's order and heel at his master's side.

An arm winds around my side, making me flinch and I look up into Spade's stern expression. He watches me closely, his piercing blue eyes seeming to burst out of his mocha skin, the rigid lines of his Mohawk complimenting the rest of his angular face. He nudges me along the hallway when I don't instantly fall into line. I don't like being on the outside, unsure of what's going on. I've been that way my whole life and it has never ended well before. Apprehension twists at my gut, Angus appearing near the elevator to shout for me to run for the fucking hills. But I won't, wherever The Gambler's Monarchs are, that's where I've decided I want to be. The revelation both shocks me and fills me with an unfamiliar warmth.

With the silver fox at the back, we all squeeze into the elevator and the closing doors seal my fate. A cage of bodies press in on me from all sides; firm, ripped bodies I've been exploring these past few weeks whether Malik has agreed to it or not. Ace doesn't look me in the eye and Jack pretends he's sleep fucking, but I'll take it. They reward me in other ways. Spade and Malik, on the other hand, couldn't be more forthcoming in their desires. Forthcoming, backcoming, just cumming every which way.

The doors open, presenting pure darkness until the overhead lights flick on one by one down the length of the underground room. It's huge with cream walls and expensive wood flooring, yet there's only one item inside. A quad bike. Easing me into the room, my boots thump heavily as the silver fox slinks into the corner to give us some privacy. He even turns away, as if that will instantly deafen him but I don't care either way. It's the quad that has me captivated.

She's fucking beautiful. An Artic Cat, in hot pink with a love heart vinyl on the rear. 'Adore me', it says. I run my fingers over the handlebars and cushioned leather seat and then slut-drop to admire the four monster sized tyres. Regaining my stance, I now pull my attention to the black leather jacket hung over the fuel tank, an embroidered playing card displayed on the back. The Queen of Hearts, just like I planned to use on my revenge pranks before Jasper intervened.

"I don't...is this..." I round the bike to find all four men staring at me intently. Despite staying with them the best part of a month, I rarely see them all together like this, aside from poker nights when they're cursing each other out and making snide comments. The men before me now are shoulder to shoulder, united as a crew. No, as a family. Malik steps forward, separating himself as the leader and spokesmen for the rest.

"We want you to join us, and be ours." He nods as if sorting a business deal but I stopped listening after 'we want you'. Those three words echo around my mind, varying in volumes until Angus is screaming them in my ears. He's already taken his position on the quad, trying to stretch his stubby arms towards the handles. Dragging my eyes from him, I look from each set staring at me to the next. Chocolate brown, hauntedly dark, piercing blue and emerald green, although Jack's don't hold the same determination as the rest. My mood dampens, a slight frown pulling at my lips.

"They need to say it," I jerk my head to the others while holding Malik's gaze. "I won't be another demand you give that they later blame me for." He seems to understand, crossing the space between us to stand on my left. Brushing his lips over my ear, he places a kiss on my cheekbones before whispering.

"I want you." Shivers roll down my back. Spade is next to round the quad, with a limp in his step but no crutches in sight. He copies Malik's words, trailing his fingers across my lower back. I keep my head held high, my composure unwavering but inside, I'm a wreck. The little girl in me that missed out on a lifetime of cuddles and kind words is creeping to the surface, begging to hear them say those words over and over.

Ace moves then, approaching the front of the bike separating us. He looks down thoughtfully, wiping an invisible spec of dust from the glossy paint. When his head lifts to mine, a sea of emotion swims in his eyes and a tsunami of pain I can't comprehend claim his features.

"It's not a question of if I want you Candy, but if you'll have me." A visceral pain as sharp as a blade slices through my being then, the weak part of me wanting to climb over the bike and cradle him in my arms. He's foolish to think I haven't done worse, the difference is I swapped out my conscience for a gummy fucker that spurs me on. Ace will never forgive himself for the things he's done in the past, and I doubt he'd believe I could too. So instead of wasting my breath, I take Ace's hand in mine and brush my thumb over his knuckles.

"You're not a monster amongst us Ace, you're just another misguided soul doing the best with what we've got. You won't hurt me again, and if you do, I'll gut you for body parts to sell on the black market in your sleep." If that's not romantic, I don't know what is. Half a smile pulls at Ace's mouth and he lifts my hand to place a kiss on the back.

"Deal." He joins Malik's side and the four of us now face Jack across the room. He sighs, dragging his feet across the wood as if he'd rather be anywhere else than here. It cuts me deep that he still hasn't found something to like about me. I mean, I know I'm annoying, but I always thought it was in an adorable way. Not to Jack. The small time I spent believing he was falling for me continues to mess with my head, taunting me with how we could have been. I yearn for his affection, for him to want me as much as his twin apparently does.

"It's okay Jack," I mutter, failing to hide my disappointment.

"No Crazy Girl, it's not," he grumbles. I look away, not needing to see my incoming rejection as well as hear it. Spade's hand grips my side, pulling me into him in an attempt to shield me and I smile sadly. Surely he knows by now rejection is a daily occurrence for me, yet I've never seemed to quite master accepting it. "The way I've been behaving is anything but okay." My eyes flick up to Jack's tormented green ones, my breath hanging on his next words.

"Candy, I want you so bad, it hurts to look at you. I wanted you from the second you took down Malik with your bat and shot Spade like a badass. But wanting you is what allowed my….Jasper to use you as a weapon against us. I've tried to push you away and keep you at a distance, hoping it'd spare you from our family shit, but you're fucking relentless." Jack chuckles, gaining some agreement from the men beside me. "Truth is, you're one of us and have been from the start. We're all just too stubborn to give into our own desires and admit it."

Picking up the leather jacket, Jack moves towards us to slide my arms into the sleeves. His fingers caress my nape as he flicks up the collar, the pressure of his hand pressing over the Queen of Hearts heating my back. I bite down on my lower lip, holding back the hurricane of emotions whirring within me.

"Don't you dare," Angus snarls at me. I see a glistening tear roll down his cheek before he can cover it up, his voice breaking. "Don't you fucking dare cry now!" I don't know what I'm going to do. Cry. Explode. Faint. Something is coming for sure, these usual feelings more than I can handle all at once.

The heat all around me disperses, causing me to look around in panic as to where everyone is going. Ace, Spade and Jack smile lovingly at each other and then me as they leave Malik and me to a moment of privacy. I follow them with my eyes all the way to the elevator, already wondering when they'll come back. Shit, I didn't even say I wanted them back. I open my mouth but the doors close and I've missed my chance.

Strong hands turn me by the shoulders, soft lips pressing against mine gently. Malik holds the sides of my face, kissing me like I'm delicate enough to shatter with even the slightest hint of force. He's never kissed me like this before. Usually, it's rushed. Desperate. Dominating. His tongue darts out, wetting our lips but not breaching my mouth. His rich cologne fills my lungs on my next inhale, my hands gripping onto his tie so he can't back away. Our mouths mesh together slowly, sensually creating a physical bond between us. My body pulses with electricity, sparking a belief in me I haven't had before. I'm good enough. Not just for Malik, but for all of them. Today isn't just about a quad bike or a jacket, it's an initiation. A fresh start as a member of their crew, a welcoming into a special spot in their hearts. In short, everything I've ever wanted all at once.

"I don't know what to say," I breathe shakily the next time we come up for air. Malik looks at the quad bike thoughtfully, his arms pulling me closer into his body as if he can't bear to let me go.

"It's hard to know what would suit you," Malik says quietly. He fiddles with his shirt cuffs behind my back, his throat bobbing against my face as he swallows hard. Is he…nervous? I beam into his collar bone, my smile stretching from ear to ear as I hook my arms around his waist.

"Well that's easy. A dick in each hand and orifice and we're good to go."

"Oh my," the silver fox gasps from somewhere across the room. I'd clean forgot he was even here.

"But it's perfect," I continue to answer Malik as if we're alone. "Beyond perfect. And it's mine!" I squeal, suddenly realising I haven't tried my bike out yet. My. New. Quad. Bike! Seeming to read my mind, Malik helps me on and then surprises me by jumping onto the back. A whirring sounds and I twist to see the silver fox has pressed a button for a secret door at the rear to open. Sunlight bleeds inside, filling my chest with excitement. Oh, hell yeah.

Twisting the key in the ignition, I rev hard and spin us before catapulting towards the exit. An inclining ramp takes us back to level ground, the brightness of daylight temporarily blinding me. A horn blares and I swerve away from a car pulling into the car park just in time, my vision clearing through my constant blinking. Steering around the shitty Ford, I give him my middle finger and then take to the main road. Heading in the opposite direction to the freeway, I'm called towards a green landscape up ahead and the sounds of motorbikes gaining on us makes me whoop loudly.

Three bikes pull up either side of the quad, their fearless riders falling into formation around me. This time, I don't hold back the tears that stream from my eyes but at least I can blame it on the wind. At last, and in the most unlikely of places, I've found a home, a family and a place to belong. It doesn't get better than this.

JESTER

"Well, isn't that touching?" I mutter to myself. I sit in the old Ford I've hotwired for today, watching Candy ride her new quad bike into the sunset in my rear-view mirror. She has no idea how hard it must be for Malik to give up control and let her drive, but that's why she's quickly becoming his greatest weakness. The rest of the men I used to call my brothers flock into the car park, paying me no mind in my sunglasses as they jump on their bikes to follow like obedient little puppies. Idiots.

"How'd you know they'd be here?" a shrill voice asks from the passenger seat. To be honest, every time Tanya speaks, my dick curls up into my body a little more and begs me not to force him into her again, but needs vs. must. I need to bring down Malik for good so he must pleasure our best asset. Aside from Candy that is. She doesn't realise how helpful she's become to me – and not only because I close my eyes and picture her on the end of my cock each time I give in to Tanya's demands.

"Because Malik is predictable. Too set in his ways for his own good. It makes keeping tabs on him so easy, it's quickly becoming tedious." I sigh, flopping back into the driver's seat. My phone starts to vibrate in my jean pocket and when I fish it out, I see Graham's name flashing on the screen. Answering the call, I drape myself over the wheel to get a better look at the silver hair and bearded man standing in the doorway, his own phone pressed to his ear.

"They've just left, Mr Conway."

"Yes, I can see that Graham. Tell me everything." For the next ten minutes, I listen intently as Graham relays how Candy was given her own version of the Gambler's Monarch's jacket and has been welcomed into my old gang with loving arms. My hand tightens around the steering wheel until my knuckles have turned white and my teeth grind together. She's one of them now. Firmly in their grasp, yet it's not the fact she's a fully-fledged Monarch that angers me. It's that they get to share her, touch her, have her, fuck her whenever they want.

I slam my hand on the wheel, accidentally setting off the horn. Throwing the shades off my face, I end the call before I break my phone and claw at my hair. Images of their hands on her assault my mind, her sweet cries of pleasure filling my old bedroom. And Malik wins again. The self-proclaimed King of his carefully orchestrated world. Snuggling up at night with the only woman who has held my attention for more than five minutes. Who fills my days with jealousy and my nights with dreams of how I'd take her in every way I can imagine until she's screaming my name as if no other exists. Jasper, Jasper, *Jasper*.

"Jasper!" That high-pitched voice breaks through my imagination again, making my toes curl in disgust. Fuck my life. "Are we going after them or not?!" I don't bother answering her, slamming my foot onto the accelerator and skidding out of the parking lot. An army of cars follow, the hired help having arrived hours prior and waiting patiently for my signal. Well here's the signal boys, it's time to end this.

I speed along the road, keeping my eyes on the horizon. I can't see them anymore and if it had been Malik leading the parade, I'd have been able to hazard a guess as to where he might have headed. However, since it's Candy in charge now, she literally could go anywhere or do any fucking thing. Green fields span either side of the road so I continue on, hoping she doesn't come to an intersection before I manage to catch up.

Tanya has not stopped fucking talking, asking me questions I don't answer and making sarcastic comments to herself. I've mastered the art of tuning her out. My eyes are frantic, despite having nothing to look at. We pass a line of trees separating the field on the right from the glimmering lake hidden behind it. Tanya notices blackened, tyre marks on the road at the same time I spot a bright, pink head bobbing in the water. Twisting the wheel sharply, the cars behind follow me onto a thin, dirt track around the back of the lake and there we find the bikes.

Malik and Spade jolt at our arrival, scrambling for weapons in a backpack on the ground. I jump out of my seat and level my MK47 on Malik at the same time he aims a pathetic pistol at me. I keep my eyes trained on him, but my other senses are attuned to Candy's laughter and squeals from within the lake. It takes every ounce of restraint not to look, needing to know what Ace and Jack are doing to get such a reaction from her. The sounds die suddenly, probably having something to do with the hordes of armed men I hired for today closing in on them, the semi-automatic in my hands or maybe just me being here at all.

"Are we going to keep doing this, Jester?" Spade drawls until Malik elbows him in the ribs. "Ahh, I mean Jasper. You obviously aren't going to kill any of us or you would have already." I blow a heavy exhale through my nose, hating the sound of my old nickname on Spade's lips as much as I hate Malik for banning them from calling me by it.

"The jury's still out on him," I narrow my eyes on my ex-leader. His tie is loose and his top button popped open, his sleeves rolled up to the elbow and shirt untucked. It's like arriving in an alternative universe where nothing is as it should be. And then there's her.

"Come on boys, there's no need to fight. There's plenty of me to go around," Candy giggles. We all turn to scowl at her, our raised gun temporarily forgotten at the sight before us. Flanked by Ace and Jack in their boxers, she walks out the water, gloriously naked, unashamed and fucking stunning in every way. The quirky tattoos, her lithe muscles, those pert breasts I ache to squeeze.

Blood rushes to my dick, my eyes drinking her in like a shimmering mirage. Ace and Spade lunge into action, dragging an oversized, black t-shirt over her head to cover her up and a growl traps in my throat. As much comfort as hiding her body is, I'm the only one who should be touching her. At all. I had her first, she belongs to me.

"Finally picked your latest victim I see," I comment to Malik, keeping my eyes on Candy's.

"What do you even want Jasper? Not even you are stupid enough to blow through all of the money you stole already." I smirk at Malik before remembering the raw scar on my face still tugs when I do that. The gash runs from my temple to my dimple on the right side of my face, a permanent reminder that my loyalty to my brothers wasn't reciprocated. Well today they realise that everything I have done was for them, for all of us.

"I'm not the thief here Malik, you are. You stole our futures, but by taking your precious money, I took away your strength and your power to hurt anyone else." I run my tongue over my teeth, my gaze settling on Jack's at last. The disdain he holds for me breaks the last thread of hope I had at connecting with my twin again. "To answer your question, what I want is for you to tell them everything."

Silence echoes through the circle we've found ourselves in, no one daring to stand down first. Fine then. I drop my semi-automatic, the weight of it giving me a dead arm. It doesn't matter anyway, if Malik was stupid enough to shoot, I have at least forty guys behind me who won't get their bank transfers from Tanya in the cab if they don't retaliate instantly. On Malik only, the rest get to walk away no matter what. That's the deal.

"No?" I ask when Malik doesn't speak up. "Shame, maybe

you'd have had a slither at a chance of explaining yourself if you did it. I'm not surprised you copped out like usual."

"I've had enough of this," Jack states, walking through the circle to grab a gun from the backpack. Aiming it downwards, he shoots a bullet at my foot, missing by merely a few millimetres. He literally never learns, even after years of archery practice where I showed him how to not shoot just to the left. Jack seems more frustrated with himself than me, clawing a hand into his hair the same way I do. "Just say what you want to say already?! I'm bored of you turning up everything when things start going well." I raise an eyebrow at Candy, noticing how she's halfway between me and them. Maybe there's hope yet.

"Okie dokie. It's all fake. You're welcome." I turn towards the truck, surprised it's the ever-obedient Ace who speaks up to stop me.

"What's all fake?"

"Mmmm? Oh, just everything Malik told us. He didn't find us by some happy accident, he picked us. Carefully choreographed the incidents that brought us to him."

"That's enough," Malik growls at me, flicking the safety off on his pistol.

"Oh it's nowhere near enough. You had your chance to speak, but you didn't." Crossing the circle, I approach Spade first, his story being the easiest. "The casinos where you racked up those debts where owned by friends of his parents and you didn't lose half as much as they lead you to believe. They tricked you and beat you for it, just so King Malik could swoop in and save you." Spade's blue eyes narrow, flicking towards Malik for confirmation. I chuckle when he can't deny it, moving over to my twin.

"And then there's us, darling brother. We didn't piss off the cartel, they hadn't even heard of us. Malik hired men to chase us straight towards him, these men in fact." I point to the sea of raised guns, slinging an arm over Jack's shoulder. It's poetic really, and exactly why these men were so eager to help me in my revenge scheme. Jack and I injured many of them once, even killed a few, all for Malik's benefit.

"Understandably, they wanted their pound of flesh in return and I took as many beatings as I could on your behalf, but they wanted just one with you. Hence your kidnapping. I was going to return you straight after our debts are well and truly paid." I tilt my head in Malik's direction, noting how the vein protruding from his head is fit to burst. Perfect.

"Well, how about you pick up the fucking phone and just tell me next time," Jack shrugs me off and stalks over to Malik's Harley Davidson. I wave my hand to the men, telling them to move out of his way before he mows them all down. We both know if I'd tried to tell him, he wouldn't have listened and now he just needs some space to think. Candy is on my other side, the fierceness she exudes begging for my attention but I can't give it to her right now. I'm enjoying this moment way too much.

"And me? How could Malik have faked me killing someone?" Ace scoffs. I walk over to the truck, hopping up onto the hood and nestling my head into my hands.

"Ooh, you might want to get comfortable, Ace. This is my favourite one," I smirk despite the discomfort it causes me. Ace only moves to cross his arms and side step marginally to get closer to Candy, pulling from her strength as uncertainty floods his vision. "Malik here hacked into your counsellor records and found your triggers. The whole night was a set up which started with your drink being spiked in the bar. Malik fed you your worst nightmare and your mind created the corresponding images. Isn't that hilarious?" I laugh out loud.

"You did what?" Spade gasps, turning on his leader and so-called friend. I must admit, the day I clicked on the wrong file on Malik's computer and let my curiosity get the better of me, I was livid. Beyond fucking furious for Ace mostly. But I needed evidence, I had to know if it was real before I freaked out the others. I transferred myself the entire contents of his off-shore account and went in search of the casino owners, hitmen, bar staff.

Bribing any and everyone I could. I'd been too wrapped up in my investigations, I'd never even considered the lies of betrayal Malik would feed the others and I'd find myself with a target on my head if I returned.

I lived for these men, I'd have died for them too, but not at their own hands. Not when I knew the truth. We were all part of Malik's sick game because we were easily influenced. Gullible, naïve and malleable to become the puppets Malik desired. But their instant hatred, especially with how easily Jack turned on me, sparked my own. They deserted me long before I deserted them. I'd never been alone before, always having Jack by my side, which made hiding in the shadows and waiting for my chance so much more difficult. And then there was Candy. Sweet, sassy Candy and the world of jealousy she's ignited in me. Granted from there on….shit went a little too far.

Refocusing on the scene before me, Spade is standing with his chest heaving and fists clenched, but the attack on Malik I was hoping for doesn't come. Why? Why aren't they turning on him as quickly as they turned on me? Instead, Spade grabs a vacant Ace by the arm and drags him over to their bikes, ordering him to get on. I hop down from the truck, shouting for them to wait but the roars of the bikes drown me out and I'm forced to jump out of the way before they mow me down. I watch them go, my mouth hanging open. Sure, take some time guys. Plan your payback carefully, buy some machetes or a tree grinder machine or some shit.

A movement of pink shifts in my peripheral vision, easing my rising panic. This is the moment Candy runs into my arms and realises I did have good motives to begin with, even if they did get a little lost. Turning, I see her walking away from me to approach Malik, speaking too softly for me to hear. I wait, watching for the moment her head shifts and then I see Malik. That face right there, that's what I've been waiting for all this time. The utter desolation of a lonely man who ruined our lives and led us to believe he saved us. I just wish the porcelain face beside him didn't sully this moment.

Candy twists to look at me, her eyebrows pulled together in confusion and her wide brown eyes calling to a part of my soul. For a moment, she'd looked so happy, so full of life flying down the road on her quad bike in her Monarch jacket. Worlds away from the misery in her expression now, but that's what trusting Malik does to you. Gives you what you thought you wanted and then rips out from beneath your feet until you feel like you never stop falling.

Unfortunately, Candy interlocks her fingers with Malik's and seals her choice. After everything she's just heard, when I'm clearly hanging around to whisk her away, she chooses him. I'd have dropped everything; my anger, this vendetta, the past, just to give her the world. I raise an eyebrow, waiting to see if she'll change her mind but all I get in return is a defiant rise to her chin. Too bad, 'cause now I'll have to destroy them both.

ACKNOWLEDGMENTS

They say people come into your life when you most need them, and I've never fully believed it before Sam. Reader turned personal PA for me, Sam appeared when I was ready to give up on both myself and my dreams. I can now say, hand on heart, I wouldn't have been able to let Candy burst free from the cage of my mind and spread her assets all over these smut-filled pages without Sam's guidance, support and friendship. Take a good look Mrs O'Neill, this one is for you.

Thanks to Jessica for creating the amazing artwork that inspired such an awesome, crazy bunch of characters. You have a real talent, girl!

Thanks to Tiffany for working flat out, and going without sleep so I could get Candy out in time. You are amazing.

Thanks to Emma for working with me to bring the inside of my books to life, I love the designs so much. And co-writing with you is so much fun, I can't wait for people to read all our words.

To all my ARC - thank you for reading and reviewing - I appreciate you all so much.

To my Street Moles, for sharing teasers, recommending my book, and generally making sure people hear all about Candy. You guys rock!

Finally, to each and every one of you. Thank you for downloading and for reading. Your continued support means the world to me. I can't wait for you to see what I have planned next.

ABOUT MADDISON COLE

Maddison is a married mum of two, and a serial daydreamer. As a huge fan of all romance troupes, from RH to Omegaverse, she finally decided to put pen to paper (finger to keyboard doesn't sound as poetic) and write her own.

As a child, life was moving around the UK and a short stint in the Caribbean, before Maddison has found herself back in the south east of England where she is now happily settled. With a double award in applied arts and an A-level in art history, Maddison is an average musical-loving, Disney-obsessed, jive-dancer with a dark passion for steamy fantasy books.

FOLLOW MADDISON COLE

If you want to be the first person to find out about my new releases, exclusive reveals and announcements, giveaways, and so much more, then you need to follow in any or all of the places below.

Sign up to my newsletter here:

http://eepurl.com/hx3Zqr

Also, make sure to join my Facebook readers group, Cole's Reading Moles here:

Coles Reading Moles Facebook Group

You can also find me on Tik Tok here:

- facebook.com/maddison.cole.314
- instagram.com/maddison_cole_author
- amazon.com/author/B086ZQ6SW4
- bookbub.com/authors/maddison-cole
- tiktok.com/@coles_moles
- goodreads.com/authormaddisoncole

ALSO BY MADDISON COLE

ALL MY PRETTY PSYCHOS
Paranormal RH with ghosts and demons

Queen of Crazy
https://amzn.to/3O4biQt

Kings of Madness
https://amzn.to/3HzvBCY

Hoax: The Untold Story (novella)
https://amzn.to/3xAJhcA

Reign of Chaos (pre-order)
https://amzn.to/3b95PcI

.

I LOVE CANDY
Dark Humor RH - Completed

Findin' Candy (novella)
https://amzn.to/3bcueOp

Crushin' Candy
https://amzn.to/3n0TASf

Smashin' Candy
https://amzn.to/3Oniuai

Friggin' Candy
https://amzn.to/3QwlmUb

The Complete Candy Boxset
https://amzn.to/3t2dqiW.

.

THE WAR AT WAVERSEA
Basketball College MFM Menage - Completed

Perfectly Powerless
https://amzn.to/3OqHTQp

Handsomely Heartless
https://amzn.to/3tMoRfu

Beautifully Boundless
https://amzn.to/3MYiiNG

.

MOON BOUND
Vampire/Shifters Fated Mates Standalones

Exiled Heir
https://amzn.to/3OtlqSD

Privileged Heir
https://amzn.to/3mYwQ5g

.

WILLOWMEAD ACADEMY (CO-WRITTEN WITH EMMA LUNA)

Sexy Student - Teacher Taboo Age Gap Standalone

Life Lessons
https://amzn.to/3tL8eAX

.

A WONDERLUST ADVENTURE: A DERANGED DUET
Retelling of Alice - twenty years on

My Tweedle Boys (pre-order)
https://amzn.to/3wRIqVd

Our Malice (TBC)

.

VICES AND HEDONISM SHARED WORLD
A Reverse Harem MMA Romance

A Night of Pleasure and Wrath
https://amzn.to/3Rgg0fC

.

FINDING LOVE AFTER DEATH (CO-WRITTEN WITH EMMALEIGH WYNTERS)

Haunted by Desire
https://amzn.to/3BaTlvI

Printed in Great Britain
by Amazon